Naughty,
Naughty

Naughty, Naughty

Susan Johnson

Adrianne Lee

Leandra Logan

Anne Marie Winston

St. Martins s Press

NAUGHTY, NAUGHTY

ISBN: 0-7394-0478-4

Printed in the United States of America

St. Martin's Paperbacks are published by St. Martin's Press,
175 Fifth Avenue, New York, N.Y. 10010.

CONTENTS

Naughty, Naughty

A Tempting Wager

Susan Johnson

VIENNA, FEBRUARY 1815

"Rumor has it he can make love for hours on end." The Comtesse de Polignac's fair brows lifted marginally in sportive acknowledgment. "Apparently he's quite astonishing . . ." Her luscious mouth curved into a mischievous smile.

"The Duchesse de Montebello insinuates days," the young Baroness Ferron interposed with a wicked grin. "And she should know. Such delicious stamina might be worth more than the diamond necklace."

"I'll take both." The Princesse de Boissy lifted her teacup to the group of women discussing a piquant wager having to do with Simon Mar, Marquis of Narne, the most profligate rake on seven continents, a member of the English delegation to the Congress of Vienna, and to date unprecedentedly celibate in the Austrian capital.

"You always were greedy."

"Life is short, darling Emilie." The princesse cast a glance at the Duchesse de Ouvrard, Talleyrand's latest mistress. "As we know too well." The ladies, all members of the ancien régime now returned to France with the restoration of the Bourbons, had lost many of their family to the Revolution's guillotine.

"Pray, no depressing thoughts," the baroness chided. "I

much prefer contemplation of the notorious Simon Mar in my bed.''

''Hear, hear.'' The comtesse raised her sherry glass to the group. ''To the pleasures of life.''

''Making up for lost time, Georgie?''

''Definitely making up for lost time.''

''At least your husband was rich.''

''It wasn't enough, believe me.'' Georgette St. Germain, a comtesse in her own right, had been married at fifteen to a rich financier, old enough to be her grandfather. He had been a mean-spirited, repulsive man, and her seven years of marriage had been a durance vile. ''Are we clear on the details, then?'' she briskly interposed, quick to change the subject from anything having to do with her baleful marriage. ''Whoever lures Simon Mar into their boudoir wins the diamond earrings. And the matching necklace if he stays the night once he's informed of the wager. The highest number has the first chance to win.''

''He has a preference for redheads, I hear,'' the pretty baroness said with a smile and a toss of her titian curls.

''Lady Buchan had dark hair and their amour lasted the longest of his liaisons,'' the comtesse reminded her.

''He has no preference save beauty and availability. Talleyrand is quite envious of his reputation for vice.''

''And of his youth, I expect,'' the princesse said.

Emilie dipped her head in acknowledgment. ''Which doubtless contributes to Mar's reputation for stamina.'' Talleyrand, her current protector, a former bishop, rake extraordinaire, foreign minister through all the upheavals of French society, was sixty-one.

''Why is he admitted into the inner circle of negotiations at his age?'' the baroness asked. ''The ministers are all much older.''

''Family connections,'' the princesse pointed out with a knowing glance.

''And intelligence. The English need his brains, Talleyrand says, to keep the Russians at bay.''

"He's also tall, dark, handsome, and was a bold, audacious officer during the Peninsular War—"

"Wealthy as Croesus, don't forget that," the princesse noted. Her ancient family was known for their prosperous marriages.

"And shamelessly talented in the boudoir," the baroness went on with an arch smile. "Truly a paragon of virtues."

"But celibate during his sojourn in Vienna," Emilie reminded them.

"Perhaps he has a mistress tucked away somewhere." Georgette gazed at her friend from under her pale lashes.

"In this city of gossip and spies?" Emilie waved her hand in dismissal. "Impossible."

"Is he nursing a broken heart?"

The princesse's trill of laughter rippled through the sun-filled room. "He doesn't have a heart, my darlings." Her fine blue eyes sparkled with amusement. "But he has more than enough other charms to make up for that deficit."

"So?" Georgette softly murmured. "Are we all ready for tonight's entertainment at the Schönbrunn?"

"The highest number wins?" The baroness looked at everyone in turn. "Are we agreed?" And at their approving nods, she rose, walked to a delicate bonheur du jour, and drawing out a sheet of paper from the drawer, quickly wrote down four numbers. Tearing the paper into fourths as she returned to the tea table, she shuffled the bits of paper and tossed them into her empty cup.

As each lady drew a scrap of paper from the cup, she placed it number up on the inlaid tabletop.

The focus of attention a moment later, Georgette found herself blushing.

"Soixante-neuf," the princesse purred. "How appropriate. I envy you your evening's pleasure."

Juliette had deliberately written low numbers on the other scraps of paper so there would be no arguments over the winner. Simon Mar was too intriguing to be generously shared.

"I'm not so sure he's accessible."

Georgette's demur brought various looks of astonishment from her friends. "Are you backing out?" Emilie inquired with a searching glance.

"No . . . no. Only—that is, do you suppose he's ill?"

"I'd gladly take your number and find out for myself," the princesse offered with a sportive wink. "And I do adore diamonds."

"Now I needn't sleep with him if I choose. The wager is only to bring him to my boudoir for the earrings."

"How innocent you sound, Georgie, as though you hadn't lived through a hellish marriage—and taken solace in your particular style of independence since."

"I'm just leaving my options open. Who knows how I'll feel."

"Or how he'll feel," the baroness drolly said. "But do what you wish, darling," Juliette went on. Georgie was astonishingly innocent at times despite the misfortunes and miseries in her past. "All you have to do is bring Mar into your boudoir. And if you're not successful, next highest number tries tomorrow."

"We'll all be watching you this evening, Georgie, darling," the princesse murmured. "Whatever will you wear to catch his eye?"

It was late before the Comtesse de Polignac was able to approach the marquis alone. She'd been surrounded by admirers all evening, and Simon Mar had been the center of feminine attention, not to mention a participant in numerous political discussions with colleagues. The ball at the Schönbrunn was a glittering assemblage of nobles from all the countries of Europe; the Austrian Emperor Francis II had appeared briefly, the Russian Tsar Alexander I was still in attendance. The music and dancing filled the ornate ballroom with glittering sound and color as beautifully dressed aristocrats twirled around the room under candlelit crystal chandeliers.

"The congress dances, but it isn't going anywhere," the Prince de Ligne remarked, unjustly—for beneath the glamorous glitter of the entertainments, serious business was being carried on. Simon had already been detained by both Metternich and Chancellor von Hardenberg that evening in connection with the annexation of Saxony. The entire work of the congress was being accomplished by small committees or in meetings behind the scenes. And he'd promised von Gentz he'd see him before morning. He was tired, weary of jammed ballrooms, much too sober considering the amount of champagne he'd drunk, and still he had hours of work to do before the meeting of the Allies in the morning.

All reasons perhaps why he didn't notice the comtesse approach him.

"I was thinking about dinner tonight—just the two of us."

Simon's dark gaze swung around at the distinctive tone—a sensual purr beneath the delicate French phrasing. Veiling his surprise at the sight of the Comtesse de Polignac, he quickly surveyed the adjacent guests on the verge of the imperial ballroom.

The comtesse, gloriously blond, small and slender, rumored to be mistress to the French minister, offered him a lush, intimate smile.

As a member of the British delegation, Simon had to weigh such temptation in the context of Anglo-French relations. But she was the most beautiful woman in Vienna and he'd never been known for prudence. "Tomorrow," he said. His evening was already overbooked.

"Tonight."

"I'll have to change some plans."

"I'd like that."

He felt his body instantly respond as though she'd said something carnal. "I've been working day and night," he said, as if his sharp-set urgency required some explanation.

"I've heard. Perhaps you'd like to rest tonight."

He *had* been working too hard, he decided, suddenly tempted to drag her behind the drapes and take her standing up at the word "rest" pronounced in that provocative murmur. "Where?" he said with forced mildness.

But despite his temperate voice, the full force of his physical power was impressive at close range, Georgie reflected, a brute strength beneath his fine tailoring and practiced charm. Looking up what seemed a great distance, she smiled. "I'm staying at the Durnstein Palace."

He nodded. "It might be a few hours yet before I can get away." There was von Gentz to pacify and the delegates from Venetia and he shouldn't even be considering this.

"I'll wait up for you." But a curious frisson stirred her when it shouldn't, when she was actually questioning the judiciousness of the wager. The audacity of his bold gaze struck her with a small qualm, an unbridled sensuality beneath his well-bred replies, a nervy insolence a hint of danger perhaps. He struck her as the kind of man who lived outside the rules.

"Would you care to dance?" He found he wanted to touch her suddenly, feel the warmth of her under his hands, dominate her—a shocking notion for a man who equated sex with pleasure and games, never possession. She was so exquisitely small though, he thought as he offered her his hand.

How could she refuse if she wanted to continue the game? How could she refuse when he looked at her with such fierce urgency? And she decided as she lifted her hand to his that it was impossible for someone like Simon Mar to maintain a chaste existence. He had to have a woman hidden away somewhere in Vienna with such irrepressible lust smoldering in his eyes.

But their fingers hadn't yet touched when Chancellor von Hardenberg suddenly strode up, followed by his entourage. Bowing to Georgie, he apologized for his intrusion, but nevertheless he required Simon's attention without delay, he gruffly declared.

"Forgive me," Simon said, bowing gracefully. "Truly," he added with a faint smile. And leaning forward, his mouth brushed the curls near her ear. "Give me two hours," he whispered.

She was left trembling when he walked away, the sensation of his warm breath on her cheek shocking, intoxicating, as though he'd branded her. Shaken, disturbed by the exceptional intensity of her response, she left the ball without speaking to any of her friends. She didn't want to be questioned about the marquis when she couldn't explain what had overcome her. Nor did she wish to be teased for what seemed, even to her, an adolescent reaction to the merest touch. Walking out into the chill night, she pulled her fur-lined cloak close and moved down the lamp-lit street. As she hurried past the waiting carriages and drivers, she wondered if she were making a mistake inviting Simon Mar into her boudoir.

On the other hand, they were both sophisticated enough to understand the customs and conventions of the fashionable world. Should she change her mind, a gentleman would acquiesce. Although Simon Mar didn't seem to be the type of man who would easily acquiesce. And so she debated the various possibilities on her walk back to her apartments, coming to the sensible conclusion with time and distance from the marquis that her unusual reaction was simply the result of undue nervousness over the wager. She'd never partaken in such outlandish sport before—it was a mark of everyone's ennui after months of unending entertainments. But since this was no more than a frivolous caprice, there was no point in viewing it with unnecessary melodrama.

The marquis was just another man.

Arriving long after midnight, the two hours having stretched to three, Simon apologized as he entered her boudoir. "No one seems to sleep in Vienna," he said, shrugging out of his greatcoat and dropping it on a chair. "Forgive me for keeping you waiting." He glanced at her maid, asleep on a chaise.

"I'm afraid I have a confession," Georgette murmured, keeping her voice low in order not to wake the servant she'd retained as a witness for the wager. She *had* decided on prudence in the interval since she'd arrived home, her concern not so much for the impropriety as for becoming involved with a man who affected her so markedly. Mar was a man of profligate tastes; hardly a candidate for her curiously ardent enthusiasm. "I invited you here only because of a wager," she calmly said, her odd emotions subdued. She went on to explain the particulars and offer her regrets for bringing him out so late at night.

The marquis stood motionless beside the chair where he'd thrown his coat until she finished speaking. "So you have the earrings at least," he pleasantly observed. "Since I'm here though," he blandly went on, unbuttoning his jacket, "there's no point in you losing out on the diamond necklace."

"You misunderstand," she coolly said, moving back a step.

"I walked away from the chancellor of Prussia and two other delegations to come here. Perhaps *you* don't understand," he softly countered, shrugging out of his jacket and tossing it on top of his coat. He smiled faintly as he unfastened his white silk waistcoat.

"I'll wake my maid," she threatened. "You can't do this."

"Why don't I wake her." And with an authority that reminded her of his commanding position in Vienna, her maid was wakened and quickly dismissed.

"I could have made a scene," she noted as he turned from shutting the door, her gaze hot with temper.

"Why didn't you?" he asked, although he knew why even if she didn't. How beautiful she was in the candlelight, haughty and full of fire, her pale hair a silken nimbus framing her exquisite face, her ivory silk ball gown a perfect foil for her nymphlike delicacy.

She met his mild gaze with a taut, heated look, and when she spoke, her voice was tight with restraint. "Do you want the truth?"

He smiled. "A unique concept in Vienna at the moment. Please do. I'd find it refreshing."

She exhaled softly before she answered, her thoughts in tumult. Honesty in boudoir assignations was not only rare but indecorous. "I find myself unduly tempted by you, much too fascinated and intrigued. As we both know, such overwrought emotion is a stumbling block in situations like this. So I thought it best to avoid complications."

"Such as?" He spoke so quietly that even in the hushed room, she barely heard him.

The odd tenderness in his tone caused her pulse to quicken. "Such as ardent longing—perhaps fondness." Her smile was rueful; such outrageous candor was unheard of. "You must find the notion as ludicrous as I since both of us understand the parameters of amour. So you see," she murmured, "it would really be better if you left before I embarrass myself completely."

"I prefer staying." He shrugged negligently. "Don't ask me why. I wouldn't have an answer."

"If we're being plainspoken," she said, thinking it was much too late for tact and scruple, "I have another question. Why have you avoided liaisons in Vienna?"

"How do you know I have?"

"Gossip, of course—what else? Although my friends and I were debating this afternoon whether you might have a mistress hidden away somewhere."

"I don't." He grinned, looking suddenly boyish in his shirtsleeves, half undressed. "Would you like the position?"

"I doubt it would be worthwhile," she lightly replied. "You're much too busy."

"Mmmm," he said, studying her with a razor-sharp look.

"Don't look at me like that. I was only teasing."

He seemed to refocus his thoughts and his smile this time was practiced and full of grace. "Since we have a few hours before dawn and I've managed to elude all the delegations, perhaps we could discuss the suitability of a friendship"—he glanced at the bed—"in more comfortable surroundings."

"And if I said no?"

"Then I'd have to seduce you with my charm," he replied, smiling faintly.

"I find myself highly susceptible without any further charm."

"How nice."

"A familiar occurrence for you, I expect."

"No, actually not. None of this is remotely familiar. I shouldn't even be here. I should be working." He shot a sidelong look at the clock on the mantel, then immediately apologized, adding, "Although I confess I tried to resist as well, chiding myself on my dereliction of duty even as I was giving my excuses to the Prussians and Venetians." He flexed his fingers, still disconcerted by his rash impulses. "So you see, I'm not exactly sure either—about any of this."

"What began for me as a playful whim has taken on"—her nostrils flared—"an unwonted turn."

"Would you be offended—"

"No," she said, her green gaze direct.

He exhaled in a sudden whoosh of air when he realized he'd been holding his breath. "I feel like a damned novice."

"Maybe it's been too long for you."

"What about you?" he sharply queried, as though he had the right to ask.

"I'm relatively chaste—considering."

"Considering what?" Blunt, curt, he found himself feeling like an affronted husband.

She laughed. "Considering the ambiguous temper of the times since the Revolution, considering a society where all the rules have suddenly disappeared. Considering my friends engage in liaisons as casually as they dance the newest waltz."

"And you don't?"

"So far—no."

He finally smiled as though his catechism had produced the proper answers. "Until now?"

"Yes, my dear Mar. Does that make you happy?"

"Strangely yes. And I hope you don't have any engagements you can't break in the next few days, because I have the feeling I'm going to want you close to me."

"You can tell already? I would have thought you difficult to satisfy."

"I am. But I recognize the rarity of these rash impulses. And it's not a question of satisfying me—I know how to do that. We together though . . ." He slowly advanced toward her and in a murmur resonating with lust added, "Let me know when you've had enough."

He hadn't even touched her and she felt as though she were on fire, the sensation so fierce, so overwhelming, she put her hand out as though to hold off the conflagration.

"Sorry," he whispered, brushing her hand aside, lifting her in his arms as though she were weightless. "You can't keep me away." And his mouth gently covered hers as he walked to the bed, his kiss swiftly turning heated, intemperate, forcing her mouth open, ravishing the sweet interior. When she moaned softly, twined her arms around his neck, and returned his feverish kiss, he murmured against her lips, "I don't know if I'm capable of foreplay the first time . . ."

"Nor I," Georgie breathed, shocked by her instant lust, blushing as he gazed down at her, thinking herself supremely foolish to succumb to the most notorious rake of the age with such wantonness.

"Next time then," he murmured, charmed by her blush, intensely aroused by her discomposure, tantalized by the erotic sorcery of her diminutive form.

Placing her on the bed, he kicked off his shoes, followed her down, swiftly pushed her silken skirts aside and settled between her legs with an inexplicable sense of homecoming. It *had* been too long, he decided in the next pulse beat, opting for logic rather than sentiment even as he experienced acute sensations beyond his memories of carnal passion. His breeches were unbuttoned in a flash and he guided himself to her sweet cleft with a murmured apology for his haste.

He needn't have apologized, he realized a second later as his fingers touched her hot, sleek labia, her arousal as intense as his; she was wet, slippery wet, lifting to meet him, her thighs opened wide. And when he first entered her, they both sighed as though they were meant to feel what they were feeling, as though they had both waited all their lives for this astonishing sensation, as though the notable events of the Congress of Vienna were only extraneous adjuncts to this tempestuous inevitability.

She clung to him, panting as he slowly forced himself deeper, her flesh yielding by degrees to his enormous erection, the friction of silken flesh on flesh, pulsing tissue merging to ravish their senses. The achingly sweet penetration seemed for those hovering moments to refocus the universe to a microcosm of raw, carnal desire.

And when at last, fully submerged, he rested inside her, they both held their breaths. A wild, galvanic feeling infused every nerve and cell and pulsing vein, shameless lust beat at their brains; the rhythm of the universe was suspended. Until . . . reluctantly they had to breathe again and reenter the world.

"Screw politics," he whispered, gently moving inside her, his life quickly re-prioritized.

"Or me," she murmured with a beguiling smile, understanding why Simon Mar was in such demand.

"No question there." He nibbled on her lip, forcing himself deeper.

She moaned, and her arms tightened around his waist as she felt that first small pulsing prelude to orgasm—quicksilver, instantaneous . . . his sensational size an orgasmic trigger.

He felt the minute ripple too and knew it wouldn't be long until they both climaxed. She was already whimpering when he slipped his hands around her hips and settled into a slow, delicate penetration and withdrawal, watching her face and eyes, the rhythm of her breathing, gauging her arousal with the expertise of long practice. Seconds later, she uttered a faint cry and then screamed in a long, low wail that brought a faint smile to his lips.

Soon . . . soon . . . he selfishly thought and moments later, as she lay gasping beneath him, he allowed himself his own release, withdrawing at the last to come on her stomach.

Neither spoke for breathless moments, the only sound that of the fire in the grate and their own soft panting, their bodies pulsing with the rhythm of their hearts. Opening his eyes first, he gazed down on her, smiling at his good fortune.

Her lashes fluttered open, and seeing his smile, she whispered, "They can keep the diamonds."

"*I'll* give you diamonds." She was his, he inexplicably decided, struck by an aberrant craving when always in the past he wished to escape at this point.

"I'll give you all my estates and fortune," Georgie blissfully sighed.

He laughed. "I know what you mean." Lightly brushing her parted lips in a kiss, he murmured, "Maybe it's the novelty—after so long."

"Do you think so?" she whispered, her body still shimmering with a blissful glow.

"Hell no," he said, disconcerted by the irrational sensual need she evoked. Easing away, he rolled on his back and raked his fingers through his dark, tousled hair. "I don't know what the hell that was," he muttered.

"Could we do it again?" she purred, turning to half lie across his chest, glancing at his undiminished erection.

His body was still in hard-driving rut, and recognizing the impossibility of denying such fierce desire, he dismissed introspection in favor of more pleasant activities. Pulling her close, he murmured with a grin, "We can do it as often as you like."

Gratified, she smiled at him. "Or until the Prussian delegation searches you out."

He grimaced at her reminder, knowing how limited his time was. But after only the merest hesitation, the gentle pressure of her soft breasts against his chest, the warmth of her soft body enveloping him, he said in unprecedented invitation, "Come home with me; I'd like you more available." His dark lashes drifted fractionally downward. "Or will Talleyrand call me out?"

"You must be thinking of Emilie."

"There was talk he had his harem in Vienna."

"Even if he does, I'm not a member."

The degree of his relief surprised him, but when he spoke, his voice was diplomatically tempered. "I'll have your maid pack your things."

"Just like that?"

He gently lifted her chin with his fingertip. "Have you felt this way before?"

She shook her head.

"Nor I. Come home with me," he offered, "and we'll have breakfast together."

"Just for everyone's peace of mind, let me say that I have no expectations beyond breakfast."

He understood she was being gracious, but he was the last man in the world who required polite deliverance from a woman. "I don't do this lightly."

"Please," she said, touching his mouth with her fingertip. "I don't require even the slightest commitment. In fact, after *my* marriage, formal commitments are suspect." She smiled. "You give me pleasure and I'm grateful, although I may not oblige your requirements for availability."

"I didn't mean that," he quickly replied. "It's just that my schedule . . ." His voice trailed away at the ungallant implications.

"Why don't I stay until I no longer wish to?"

"Agreed," he said, his palms gently stroking her shoulders. "You set the rules. I'm amenable to anything."

"So diplomatic, Mar."

"Simon."

"Simon," she whispered, liking the feel of his name on her tongue.

"I don't know your given name."

"Georgette, Georgie to my friends."

"Suddenly, the settlement of Europe holds considerably less charm. I think my secretaries can begin to learn how to deal with some of the details. I've become obsessed."

"And . . . I'm so *very* glad I met you."

"Think of the time we've wasted."

"Months."

"Fuck," he softly grumbled, his level of frustration startling for a man who routinely viewed amorous adventures with dispassion.

"Perhaps you'd have a minute or so now?" she dulcetly murmured, pushing away enough to trace the taut crest of his erection with a gently drawn fingertip.

Sucking in his breath at the libidinous jolt, he quickly looked at the clock. Regardless of his wishes, his life *was* dominated by his work. "We've almost an hour."

"Then heaven's within reach," she playfully whispered, sitting up in a rustle of silken skirts and moving to straddle his legs.

He'd never actually believed in heaven before, but the luscious Georgette St. Germain was doing much to alter his jaundiced views. He held paradise in his hands, he thought, sliding his hands beneath the folds of her skirts, lifting her bottom enough to ease her over his erection.

They both closed their eyes at the first millimeter of penetration and for that inexpressible interval as she slowly descended his rigid length, the sleek, heated friction silk on carnal silk, all thought was prisoner to sensation. Thoroughly impaled at last, she opened her eyes and smiled down at him, voluptuous, wanton, female incarnate, and he understood why nirvana had been depicted so often in terms of sexual pleasure.

Gazing at him with smoldering desire, her golden hair loose on her bare shoulders, her flaunting breasts and taut nipples straining at the sheer silk of her gown, she reached for the diamond studs on his evening shirt. "I want you naked," she whispered, "so I can feel you everywhere . . ."

With self-indulgent gratification, he obliged her, shrugging out of his shirt with the ease of much practice, bracing his feet on the bed and raising his hips to slip his breeches off. His shifting movement lifted her slight weight and she half swooned as he drove in deeper, the sudden thrusting invasion touching her to the core. Quickly grasping her around the waist, he steadied her.

"Are you all right?" he whispered, concerned he'd hurt her.

A moment passed before she opened her eyes and then another before she found the breath to speak. "Ravished," she softly sighed, "in the most blissful way." And lightly moving her hips, she more fully indulged her fevered senses.

"I'll make it better," he murmured, a half-smile lifting the corners of his mouth.

"Mmmm . . . promises . . ." she purred.

"What if I kept you like this?" he whispered, lifting her gown and sheer chemise over her head. "Fuckable—for myself alone." He slid his hands over the curve of her slender waist, his drifting movement traveling upward, his palms gently cupping the fullness of her breasts. Their plump weight filled his large palms, his erection swelling at their palpable allure.

"What if I let you?" she breathed, flame-hot desire in her eyes. "So I could feel this all the time," she murmured in sultry response, easing her hand between their bodies, her fingers stroking his erection.

For a convulsive moment violent sensation overwhelmed him, the need for ownership dominating his emotions. He would keep her, he decided, a novel impulse for him.

A passing second later he wondered if he'd drunk too much; the concept was so shocking in its implications. But despite attempts at rationalization, his odd possessive instincts persisted, lust more powerful than reason or the sensual allure of the comtesse simply more intense.

When she quickly climaxed again short moments later though, he suddenly found himself vaguely nettled at her eager, ready sexuality. How many other men had seen her like this, he resentfully thought, as if he had the right to question her past. Abruptly lifting her off, he rolled over her. "You *do* like to fuck, don't you?" he growled.

"You noticed," she breathlessly whispered, her senses still glowing.

It shouldn't matter, he thought, but it did and when he looked into her languid eyes, his own gaze was dangerously heated. "See how you like this, then," he perversely murmured, driving into her with such violence, he pushed her entire body upward on the bed.

She uttered a low, welcoming sound—half moan, half entreaty—and yielded to his fierce possession, bewitched, slavishly in thrall to the insatiable desire he roused. Clinging to him, she spread her thighs wider, rose up to meet his powerful downstroke, responded with a sensual dissipation as dizzying, as feverish as his. And seconds later, she cried out in another orgasmic ecstasy that incited such a wild, unnatural jealousy in him that he recklessly poured into her.

Shocked disbelief flared in her eyes.

He jerked back as though he'd been shot.

"You idiot!" she screamed, slapping at him in blind rage. "You stupid idiot!"

Swearing under his breath, he rolled away, passive against her attack, trying to apologize when they both knew it was too late for apologies.

"Sorry?" she raged, furiously pummeling his body. "You're sorry!" she cried, trembling. "What the hell good will that do?"

Feeling like an adolescent out of control, contrite, appalled, he wondered how he'd completely lost all constraint. Ignoring the inconceivable notion of jealousy, he thought perhaps he'd been celibate too long, or was overly fatigued after months with little sleep; perhaps he'd imbibed too much. Or possibly, he thought, surveying the showy, ostentatious comtesse, it was because she was a woman so flagrantly sexual—so unlike anyone he'd ever possessed—that she had compromised his normal discipline.

She was rosy pink, flushed from passion and anger, her luxurious breasts quivering as she struck him, every soft, bounteous curve and contour a temptation. Her pink, taut nipples beckoned, the glossy hair at the juncture of her thighs, moist and dewy, drew the eye, while her bold wantonness enticed him like the Circes of old.

But despite her ravishing appeal, there was no excuse for what he'd done. Catching her flailing hands, he held them still. "I take full responsibility—"

"Much good that will do," she bristled, struggling against his grip.

"Tell me what you want me to do." He dealt every day in compromise and resolution.

"Set the world back five minutes and readjust your damned brain."

A fleeting smile, quickly restrained, lit his face.

"It's not funny," she snapped, glaring at him.

"I know. Forgive me."

"I can't believe this," she muttered. "The one time I give in completely to impulse—look!" Her scowl deepened.

"There are ways to mitigate this," he offered. "Don't you have—some . . . ?" And as he took note of her blank look, he realized she was more naïve than he'd thought.

"What?"

"Er—something to wash—yourself."

"Such as?"

"Let me find you something useful on the way to my place."

"I'm not going." Sullen, resentful, she rued her incautious passions, his disastrous attraction, the frenzied state of her emotions.

"Don't worry. I'll take care of everything—guaranteed."

He spoke with such confidence, she scrutinized him with a hard, searching look. "You can?"

Contessa Alviari would be more than willing to help, he knew. With the congress, Vienna was filled with courtesans and sophisticated ladies, most of whom had no intention of becoming pregnant. "Absolutely. The sooner we leave, the sooner this problem will be solved."

A modicum of her tension eased. He seemed so certain. "You'll bring me home when I wish?"

"Of course. And I *am* sorry."

"I should hope so, although," she had the grace to admit, "I suppose the responsibility wasn't exclusively yours."

He didn't reply because he didn't wish to prolong the argument, but he knew she was largely accountable for his unusual response. He never lost control.

When the marquis arrived at the home of the Contessa Alviari a short time later, he knew he'd be interrupting her tête-à-tête with the tsar. Even though Alexander was sleeping with so many ladies in Vienna that gossip could scarcely keep track, the contessa was his favorite. After apologizing for intruding so late at night, Simon quickly explained his dilemma. The tsar offered his condolences with a smile, while the contessa climbed out of bed and brought Simon to her dressing room.

"Such innocence, my dear Simon," Maribella Ligure murmured, sifting through a drawer for the required articles. "Not your usual style in lovers. Although the Prussian chancellor said the lady must be very special to have garnered your attention tonight of all nights."

"Hardenberg considers all his meetings of utmost importance."

"Nevertheless, darling," the contessa noted with a sidelong glance. "Saxony is rather in the balance."

"As it has been from the start. They'll manage to discuss it adequately without me tonight."

"Who is she?"

"A French lady." His brows lifted marginally. "Civility doesn't allow me, et cetera, et cetera."

"She must be young."

He shrugged. "I don't really know."

"I assumed when you needed . . . these," she said, handing him a small leather bag.

"Inexperienced at least," he noted, taking the pouch from her.

"Why don't you just send her home?"

He paused for the smallest interval. "Good question."

"You would have in the past."

"It must be the late hour," he said with a half-smile. "My thanks, darling," he offered, not about to discuss the curious state of his feelings. "Tell Sasha he's lucky to have you."

She smiled. "He knows it." The contessa was not only beautiful but a talented diplomat. Her family had controlled the papacy for so long, their wealth was measured in small kingdoms—one of which bordered on the tsar's Balkan holdings. "Do enjoy yourself, Simon dear. You've been working much too hard."

"I will," he replied, "once I've calmed the lady's fears."

Returning to the carriage, he placed the red leather case on Georgie's lap. "Rest easy now, darling. We have an entire arsenal at our disposal."

"And you're proficient in their operation?" the comtesse asked, opening the small satchel and looking at the various appliances with curiosity.

"The applications are pretty obvious. The tsar sends his compliments, by the way. He was in bed with the contessa."

Georgie set the bag aside and stared at him. "You dared?"

"The contessa and I are old friends."

"Really?" she said, knowing she had no right to feel affront.

"We've known each other for years."

"Really?" she said again in that studiously controlled tone.

"I prefer petite blondes to the exclusion of all else," Simon said with grace.

"I know you were lovers."

" 'Were' is the correct word."

"When I shouldn't take issue anyway," she murmured, understanding the limits of Simon's exclusivity.

"Please do. My own proprietary instincts are in full flare as well. It must be kismet," he said with a smile. "Now kiss me because I need you."

She found it impossible to stay angry with him, particularly when his lips met hers and a delicious, strange warmth seeped through her senses. How curious, she thought, that intellect and emotion were so at variance when Simon Mar set out to charm. How curious that a rake who should be anathema to her could make her feel so wonderful. And stranger yet that the intoxicating heat deep inside her seemed immune to good judgment when he held her in his arms.

When he lifted her onto his lap a moment later, and she felt his flagrant erection imprinted on her flesh, all her control instantly vanished. Her body opened as if on cue, the luscious ache of wanting began to throb between her legs, and desire relegated pique to the nether regions of her mind.

"One forgets," he murmured, lifting his mouth from hers. "There are degrees and there are degrees . . ."

"I never knew," she whispered, the heat from their bodies steaming the carriage windows.

"Then I'll have to show you tonight." Slipping his hand under her skirt, he stroked her damp, pulsing cleft, a languid, deft gesture that elicited heated waves of pleasure in her toes, her brain, her hot, sleek core—everywhere. And when he slid his fingers inside, she died away in his arms as though she'd not climaxed in a decade.

He immediately began mentally modifying his morning schedule because he knew he wouldn't be sleeping anytime soon, his own desires as ravenous as hers.

When they reached the Baroque mansion serving as his base of operations in Vienna, he lifted her from the carriage and carried her up the stairs, ignoring his servants, so impatient to have her again that everything save feverish need was dismissed from his thoughts. He took the staircase at a run, his casual strength intoxicating her senses. Striding down the corridor, he covered the distance to his bedroom in record time, shoved the door open, quickly entered the room, kicked the door shut, set her down, and leaning back against the solid wood, drew her hard against his body.

"This is insane," he whispered.

"But I want you," she breathed, not caring about reason or logic, impelled by a carnal urgency so intense, she wondered for a moment at her own sanity.

He softly laughed. "Then I must oblige."

"Yes, yes, now . . ." she murmured, impatiently reaching for the buttons on his breeches, wondering if every woman responded to the notorious marquis with equal frenzy. In the next second she no longer cared; all she wanted was to be quickly gratified.

He moved with dispatch, recognizing her urgency, his own as insistent. Turning, he forced her back against the door, pushed her skirts aside, unfastened the last buttons on his breeches, and lifting her slightly, entered her.

An audible sigh was proof of their satisfaction. "We fit," he whispered, drawing her legs around his waist to gain better purchase, sliding deeper, cupping her bottom in his hands.

"Perfectly." The word was warm on his mouth, her smile felt more than seen, her arms wrapped around his neck with an agreeable tightness.

"I might as well come in you once more," he breathed.

"Somehow that appeals to me," she murmured, the ripple of her breath warm on his lips.

Her words held such blatant invitation, he quickly debated the possibility of indulging his libido more than once before they resorted to the practical measures procured from the contessa. "Then you must have what you like."

His whisper seemed to touch her to the quick. "Now," she said, molten heat in her voice.

"Now?" he teased, already feeling the first small quivering flutters in her vagina.

"An order, Mar." Even whispered, it was a command.

A sudden knock on the door vibrated against her back.

"An urgent message, Your Grace."

She restlessly stirred, disconcerted at the closeness of the servant's voice.

"Later, Malcolm." Simon's tone was mild, but it held a trenchant briskness and receding footsteps immediately sounded in the corridor outside. "Sorry," he murmured.

"Put me down." Her heated blush was evident even in the dim candlelight.

"He's gone," the marquis whispered, his lips brushing

hers. ''He's gone, he won't be back; no one will come back—''

''Simon, he *heard* us!'' Tense, agitated, she trembled under his hands. ''I can't do this.''

''You don't have to do anything.'' He moved inside her, gently, delicately, the silk of his hair brushing her chin as he trailed kisses down her throat, the fresh scent of the night air clinging to his dark curls. ''Just take me in . . . let me bury myself in you . . . let me make you climax again.''

How could she refuse with the feel of him so exquisite, so tantalizing, his rigid length stretching her, moving upward by slow pleasurable degrees. ''I'm lost,'' she whispered.

''I'll take care of you . . .''

Her voice had taken on a low-pitched languor. ''Fuck me, you mean.''

''Fuck you,'' he said with an enchanting smile.

And when she smiled back, he did what he did so well, what made him sought after and pursued by every female of passion. He brought the comtesse to climax once, twice, three times, and then carried her to his bed where he upheld his reputation for stamina with skill and utter charm, with an unbridled libido that profoundly gratified the comtesse's fevered senses.

Much later that night when they rested for a time from their amorous play, he kissed her eyes and cheeks and mouth, her ears and slender throat, and murmured affectionate, earnest, sweet words with joyful feeling, and she answered yes, yes, yes, yes, yes, with unconstrained openness to all he asked for and wanted.

It was a newfound paradise for them both, as rare to the marquis with his infamous past as it was to the artless young comtesse who had tasted life but never savored it. But as dawn broke, Simon understood they were stretching the limits of discretion in terms of conception. He reached for the small leather bag sitting on the bedside table, and placed it on Georgie's belly. "Perhaps it's time to be practical."

"Must we?" she lightly teased, reaching up to touch his mouth with her fingertip.

"Unless you're interested in motherhood, we must." But he spoke with a rare lack of panic. "You decide."

Throwing her arms over her head, she lazily stretched. "I suppose we should." She smiled at him, a smoldering warmth in her gaze. "Since we've only just met."

He chuckled. "A deterrent, I suppose."

"It must be your charm, Mar. I feel as though I've known you forever."

"Not long enough." He leaned over to kiss her mouth. "You must stay with me." Returning to his half-reclining pose beside her, he picked up the red pouch and, dangling it from his slender fingers, added, "So shall we or shall we not?"

"Oh, damn, you know there's no choice," Georgie muttered, rising to a sitting position. "Give me that. I'll pick one out and you figure out how to use it."

He was charmingly objective and impersonal in managing the undertaking, ordering hot water, taking the copper ewer from his servants at the bedroom door so no one need enter the room. After quickly washing himself, he mixed the powder Maribella had given him into a small bowl of warm water, assembling the douche apparatus without embarrassment, without embarrassing her. "Shut your eyes, if you wish," he graciously offered, moving toward the bed, "and I'll let you know when it's over."

She briefly questioned his expertise in such a highly feminine undertaking. Had he known someone that well, that intimately? And why did it matter? But a moment later she decided it was impertinent of her to view him with any degree of possession. She was here for reasons of pleasure. He was as well. This wasn't the time for nurturing any thoughts of exclusivity.

She shut her eyes.

But when the cool horn cylinder slid inside her, her lashes lifted and she grimaced slightly. "I much prefer you."

"Give me two minutes and I'll be available."

Her brows rose. "My prize for this?"

"*My* prize."

She glanced at the lightening sky outside the window. "It's almost morning though."

"I'll rearrange my schedule."

"For me?"

Such artless joy could be a man's undoing, Simon thought with not so much alarm as delight. "Only for you, sweet Georgie," he indulgently said.

She squeaked when he squeezed the soft leather bulb and flooded her vagina with warm liquid. And then the scent of jasmine and myrrh wafted through the air. "How luxurious," she whispered.

"The gates of paradise are once again virgin and fragrant," Simon teased, withdrawing the device and tossing it aside.

"You know too many women." She wrinkled her delicate nose.

"Not any more," he genially replied, wiping her dry. And it wasn't a charming lie like it always had been in the past. Wrapping up the Turkish towels he'd spread beneath her, he threw them on the floor. "Now tell me, Comtesse, how exactly do you wish to be fucked this time?"

"Surprise me," she murmured in a sultry contralto, feeling as though she were meant to be in his bed with the warmth of his gaze devouring her, with anticipation rippling through her senses and mindless pleasure her goal.

The past and future were no longer of concern.

Only the moment.

"I think the height of that table will be about right," Simon softly murmured, bending to lift her from the bed.

"Do you mind if I include you in my memoirs?" she facetiously whispered, curling her arms around his neck.

He chuckled. "If this is going into print, I'll see if I can make it memorable."

"In terms of size alone, I expect you're memorable."

"As long as you're happy, *chou-chou*." Gently depositing her on the marquetry tabletop, he ignored her comment.

"I am—terribly, greatly, wonderfully . . ." Her senses were afire, addicted to the sensual pleasures he offered. Her narrow world had expansively altered in the hours past, and feeling inexpressibly wanton, she opened her thighs, placed her index fingers on the soft, pouty tissue of her labia, and offered herself to him.

As if he weren't dangerously in rut already, he thought with a muted groan. "Now how the hell am I supposed to act the gentleman when you offer me that with such lascivious intent?"

"I'm sorry," she murmured, flirtatious and impenitent.

"Like hell you are," he growled.

"I'm all sweet and clean, my lord," she breathed, sliding the tips of her fingers inside her vagina.

It was too much for anyone's self-control, and he had little to none when it came to sexual adventure. "Then maybe I should eat you first."

A rush of pleasure streaked through her body and it took a moment before she could speak. "Be my guest."

He didn't answer her for some time, nor did he move, beset by tumultuous feeling so contrary to any he'd ever experienced, it took him a moment to regain his composure. "I'm thinking about locking you in this room," he brusquely noted.

"Would I be your sex slave?" Flagrant invitation infused her whispered query.

"Damn right."

"How nice."

" 'Nice' isn't exactly the word I had in mind. Fucking myself to death—now there's a concept." Gracefully dropping to his knees, he ran his palms down the insides of her thighs, leaned forward, and slid his tongue down her pulsing tissue.

"More . . ." A heated small whisper.

"Like this?" Exposing her clitoris with his fingertips, he gently suckled.

She pulled at his hair. "No, Simon, please don't tease me." Her entreaty was so urgent that even if he were capable of a measured pace, he would have succumbed to her pleading. And he'd long ago relinquished any semblance of dispassion with her. She was the most tantalizing inamorata he'd ever known, delectably small, gloriously beautiful and hot, so burning hot he wondered how she'd remained untouched for as long as she had.

Coming to his feet, he responded to her urgency with his own covetous desires, entering her without preliminaries, making love to her as though she *were* his sex slave—selfishly, ravenously, with uncurbed ferocity. And she met his frenzied zeal, then wildly drove the rhythm up a notch into a fevered hysteria so recklessly ardent and overwrought, she left bloody marks on his back. She came twice before he did, and forcing himself to prudence only with enormous will, he withdrew before orgasm.

But he found himself rankled at the feeling of incompletion, and that resentment translated itself into a simmering displeasure, primal and savage. Like a throwback to some barbarian age, he picked her up, tossed her over his shoulder, and stalked to the bed. Dropping her onto the rumpled covers, he said, low and heated, "You won't be leaving until I'm finished with you."

"I don't want to leave." Her skin was glowing, her gaze passion-filled, her senses boiling over with lust. "Actually, I'm considering buying *you* a carriage full of diamonds," she purred.

"Is this some kind of a contest?," His voice was harsh with challenge.

"Not for me, darling." She lounged like a sultan's favorite, lush and alluring. "I'm utterly compliant."

But if it wasn't a contest that night, it was decidedly a game, played with self-indulgence, nervy excess, with prodigality and exaltation, with sweet, languid sensuousness, as the hours passed and a measure of fatigue overcame them. And when at last they lay replete in each other's arms, the morning sun was shining brightly through the lace-hung windows.

Reluctant to leave but aware of the late hour, Simon slowly raised himself up on one elbow. "Do you want breakfast?" he gently asked. "I *do* have to bathe and start working, read my messages, have some coffee to keep me awake today. But rest if you wish—I understand."

"I'd rather have breakfast with you."

He smiled. "Good. I was being polite. But when you need to rest, ask my servants for anything at all—and sleep."

"I don't know if I can sleep. I want to touch you and look at you and listen to you and in general behave like a lovesick young girl."

"Then we'll be foolish together," he cordially replied, dropping a kiss on her small straight nose. "Although please don't refer to my behavior as lovesick in public. I'll be ridiculed mercilessly."

"Otherwise you don't mind?"

"Not in the least, *chou-chou*. People live lifetimes without ever feeling what we're feeling. I'm beginning to think there's a benevolent god after all."

"These sensations do rather shake one's sense of reality."

"A much nicer reality." Unlike the brutal, malevolent world of diplomacy, he thought.

"Like a dream," she said with a smile.

And within their newfound, enchanting wonderland, they bathed and dressed and had breakfast together as though it were the most normal thing to do. As though they'd always known each other and were deliciously in love. She read the morning papers while he perused the dozens of messages he'd received, their eyes meeting occasionally over the remains of breakfast, their smiles radiant with delight.

"In my current mood, I'm capable of taking on the world or certainly Metternich at least," Simon cheerfully said, pushing away the last of his messages. "I *will* ask you to excuse me for an hour or so. I have to meet with the tsar. Can you entertain yourself in my absence? A portion of my library is here."

"I'll be quite content. And tsars quite outrank me."

"He'll receive short shrift from me today. I've better things to do." Blowing her a kiss, he rose from the table. "With luck, this shouldn't take more than two hours."

"I'll be waiting."

His dark lashes lowered marginally. "That gives me a powerful incentive to hurry."

No more than ten minutes had passed; Georgette had scarcely finished her second cup of coffee when Simon's majordomo entered, announcing a visitor. Her shock must have been apparent for he inquired, "Should I send her away?"

She wasn't sure even such an august figure as Malcolm could intimidate the Princesse de Boissy—no one had to date. "That won't be necessary, Malcolm. The princesse and I are old friends."

"You must have won the necklace," the princesse cheerfully said, entering the breakfast room. "Along with other delectable rewards from the look on your face." She waved her hand in a sweeping gesture. "And this is your current abode."

"Do come in, Caroline," Georgie offered, her smile an indication of her happiness. "Yes, you're right. Now, how did you find me?"

"My servants had the information before I woke, you sweet naïve dear. Juliette and Emilie are right on my heels," she went on, throwing her luxurious sable wrap on a chair. "Is he as delicious as they say? Tell me everything," she purred, dropping into a gilded chair.

But before Georgie could begin to explain those details she cared to divulge, her other friends were announced, out of breath and wide-eyed.

"Chérie," Juliette breathed. "Ensconced in his home. Whatever did you do?"

"Mar never brings ladies home," Emilie softly said, gazing about the sunny breakfast room as though imprinting the details on her memory for future reference. "Talleyrand is beside himself with curiosity."

"We found we had much in common. Would you like tea or coffee?"

"Nothing, just every detail if you please," Juliette firmly replied, sitting down. "Don't leave out *anything*."

"He's very sweet," Georgie murmured.

"Sweet? Simon Mar? He's left more broken hearts than any man in Europe," Emilie protested.

"I understand; believe me, I'm not planning a protracted stay. But the present is delightful."

"That's quite obvious," the baroness playfully noted. "I believe you're actually glowing. But here—in the lion's den, so to speak. However did you manage that?"

"It was his idea. With his brutal schedule, he preferred to have me stay here."

"Readily available," Emilie said with a licentious arch of her brow.

"I'm not complaining, darlings."

And they were all singularly pleased at Georgie's blissful smile.

"How charming," the princesse said. "You're smitten at last."

"Only sensibly enjoying myself. I know better than to be smitten with Simon Mar."

"Is gossip true?" Emilie shamelessly asked. "Is he the very best?"

"Not that I'd qualify as an expert, but yes, he's very nice."

"Nice in what way?" the princesse inquired with a small smile. "Are you in love, my sweet?"

"I would never be so foolish." She knew better than to admit to such a bourgeois sentiment.

"Is *he* in love?"

"You'll have to ask him."

But none of them dared when he appeared an hour later. After walking into the breakfast room, he greeted the ladies with courtly good manners and even sat with them for a time sharing the latest gossip of the day. But when he considered the courtesies sufficiently met, he said with a gracious smile, "If you'll excuse us, ladies. I'm only home for a short interval." Rising, he offered his hand to Georgie.

She blushed before her friends' knowing glances.

Simon had never blushed in his life. "Do come and visit again," he cordially said. "Georgie will enjoy your company." And with a chivalrous bow, he escorted Georgie from the room.

"The news of our liaison will be out by afternoon," Georgie said as they walked toward his bedroom. "I hope you don't mind."

"It's already old news, darling. They wouldn't have found you otherwise."

"So nothing's private."

"I'm afraid not. Don't blush. Amorous liaisons scarcely cause a ripple with the fate of nations in the balance."

"How fortunate," she murmured ironically.

"How fortunate indeed. I prefer as little speculation on the state of our relationship as possible."

She gave him a searching glance.

Taking her hand in his, he quietly said, "Only because no one would understand. Hell, I don't even understand," he added, grinning. "The tsar was astonished when I left the meeting, but I hadn't seen you for an hour. And I apologize in advance for I'm going to be crudely expeditious now. I promise to make it up to you tonight. I've already informed Wellington I won't be at this evening's reception."

"I really missed you," she quietly said, slipping her hand into his.

"Did you now?" he murmured, scooping her up into his arms. "Maybe you could *show* me how much you missed me."

And in the days to come, they settled into an enchanting domestic arrangement so unprecedented in their lives, there were times they questioned their sanity. Simon stayed home most nights, delegating the evening sessions to his subordinates. They made love with infinite variety. At other times, they lay before the fire and simply held each other. He brought her lavish presents, jewelry, gowns, bibelots of luxury and meticulous craftsmanship. And when she protested, he told her it gave him pleasure, like the feel of her in his arms; she could give them away if she didn't want them.

They always breakfasted together, and when he kissed her good-bye and left for the day, he promised to be home before dark. The marquis was outrageously impatient in meetings now, forcing the pace of negotiations with precipitous authority, actually accomplishing a great deal more once he'd replaced conciliatory tact with his energetic approach. But pressure alone wasn't sufficient to settle the myriad disagreements at the bargaining table, and he was apprehensive, as tempers escalated, as rifts and divisive conflicts increased, that all of Europe might suffer.

Spies had already begun to bring rumors of a possible return of Napoleon. Simon had daily reports sent him on the state of the naval blockade on Elba.

Many refused to believe Napoleon could muster an army sizable enough to return him to power. But everyone speculated on the possibility. And those most prudent considered the disposition of their troops.

March 7 marked a month's anniversary for the lovers—the passing weeks had been blissful. But each day the continent moved inexorably toward conflict once again and the possibility of separation for the lovers was ever present in their thoughts. If war came, Simon would immediately leave to ready his command for action. And during the continuing negotiations in Vienna, Simon marveled at the witless, parochial views of the European monarchs, concerned only with their selfish claims, seemingly immune to the consequences of their carping disputes.

He was truly exhausted that night. The meeting of the allies had lasted over ten hours without effective results, and after he made love to Georgie, he simply held her as though she were his anchor in a world gone mad.

"This must be love," he murmured into her hair, the scent of her perfume fragrant in his nostrils.

"Or if this isn't love," she whispered, touching the warmth of his throat with her tongue, "it's certainly delicious."

"Are we too cynical?" His voice was hushed.

"We have reason to be. Nothing lasts in this world."

"Perhaps this could."

"Wouldn't that be nice? But don't make promises impossible to keep. This past month has been the happiest of my life and I'm content."

"What if we were to marry?"

"I've been married. I wouldn't recommend it."

"What if I wished to marry you?"

She propped her forearms on his chest and gazed at him. "Are you proposing?"

"What if I were?"

"So equivocal, darling," she said with a small smile. "Why don't we think about it?"

"For how long?" His voice had taken on an edge.

"Until you're sure, my dear Mar."

"Are you saying you're sure?"

"Yes, I'm sure I love you. Marriage—now that's another matter."

"What if you were to have my child?"

"But I'm not having your child."

"I could change that."

"I suppose you could. But I still wouldn't have to marry you."

"Don't be difficult," he testily murmured, his temper warming. "Do you think I ask women to marry me every day?"

"I know very well you don't. The whole world knows you don't. Let's talk about it in the morning."

"Why the morning?"

"Because I find myself craving you at the moment." She moved upward to kiss him. "Do you mind?"

He laughed. "Do I ever?"

She made a small moue. "I'm not sure I like that."

"What?" He looked at her in that innocent male way that exonerated him from all blame.

"Your audacious capacity for sex."

He laughed out loud and, still chuckling, said, "You of all people complaining? The lady who needs to be fucked a dozen times a day."

"Don't laugh at me," she objected, playfully jabbing at him with her finger. "I'm jealous, that's all, and damn you, you're always ready for sex."

"Would you prefer I not be?"

"Of course not."

His dark lashes fell marginally. "That's what I thought."

"The point is—"

"I won't look at another woman. I haven't. I don't want to." He grinned. "You're about all I can handle."

Her gratification was plain. "You haven't even looked at another woman?"

"I've become a eunuch—except for you, of course—

and you don't strike me as the kind of woman who'd be interested in platonic love."

"Not since I've met you. I've become addicted—like a pampered sultana who lies abed and waits . . . for this," she murmured, stroking his erection.

"We're both addicted," he murmured, his hand closing over hers, lengthening her stroke. His eyes briefly closed, a soft growl resonated in his throat, eliciting a predictable sexual frisson deep inside her. His voice, the mere sight of him, was enough to shamelessly rouse her.

While his sexual accomplishments rendered her helplessly devoted to him, the idyll of the weeks past seemed so magical she forbade herself to think beyond the moment. She refused to contemplate life without him.

"Make love to me," she whispered, wanting the sense of closeness, wanting his love, wanting to never think of her past again.

She could feel his erection swell under her hand and she raised her head to look at him.

He was smiling. "He heard you."

"He wants me."

"Always." He moved swiftly as though he understood her desperation, and lying on top of her a moment later, he lowered himself between her legs. Poised to enter her, he gazed down on her. "Set a wedding date."

"Blackmail," she whispered, lifting her pelvis to meet him.

He drew back, eluding her. "Just name a time."

"I can't right now."

Guiding his penis with one hand, he nuzzled her sleek labia with the tip of his erection. "Mmm. That's hot cunt . . ."

"You're not fair." She squirmed beneath him, trying to draw him in.

"You're not giving me the right answer."

"Damn you." She tried to pull him close, her hands hard on the base of his spine.

He was unyielding. ''Anytime after tomorrow, I'm available.''

''You can't,'' she challenged, but her voice wasn't hot so much as heated—by the aching need inside her. ''You don't have a license.''

''I'll get one.'' He said it like a man who was familiar with getting what he wanted. ''And I won't fuck you until you say yes.''

Unbridled desires hovered in the air—carnal and covetous—unsatisfied.

''Next month, then, damn you,'' she whispered.

''When next month?''

''On my birthday,'' she muttered, wondering what she was doing, wondering if she'd lost her mind to agree to marry again, especially a man of his repute. But he immediately slid into her and she was so grateful, she forgot about misgivings and arched her body up to meet the rhythm of his thrusts, her aching need melting away, his perfect, deft understanding of penetration and withdrawal making her faint with pleasure.

He was shamelessly proficient, facile and ingenious, as though she deserved a reward for her accession. She clung to him, moved against him in overt demand, her impossible, insistent craving for him like swimming through a sea of sexual desire to some distant shore where he always waited to give her what she wanted. She came so many times, she was shuddering at the last, and he cradled her against his body and gently kissed her until she lay quiescent.

It was impossible, she thought, already half asleep in his arms, that she'd agreed to marry him.

He didn't speak of their wedding again, content with the bargain made, but he had a smile on his face as she fell asleep.

Simon's valet dashed into the room before morning light, without knocking, without so much as a shout in warning, and Georgie knew even before he delivered his breathless message that disaster had struck.

Simon leaped out of bed, slipped into his trousers, turned briefly to kiss her good-bye, and taking his boots and jacket from his servant, ran from the room. "I'll send you a message as soon as I know anything," he shouted.

Napoleon had landed at Antibes a week before and was marching on Paris.

Georgie was up a moment later, her own fate tied to that march on Paris. With Napoleon on French soil, the country would be in chaos once again; she had much to do. Quickly dressing, she summoned her staff and issued instructions for packing, for arranging travel funds, for closing her apartment. Her estates near Lyon could well be in danger should Napoleon requisition property on his march north. Rebellion might also break out in the provinces. She had to reach Lyon quickly to protect her home.

The funds to repurchase her family's confiscated estates had been earned in her martyrdom of a marriage and she had no intention of having them taken away from her again.

The only member of her family to survive the Revolution and the bloody terror that had swept France in 1794, she'd been saved by her nursemaid from Fouché's atrocities. She was raised quietly in the country, and her adolescent beauty had first brought her to the attention of Régnier, one of Napoleon's financiers with a country home near Lyon. When Jules Régnier had discovered the secret of her name, her aristocratic antecedents further piqued his interest. Many old régime families had become members of Napoleon's court by then; only the most rabid monarchists were still in exile. The Polignac heritage would add considerable luster to his bourgeois millions—not to mention the possibility of an heir to continue that ancient line.

Regnier's offer of marriage had been a command rather than a request and the only negotiable point was that of the young comtesse's dower portion. Fortunately, her youth and beauty were coveted almost more than her illustrious name, so the local magistrate was able to bargain for an extremely favorable settlement.

Georgie had survived the miserable marriage, counting each day of the seven long years like a prisoner in jail. But finally her elderly husband succumbed to his penchant for drink and three years ago she'd become a wealthy young widow.

It took some time to purchase all her family estates, the properties having been sold to various buyers. The final hectare was in her hands just as last year's spring plowing had commenced.

And no one, not Napoleon, not God himself, was going to take away what was hers. She'd earned it.

When Simon returned late that morning, she was prepared to leave, her carriage packed and waiting in the drive.

"What the hell do you think you're doing?" he demanded, a scowl drawing his dark brows together as he entered the library where she was dashing off hasty notes to her friends. He'd seen the carriage.

"I have to return to France to protect my estates."

"Not with Napoleon on the march. I forbid it."

She stiffened at his fiat, noxious memory recalling similar orders from her husband. Putting down her pen, she turned to him, her expression cool. "You can't."

"Try me." The meetings today had been especially acrimonious and dilatory and his temper was badly frayed.

"Don't threaten me, Simon. You're in no position to forbid me anything."

"I'll *find* someone to protect your property."

She rose from her chair and faced him, resolve plain on her face. "I need to be there personally. My name means something in Lyon."

"You're not capable of defending yourself against Napoleon."

"I went through hell for that land," she bitterly retorted.

"If I could live through that, I can handle Napoleon. He's a friend of sorts."

"I see." His words were clipped. Stripping off his gloves, he tossed them down like a gauntlet. "Have you slept with him?"

"I don't answer to you."

"Yes or no, dammit."

"No." Drawing herself up in haughty rebuff, she said, curt and cold, "Satisfied?"

Satisfaction was not Simon's current state of mind. He ignored her question. He was furious enough to consider locking her in his bedroom and keeping her prisoner. But the moment quickly passed, and recognizing the futility of a direct attack, he substituted diplomacy for fiat. "Look, darling," he politely suggested, "let me talk to Talleyrand. Certainly he can put together a troop to protect your estates."

"Surely you're not that naïve. Talleyrand only protects himself."

"Then I'll find someone else. Jesus, Georgie, you could be killed."

"My life's been at risk a dozen times since the Revolution. I watched my mother and father dragged away by Fouché's dragoons. The only vestige of my family left me is my childhood home and I won't lose it."

"Surely your steward will protect your property."

"Against Napoleon or a mob? I can't expect that of him."

"And yet you can protect it."

"My family's lived near Lyon for centuries. There are those loyal to me. I'll be fine, darling," she said in a conciliatory tone. "I'll send you word of my safe arrival."

"I won't be here."

There was a finality in his voice that frightened her, although they'd both known that if war came, he'd leave. The last remnants of her anger drained away. "When do you go?"

"In the morning."

"It's starting all over again, isn't it?" A sudden chill ran down her spine. Her whole life had been lived in the midst of revolution or war.

"This shouldn't last long." What was he going to do without her? he wondered.

"You could die," she breathed, tears welling in her eyes.

She was in his arms a second later and they clung to each other with a quiet desperation. "How long do we have?" Georgie whispered.

"We leave at dawn."

It was over, she thought, an all too familiar sense of abandonment washing over her. "Thank you for the happiest days of my life," she murmured, wanting him to know how much he'd given her.

"You have to come with me. I'll find some way. We'll be married in Brussels." He wished there were some way to marry her now but it was impossible with the delegation already on the move.

She gazed up at him, anguish in her eyes. "I have to go to Lyon first."

"I can't change your mind?"

"Please, Simon. I've suffered for this land."

"The government is already preparing to flee Paris, the Faubourg St. Germain is almost empty. France is in chaos and yet you'd go?"

"I must."

The sudden silence was strained.

"I'll make you a bargain."

Anything, she wanted to say, if I can keep you, but she understood the limitations constraining their actions. "I'm listening," she softly said.

"Promise me to take a troop of guards with you; I'll find enough French soldiers to protect your properties. Once you've assured yourself your estates are defended, come to me in Brussels."

He wasn't ordering her or forbidding her; he recognized what she had to do. "I see why you're in demand at the bargaining table." There was pleasure in knowing she might see him again.

"You'll do it?"

She nodded.

He smiled for the first time since he'd seen her carriage in the drive. "Give me an hour to assemble a guard for you. I'll talk to Talleyrand. After that we'll have the rest of the evening to ourselves."

He didn't say it was the last night, but they both understood.

"Let me come with you." She didn't want to miss a moment with him.

"Be polite to Talleyrand," he enjoined.

"Must you see him? He's unscrupulous to the marrow."

"He knows how to get things done."

"Diplomacy—the art of the possible," she murmured with a faint moue.

"And of the quid pro quo. He needs me to see that he retains his position as minister."

Talleyrand was utterly charming. A polished courtier, intelligent, a devotee of beautiful women, he offered Georgie the full scope of his mannered grace. The troops were promptly guaranteed; they would be mounted and ready to ride at dawn. And while Simon discussed the details of the armaments in Belgium with the French minister, Emilie invited Georgie into her sitting room for a hasty cup of tea.

"You're a fool to ride into France," she chastised.

"I'll be protected and it won't be for long," Georgie replied. "Are you and Talleyrand traveling to Brussels too?"

"Not at the moment. The congress won't adjourn for two weeks yet. Do be careful, Georgie. Good God, royalists are fair game again in France."

"I'm neutral."

"You're braver than I, darling."

"You didn't lose as much as I in the Revolution. It makes one more selfish, perhaps, of what remains. Simon's off to war though," she softly added. "I'm more terrified of that."

"But you're following him to Brussels."

Georgie nodded. "Soon, I hope."

"I'll pray for you both," Emilie said, "although don't tell Talleyrand. He's the most unspiritual man alive."

Time sped by at lightning speed that night, until Simon finally covered the clock and left orders with his batman to call him at five.

"I've never been so unhappy," he murmured, stroking Georgie's hair. "I wish you could come with me."

"You know I can't, at least not yet."

He sighed. "That damned Napoleon is screwing up my life."

"Your love life," she lightly corrected, not wishing to fall into despondency when neither of them had choices.

"My *life*, darling," he said with gravity, "and if you weren't so impossible, I could have seen that we were married before this happened."

"The peace might be maintained—you don't know. And your family would disown you if you married so frivolously—"

"Damned poor excuses, darling," he interposed. "Peace is highly unlikely and my family can go to hell if they don't like what I do." But he understood her skittishness about marriage. Talleyrand had enlightened him concerning Georgie's late husband. The man deserved to be shot. Luckily he was dead, so that necessity no longer required his attention. "Brussels in a month will suit me for a marriage date," he genially declared. "I'll arrange the guest list," he added with a grin.

"Don't, darling—let's not talk of . . . you know . . ." she evasively murmured, "until the political situation is resolved. It's not that I don't love you—you know that, don't you?''

Her diffidence, the flickering apprehension in her eyes, made him want to dig up Régnier's grave and kill the bastard again. ''I know.'' He drew her closer, as if he could protect her from her memories. ''And *you* know I love you more than life itself.''

''Don't say that. Don't talk of dying or war or any of the awful possibilities. Please, Simon, I can hardly bear leaving you.''

''Then I'll say instead that I'll see you in Brussels in a month.''

She half turned in his arms to smile up at him. ''Thank you. I love you vastly.''

''How vastly?'' he whispered, rolling over her, balancing himself on his elbows, dipping his head to kiss her rosy mouth.

''So vastly that words are insufficient. The thought of you makes me smile a thousand times a day.''

''Only a thousand?'' he teased.

''When I've never thought of any man before.''

''I'm chastened and delighted,'' he whispered, stroking the silken flesh of her throat with a gentle fingertip. ''And so deeply in love . . .''

''Me too, always and always,'' she said with childlike candor. ''Vienna will be forever in my memory.''

''You'll like Yorkshire as well,'' he softly declared. ''We'll raise our children there—at least part of the time,'' he pleasantly added.

''You haven't asked me if I want children.'' Her voice was purposely playful, the poignancy of loss too close, too devastating.

''I don't have to. I saw you crying when your courses came a while ago. You want a child.''

She quirked a brow at him. ''Are you my father confessor now?''

''No, just observant. You look at every baby you see

with such longing, I was contemplating obliging you on more than one occasion this past month."

"Thank you, then, for honoring my wishes."

He grinned. "Last chance until you come to Brussels."

"Are you asking?" His dark eyes were only inches away, his powerful body poised over hers, temptation incarnate, the bold readiness of his erection brushing her thigh.

"Do you want me to?" Her hesitation, her inability to refuse, were answer enough, but he loved her too much to make her unhappy; he wished her to be as certain as he.

She nodded.

"Would you have my child and be my wife—in any order you prefer?" he softly queried.

She nodded again, incapable of articulating the state of her longing with their future so grim.

"You're sure?" he gently asked, her continued muteness disconcerting.

"I'm sure," she finally said, her eyes liquid with emotion. "Even though my life since childhood has only equipped me for uncertainty."

"Of one thing you can be certain. I'll always love you."

"Thank you." Her tears spilled over and in a hiccupy whisper she said, "Thank you, too, for showing me the wonder of love."

"Everlasting love." He kissed away the wetness on her cheeks. "With our children beside us, in Lyon or Yorkshire, in the Sandwich Isles for all I care, so long as we're together."

"How can you say that when we don't know—"

"We'll stop Napoleon," he confidently declared. "He can't last more than a few months. And then I'll take you to England and introduce you to those in my family I want you to meet. On second thought, perhaps just my sister," he said with a faint smile.

"You don't get along—"

"They don't get along with me," he bluntly said. "And

they are not the topic of conversation I care to discuss before leaving you. I prefer pleasant subjects, such as the date of your arrival in Brussels."

"Soon, soon," she murmured, reaching up to kiss him, wanting to forget everything but pleasure. "And when I see you again, we'll decide on our children's names."

"Then I'd better get to business," he roguishly drawled.

"Please do," she whispered.

"I can't think of a nicer gift for my leave-taking."

"Nor I."

"I should be gentle, I suppose, on this momentous occasion."

"Don't you dare."

He laughed. "So delectably wanton."

"I learned it all from you."

His smile flashed white. "I wish I could take credit, darling, but I think your hot little pussy has a mind of its own."

"Like now when it wants to feel you."

"Like that," he murmured, smiling, easing her legs farther apart, sliding between her thighs until his erection nudged her pulsing labia. "This will have to last us both," he whispered, a husky tremor in his voice as he slowly slid inside her. "For a month." He kissed the hollow at the base of her throat at the same moment his rigid length touched the mouth of her womb and they both felt an unbelievable desire in their bones and in their souls, the irrepressible abridgement of their time together reinventing feeling and response. And they made love to each other as though they were the last people on the face of the earth, as though they were about to be cast out into the wilderness.

She trembled and cried and clung to him and he whispered over and over again, his voice muffled against her hair, "Don't cry, don't cry, I love you." Their bodies melted into each other with each thrust and withdrawal, like a molten fusing, as if the forbidden mating were more sexually intense than casual lovemaking.

And when their orgasms broke and consciousness briefly disappeared, when he released his seed in her, for a mindless moment the coming war vanished from their thoughts, and fear and danger slipped away. They were only a man and a woman deeply in love.

"You're mine," he breathed when he'd recovered his powers of speech, a biblical sense of consummation seizing his mind as if he were Adam to her Eve and his mission was to populate the world.

Still unable to find sufficient breath to speak, Georgie gazed up from under languid lashes at the father of her child, the certainty so absolute, she basked in the new-felt bliss of motherhood. "He'll have dark hair like you," she murmured in a wisp of sound.

"Or she," he smilingly replied.

"How can I love you this much?"

"Because you're my life, because we found each other in this teeming, unsanctified world, and I'll always be with you."

"Thank you," she simply said, knowing her emptiness was forever gone.

"Thank you for drawing the high number," he murmured. A practical man at heart, he understood mystical forces had been at play as well the night they'd met.

"I won you, didn't I?" Her smile lit up the room.

"You won me heart, soul, and cavalry boots."

"And you'll come back to me."

"I'll never leave you," he whispered, "but I'll see you again in Brussels."

He made her forget her fear for the brief time they had left. He teased her and kissed her and made love to her with lighthearted abandon, and when his batman came at five, she was able to bid him good-bye with a smile.

Which was his intention.

He wanted to remember her smiling if he shouldn't return from the coming conflict. He didn't want his last memory of her to be one of her in tears.

When Georgie arrived at her estate, she found that Napoleon had only recently left Lyon. He'd been there long enough to issue a proclamation dissolving the two houses of Louis XVIII's parliament and promising to convene a constitutional assembly. But haste was required to reach Paris where he could count on the army forces, for his landing at Antibes had thrown the country into turmoil. Napoleon had had to resort to a disguise to safely pass through Provence; the province was in a state of near-rebellion at the news of his return. In the Vendée a general insurrection was stirring as opposition groups resisted his arrival. Not a single segment of the population could be counted on for loyalty.

The populace of Lyon was left in political disarray after his departure, conflicting interests trying to anticipate the final result of Napoleon's nervy gamble. Grateful for Simon's insistence on a guard troop, Georgie had the advantage of a secure position while reports of uprisings and discontent flew around her. She felt a degree of peace in the political tumult; her estate was a place of refuge for her. Within the walls of her château and gardens, Georgie could forget for a time that war might erupt again.

Immediately upon his arrival in Brussels, Simon began organizing the disembarking Anglo, Dutch, and German units. Only 10,000 British troops were initially in place. Ten weeks later the British forces had increased to 35,000—together with additional Hanoverian and Dutch–Belgian levies. Although most of the non-British troops were untrained recruits, Wellington had 107,000 combatants under his command. This army was spread along a front extending from Ghent to Mons. Their Prussian allies under Blücher, 116,000 strong, held the Meuse Valley from Charleroi to Liège. With this untried force under individual commands from several countries, the only troops Wellington could rely on were his British soldiers. In contrast, Napoleon led an army of seasoned soldiers, devoted to him, unalloyed by foreign elements.

And he desperately needed a victory to maintain his throne.

In the weeks since Georgie had returned to Lyon, political discussion wasn't exclusively of war. There were rumors as well that peace might be restored. Napoleon for a time had hoped the allies would allow him to retain his throne. When that hope died, the French National Guard was called up. Naval units and part of the constabulary were assigned to army service and several thousand working men from the Lyon and Paris regions were put under arms. When only half the National Guardsmen answered the call—several provinces ignored it altogether—conscription was required to bring the French army up to strength.

With conscription notices posted throughout France, Georgie's guard was required to leave her and any hope she might have nurtured for a peaceful resolution abruptly died. She'd stayed in Lyon, hoping for a diplomatic solution, protecting her properties during the unstable period following Napoleon's return. But there was no longer time to be concerned with the safety of her properties; whether she lost her estates during the coming war suddenly wasn't of consequence. If she didn't join Simon in Brussels soon, she might never see him again. She'd stayed in Lyon, hoping for peace, but hope could no longer hold back the deluge.

She had her carriage readied.

On June 14, when the French crossed the Belgian frontier and occupied Charleroi, post chaises were no longer allowed to pass the border posts. Unable to cross into Belgium, Georgie hired a local guide and horses to secretly take her to Brussels. Traveling little-used trails, they entered Belgium and after riding most of the day reached

Brussels on the afternoon of June 15. The city was jammed with troops, auxiliary military units, and thousands of English sightseers who had come to view the campaign as if it were a pageant for their entertainment.

Commencing her inquiry for Wellington's staff at the Hôtel d'Angleterre, she was told that many British officers were billeted at the Hôtel d'Aremberg. Moving through the congested streets with only the small satchel she'd taken on horseback, she arrived at the hotel, hot, tired, and covered with dust after days of travel.

Only to discover Simon was gone.

"Will he be back?" she nervously asked. Or if not, did they know someone who might be aware of the marquis's plans?

"But yes, mademoiselle," the clerk graciously replied. Her agitation was plain; he had seen many wives and lovers in similar straits that day. "Almost certainly the colonel will return, for his batman stayed behind." Since an officer rarely went on campaign without his valet, Georgie was encouraged. Arriving at Simon's rooms, however, she found Morris missing as well. Moving through his small quarters, she tried to find some clue to their whereabouts, some indication that either or both men would return. But the small apartment was almost bare of Simon's effects; only a minimum of personal articles were evident.

As she waited, twilight fell, shadows filled the rooms, and her apprehension grew. She'd arrived too late, she fearfully thought, pacing between the windows facing the street and the door. She should have left Lyon sooner. And while she tried to rationalize away Simon's absence with a thousand different excuses and possibilities, her anxieties rose.

What if she really couldn't find him?

Moving to the windows, she debated her options as she gazed down at a city teeming with soldiers. The street below was filled with marching troops, with munitions wagons, artillery caissons, all the signs of approaching combat glaringly in review. Was there any hope of finding him if he didn't return? Had he already left for the battlefield? If she left the hotel to search for him, was there any more than a remote chance she'd stumble on him in the crowds outside?

Why had she waited so long? she chided herself. Why hadn't she been more heedful of the rapidly changing political scene? Why had she been so willing to selfishly hope for peace in the quiet of her country home?

Turning away from the terrifying display of war readiness outside the windows, she sat down and tried to calmly assess the situation. But her mind refused to compose itself and she was up on her feet only moments later, pacing once again, increasingly frightened, disheartened. What if she never saw him again? What if Simon never knew?

She was near tears when the door opened and Simon's batman walked into the room. Greeting her with a smile, he immediately allayed her fears, even his tone blessedly serene. Simon had ridden to Mont St. Jean, but was expected to return in time for the Duchess of Richmond's ball that evening.

''Thank God,'' Georgie exclaimed and burst into tears.

Moving to comfort her, Morris offered her tea and discreet solace as he escorted her to a chair. ''The marquis should be back very soon, my lady. Any minute, I'd warrant. In the meantime, I'll brew up a nice cup of tea for you.''

''Thank you, Morris,'' Georgie murmured, brushing away her tears with her fingertips, half smiling at the English panacea for every ill. The thought of a hot cup of tea in the sultry heat was something only an Englishman would relish. ''And forgive my outburst, but I was terrified I'd missed the marquis.''

''Never you mind, my lady. Everything will be all right now that you're here. The marquis has missed you something terrible, my lady.''

Offering him a shaky smile, she took a steadying breath.

"Then I'm glad I came. I wasn't sure he'd have time to think of me with all his duties."

"He did that, he did," his valet firmly replied. "There wasn't a day went by, his lordship didn't talk of you."

A short time later, she recognized the rhythm of Simon's footsteps in the corridor outside, the familiar sound of his long-legged gait and she was halfway to the door, running, when he opened it.

He stood in the doorway for only the briefest second at the sight of her and then, smiling broadly, he caught her as she flung herself into his arms.

"Finally," he murmured, holding her tight.

"They'd closed the border." She looked up at him, her eyes bright with tears.

"I know. I'd given up hope of seeing you."

"I wrote."

"Two of your letters got through."

"Only two? Yours all came."

He had connections through Talleyrand, but he didn't mention that, only saying, "The post has been uncertain for weeks now. But you're here and that's all the matters."

"Despite the upheavals in Lyon, I couldn't wait any longer once the conscription notices went up."

"Napoleon's here already."

Fear flared in her eyes. "When do you have to go?"

"As soon as we're married." Grasping her around the waist, he pushed her slightly away and his gaze drifted slowly down her body, observing the subtle changes evident to his critical eye. "You should have have told me about the baby. I would have sent someone to fetch you."

"I couldn't come at first. I kept thinking the war would be averted. But when it was clear Napoleon was marching north, I came to tell you."

"I'm pleased, more than pleased . . . although I think I always knew."

"The divine seer," she teased.

"Something like that," he mildly replied, even though

he'd always considered himself an eminently practical man. Glancing away for a moment, he called for Morris, who had discreetly moved into the other room at Simon's approach. And when his batman appeared in the doorway, he said, "Find a priest to marry us and take a message to Wellington. I don't need his permission, but it's a courtesy."

"You're making me nervous," Georgie said as Morris left the room. "With this haste."

"I don't want to alarm you, darling, but I'm leaving within the hour."

"So soon?" she cried. "Morris said you were going to the duchess's ball tonight."

"Plans have changed. I have messages to deliver for Wellington."

"When will you be back?" Panic infused her voice.

"Tomorrow. Probably tomorrow." A battle had been fought the previous day at Quatre Bras with inconclusive results, but at least Wellington's troops had held their own. Southeast of Ligny, however, the Prussian army under Blücher, with a force stronger and larger than Wellington's, had met the right wing of Napoleon's army and had been defeated and forced to retire to the north. The allied forces were currently in retreat while reinforcements were being sent up to the new front selected by Wellington at a site called Waterloo. Simon, along with the other aides-decamp, was off tonight to bring written orders to Wellington's commanders in the field: to stand and give battle. "In the meantime, though," he went on, "directly we're married, I want you to go to safety in Antwerp. Morris will accompany you there."

"I don't want to. Let me wait for you here."

"Napoleon's too close to Brussels."

"And he might be victorious."

"No, he won't be," Simon firmly replied. "But I can't take the chance you might be hurt by artillery. All the women and children are being evacuated to Antwerp."

"What if I refuse? I've only just seen you and—"

"I'll be back soon—tomorrow, the next day at the latest." The battle would be over by nightfall tomorrow, he knew. Neither army could sustain a long engagement. Blücher was in retreat, both armies were fatigued after two days of long marches and fighting, and neither had fresh reserves that could be called in to turn the tide of battle. "Wait for me in Antwerp. Darling, please, I don't have time to argue."

She saw the gravity in his eyes, could see the lines of fatigue etched on his face, and understood that battlefield orders superseded her needs. "If you wish," she evasively replied.

"Thank you." He pulled her close. "I need to know you're safe while I'm gone, that our child is safe."

"I wish I'd come sooner, so we'd have some time . . ."

"You're here now; I'm content." His relief was profound but he didn't wish to alarm her. How close it had been, he thought—an hour later and he might never have known of his child, might never have had the chance to marry Georgie. "Come, darling, sit with me for a moment while I write a few orders for Morris." Leading her to a chair, he sat at the small mahogany desk, and with an occasional smile for her as he wrote, he specified the necessary changes in a new codicil to his will. To his new wife and unborn child, he left the entirety of his estates, titles, and fortune.

Morris returned with a priest and witnesses so promptly Simon wasn't completely finished with his letter to his sister introducing his new wife, explaining what he could of his sudden marriage. Ending his message abruptly, he sealed his correspondence, handed it to Morris, and rising, offered his hand to Georgie with a graceful bow. "Come, be my wife," he said, "and make me the happiest man in the world."

"Gladly," she murmured, smiling at him with tears in

her eyes. And in that moment all the misery in her past vanished.

Their marriage was swift, Simon's need to deliver Wellington's orders pressing, each minute of delay perhaps a matter of life or death, defeat or victory tomorrow. Once the brief ceremony was over, the necessary papers signed, the courtesies exchanged, Simon saw everyone out so he could have a few moments alone with Georgie before he left.

"I'll try not to cry." she said, watching him walk across the room toward her, his jingling cavalry spurs a potent reminder that he was off to war.

"I'll try too," he said with a half-smile. "It's not every day I leave my wife and unborn child." Reaching her, his arms closed around her and he gently drew her near, wanting to remember the feel and look of her, the taste and scent of her against his unknown future.

"You won't be gone for long." Blind hope glowed in her eyes.

"No, not for long." He prayed the fates were kind to him tomorrow, but he understood the risks. "Mind Morris now. He has whatever papers you need, funds, instructions for procuring an apartment in Antwerp. Rely on him."

She nodded, not wishing to openly lie. But she had no intention of leaving Brussels when she could be close to Simon if she stayed.

"Do you need anything now?"

"Your body next to mine," she softly said, smiling.

"Give me a few hours," he murmured, bending to brush a kiss across her mouth, "and you'll have your wish."

"We'll be waiting."

"I like the sound of that. We." His dark brows rose in winsome delight. "Think of some names while I'm gone."

"When you come back." Her words were an invocation of hope.

"When I come back," he softly agreed. His kiss this time was one of farewell, wistful with longing. And when his mouth lifted from hers, he looked at her for a taut, anguished moment, heart-stricken. "Remember me," he whispered, and then abruptly turning, he strode away.

"Every memory, every touch, every kiss," she whispered, watching him cross the room.

He didn't look back; the door shut with a soft click.

Morris found her standing in the center of the room, unmoving, as though the shock of Simon's departure had rendered her motionless. He approached her with diffidence, not sure she wasn't in the grip of hysteria. "We must leave, my lady," he quietly said, coming within a few feet of her.

Her gaze abruptly altered, came alive. "I'm not going anywhere, Morris. Kindly have my satchel unpacked."

"The marquis wishes you to leave for Antwerp, my lady." He spoke with caution.

"The marquis is gone. You go to Antwerp, Morris, if you wish. I'm staying in Brussels until my husband returns."

"You're sure, my lady? The marquis was quite—"

Her gaze, sharp as a knife blade, arrested him in midsentence. "Do I look unsure?"

"No, my lady," he replied with deference, suddenly cognizant that the new marchioness was as strong-willed as her husband.

"Would you like some supper brought up?"

"Thank you, I would. And if you'd locate the Comte de Dreux-Brèze for me and tell him I'm in the city, awaiting his call, I'd appreciate it."

A woman of dispatch, Morris thought, as he left to fulfill his assignments. The comte was an influential émigré, well connected with the military commanders. He'd have a thorough grasp of the campaign.

While the Comte de Dreux-Brèze was apprising Georgie of the campaign to date, the general positions of both armies, and the possible strategies in place for the coming battle,

Simon was riding hard through the forest of Soignes on the road to Waterloo. While the movement orders he was carrying were to stand and fight the next day, Wellington still hadn't conclusively decided whether to do battle or retreat. The duke didn't feel strong enough to stop Napoleon on the road to Brussels unless he could count on Prussian help. The Prussian army at Ligny had been badly mauled, but unless Wellington could count on the assistance of one Prussian corps, he was planning on abandoning Brussels and retreating beyond the Scheldt.

Not until two in the morning—almost the hour when a retreat had to be ordered—did a Prussian aide come riding in with Blücher's answer. Blücher himself, although wounded, would lead his corps and come to Wellington's aid. On that assurance Wellington's decision was made.

His movement orders stood.

On the morning of June 18 on a ridge two and a half miles south of Waterloo, overlooking a series of small valleys, the allied forces formed their battle line. The troops stood literally shoulder to shoulder—twenty-one inches was the standard interval for infantry, thirty-six inches for cavalry—waiting for the order to advance.

By eleven o'clock in the morning, 140,000 men—73,000 of Napoleon's and 67,000 of Wellington's—waited for Napoleon's long-delayed orders. At a respectful distance, his staff awaited his commands. One of them, surveying him, thought he was in a stupor.

Uncertain of his allied forces' steadiness and nerve, Wellington awaited Napoleon's pleasure. He would defend, not attack.

Finally toward noon, Napoleon gave an order, not for an attack in strength on the British line, but for an opening diversion against the outpost in the Château de Hougoumont.

On the far left of the French line, the artillery opened fire. British artillery on the ridge above Hougoumont began to reply and the troops that would decide the fate of Europe were soon engaged.

Six hours of fierce, bloody, hand-to-hand fighting later, both armies were exhausted and the center of Wellington's line couldn't possibly hold against another French advance. When the duke himself rode into the breach at the head of the Brunswickers, his officers all gave him the same report: their forces were so cut up after the long day of battle, they couldn't hold their positions. Wellington had nothing to offer them—no reinforcements, no retreat, no alternative but to stand where they were till they died.

Everyone waited for the drumbeats of the pas de charge that would signal a new French attack—one they wouldn't be able to withstand.

"Night or the Prussians must come," the duke was heard to say. Blücher had still not arrived.

In Brussels, the heavy and incessant firing was heard all day that Sunday, shaking the doors and windows, encouraging those English who hadn't yet left for Antwerp to depart. Georgie stood at the windows facing the street most of the day, watching the wounded stream into the city, seeing numerous allied units passing down the thoroughfare, the returning soldiers spreading the rumor that Wellington's entire army was in retreat.

Morris pleaded with her to leave for Antwerp, but she refused. Having followed the marquis throughout the Peninsular Campaign, Morris had no personal fears for safety. But he didn't relish the marquis's wrath if he discovered his wife had been in jeopardy. "Consider Lord Mar's wishes," he cajoled.

"Only when he's safe again. Don't worry, Morris, I'll see that his lordship understands my decision was made against your strong protests."

Resigned against further argument, Simon's valet saw that they had all the latest information coming back from the battlefield. Moving from headquarters to barracks, from

English to Dutch to Prussian command posts, he gathered every tidbit of rumor and gossip that filtered back into the city. And everywhere he went, he asked for news of the marquis.

Late in the afternoon, the rumors of retreat became more prevalent. Crowds of wounded, deserters, and prisoners were pouring into the city. They all said Wellington was in full retreat and no one was able to contradict the reports.

To those at the center of the allied line near La Haye Sainte, it was plain the ultimate crisis had come. It was seven o'clock, and if the French advanced, Wellington's army was lost.

France's General Ney also knew the moment for the final blow had come—the fire of Wellington's army was weakening—but he had nothing left with which to deliver the blow. His surviving troops were exhausted, in shock, and Napoleon wouldn't release the reserve units of his Imperial Guard.

At half past seven, the sun was low behind the woods of Hougoumont, shining crimson through the smoke of battle. Napoleon had finally ordered five battalions of the Garde Impériale into battle with himself in the lead. But in that same half hour, a Prussian corps under von Zieten had reinforced the worst gaps in Wellington's center.

At seven o'clock, the Garde could have marched straight through the British lines.

At half past seven, the issue was once again in balance.

Napoleon didn't ride in front of his Garde very far. He left them at the bottom of the valley and Ney led the charge, thousands of Frenchmen advancing into the British guns. The British had had an hour to rest, reinforcements had strengthened their line, and they met the French advance with steady nerves, with cannon shot and musket ball, with round shot and grapeshot, their fierce defense tearing great holes in the close-packed columns of Napoleon's troops. Not one soldier in the front ranks of the advancing French survived. A second volley followed, a third and fourth, and in only minutes the smoke of gunpowder filled the air and the ground was littered with dead and desperately wounded.

Under the annihilating defense, the French broke and ran.

"The Garde is retreating." The cry spread almost instantly and only minutes after the rout of the Garde began, Wellington snapped his telescope shut, took off his hat, and waved it.

Everyone who could see him understood.

Wellington's aides-de-camp still fit for action left with orders to his field commanders: pursue the retreating French. Simon delivered the new commands to von Zieten's unit, and once the Prussian general had read the orders, he watched as Wellington's young aide-de-camp said, "Sorry, sir," and slowly crumpled to the ground. The marquis was unconscious before he landed on the slate flags at the doorway to von Zieten's headquarters.

Simon had been wounded in the hip early that morning, but fearing he'd be invalided out, hadn't mentioned it to anyone. Finally succumbing to loss of blood and fatigue, he was carried unconscious to a nearby cottage and left in the care of a Prussian sergeant. Von Zieten was gone by midnight, his troops and headquarters miles east, and Simon was left behind as the victorious allied army pursued the retreating French.

By midnight, when the marquis hadn't returned, the duke and his fellow officers gave him up for dead.

The first casualty list, showing only senior officers, reached Brussels the morning after the battle. Simon was listed as missing in action in the duke's dispatch. Morris debated how best to break the news to the marchioness, but she would have to be told, for he was leaving to search for Simon's body.

Her face turned ashen at the news, but almost immediately she squared her shoulders and took a steadying breath. "I'm going with you."

"The marquis would horsewhip me. A battlefield's no place for a lady."

"Then I'll go myself." Twin spots of color flared on her cheeks. "Do you understand? I won't wait here, not knowing." Her voice trembled slightly for a moment, but she immediately brought it under control. "Now you can find me a mount or I'll find my own." Without waiting for an answer, she turned and walked into the bedroom to put on her riding boots.

"Let me go round to headquarters one more time to see if any new reports have come in."

She spun around in the doorway to the bedroom. "If you're not back in an hour, I'll leave without you."

Her tone of voice, her expression, were unequivocal. He knew she meant what she said.

When he returned a brief half hour later, he had no new information, but he'd spoken to two officers who'd seen Simon before he left on his last mission for the duke. "The horses are ready, my lady. And two of the marquis's fellow officers said they last saw him at La Haye Sainte. He was on his way to Genappe."

During the morning, almost all of Wellington's army had moved away to the south, leaving only the dead and wounded on the battlefield, the carnage, cries of the dying, the gruesome smells of death. With daylight, the peasants had begun to congregate and were busily looting the dead, often killing the wounded before stripping them, some already staggering under enormous loads of clothes, firearms, swords, and bundles of medals and decorations. Sightseers were gathering too, many holding perfumed handkerchiefs to their noses and delicately stepping over the bodies of the dead as they viewed the battlefield.

The road was jammed with wounded men in carts, each one of which they searched in hopes of finding Simon. Morris gave away all their water within a mile of Brussels, tending to the wounded tormented by thirst. After the canteens were replenished at a churchyard, within minutes they were empty again. Their journey to Waterloo was slow and agonizing; they passed so many dead and dying, men and horses lying in piles and masses in the fields. It was a charnel house, a vision of hell, and with tears of despair streaming down her cheeks, Georgie wondered how they'd ever find Simon in the appalling carnage.

They'd traveled all day, their passage torturously slow because of the clogged roads, and it was near evening when they arrived at Genappe, the summer twilight almost too beautiful for the scene of desolation. In every hamlet and cottage, every farmhouse and bivouac since leaving Brussels, they'd inquired whether an English officer of Simon's description had been seen yesterday. And so fruitless had been their search, they sat their mounts dumbfounded for a moment when the wounded soldier seated on the ground outside the village inn replied affirmatively to their question. "The colonel fell right before me eyes, collapsed in a heap right over there." He pointed the rough branch he was using as a crutch at the doorway to the inn.

Morris found his voice first. "Where was he taken?"

"They carried him away."

"I don't wish to add to your suffering, my lady, but you should prepare yourself for the worst," Morris quietly said. "His lordship could have been taken anywhere. We don't know how badly he was wounded. And no one has medicines or care . . ."

"I know." She'd seen so much human torment and agony today, it was impossible to have much hope. "If we could find his body at least . . . so he could be taken home . . ." She couldn't speak for a moment, her tears spilling over. But she brushed away her tears a second later, reminding herself that she had not endured what the soldiers had yesterday, what Simon had. Her voice when she spoke was resolute. "We'll offer a reward for information. Tell the innkeeper. And hurry, Morris. It will soon be dark."

Some peasant could have killed and robbed the marquis

last night, his body already buried, Morris thought. But the marchioness was right. Another night would only add to the difficulty of finding his remains. If any information were available, a liberal reward would bring it to them quickly.

Georgie didn't dismount, but sat her horse while Morris relayed the message to the innkeeper. Time was precious with the sun setting, but she felt mildly heartened—even knowing what the brutal outcome might be—as though she were finally close to Simon.

"A wounded man was taken outside the village. It could be Simon," Morris briskly said, as he exited the inn, a peasant at his heels. "This man will lead the way."

Georgie's heart began racing as though she'd run a dozen miles.

"Don't get your hopes up, my lady," Morris cautioned as he mounted. "All he knows is that the officer is English."

"Is he alive? Don't spare me. I want to know."

"He was alive last night. But the man's been out looting all day."

"Please, God," Georgie whispered, her pulse rate jumping, "please let it be Simon."

"I've sent for the local doctor. For ten thousand francs he might leave his overcrowded infirmary for an hour."

"Offer him more. I want him with us."

Morris shouted briefly to the innkeeper as they rode away. "He should be on our heels," he said.

"Do you think it's Simon?" Every hope, every dream, every impossible wish, trembled in her words.

"If it is the marquis, he'll be alive, my lady. There's not shot nor enemy that can take him down," Morris proudly said. "He fought through the worst of the Peninsula War and if that hell couldn't kill him, this won't."

"Thank you, Morris." She was grateful for his reassurance, his words inspiring her with renewed hope after the awful scenes they'd been witness to today. "The marquis is fortunate to have you to care for him."

"My family's been valet to a dozen Lord Mars, my lady. We'll find him, we will." But the question was, In what state?

The hovel they were brought to inspired a new dread when they viewed it; the shelter was rough, dirty, hardly more than a hut. But Georgie called out his name as she dismounted.

The blissful sound of Simon's voice echoed back in reply. It lacked its usual strength, but it was surely his, and as Georgie ran toward the thatched shelter, she cried out his name, half laughing, half crying, dizzy with thanksgiving and relief.

She stood for a moment in the doorway, the interior so dark, she couldn't see.

"You look wonderful," Simon whispered, his voice coming from the far wall.

Offering up prayers of thanks, knowing she would forever believe in miracles, she ran to him and knelt beside the pallet of straw where he lay. Taking his face gently between her hands, she tenderly kissed him.

"I'll be fine now," he whispered, a teasing note in the raspy tone.

"Do you need water, sir?" Morris inquired, kneeling down to hand him his opened canteen, taking note of the loaded pistol beside him.

"It would be most welcome." He hadn't had water since morning. Taking the canteen from Morris, Simon raised it to his mouth with a shaking hand.

"You need a doctor," Georgie fearfully said, his weakness terrifying her.

"A Prussian guarded me last night, but he left this morning," Simon murmured, his fingers easing open as Morris took the canteen from him, and holding it to his mouth, offered him another drink. After swallowing, Simon shut his eyes as though his strength were depleted, and Georgie looked at Morris in distress.

''We're going to move you, sir,'' Morris declared, ''to the inn in the village.''

''Musket ball in my hip,'' Simon whispered, his eyes fluttering open long enough to send Morris a silent message. ''Has to come out . . .''

''Yes, sir.''

''No doctors . . .'' His voice trailed away in a wisp of sound.

''Yes, sir, I understand, sir.''

''You can't!'' Georgie exclaimed, but after a hard warning look from Morris, she lapsed into silence.

Simon fainted when he was lifted into a farm cart brought by the doctor. Once he was settled into a clean bed at the inn, Morris allowed the doctor to examine him. The wound was ragged and inflamed and when the doctor said, ''Lord Mar should be bled to release the bad toxins,'' Simon shook his head.

Morris thanked the doctor, paid him, and escorted him from the room.

''I've bled as much as I can afford to in the last two days,'' Simon said with a faint smile, feeling slightly stronger after some broth and scrambled eggs. ''I'll expect you to operate with a minimum of blood loss, Morris.''

''Yes, sir, I'll do my best, sir. Brandy or laudanum, sir?''

''Brandy. And I don't expect you to watch, darling. This is beyond the bounds of wifely duties.''

She was so jubilant he was alive, there were no duties outside her wifely purview. ''I'm perfectly willing to serve as assistant if Morris needs me.''

''Then I'm in the best of hands. Let's get this damned thing over with.''

The marquis swallowed half a glass of brandy and nodded his head to Morris.

Georgie turned white at the first incision of Morris's

scalpel and immediately sat down before she fainted. During the operation, Simon neither moved nor complained and when the musket ball was finally removed in pieces, the wound washed in brandy, and the incision sewn up, he thanked Morris as though he'd done some normal duty for him. But he fell into a restless sleep almost immediately and when he woke later that night, he asked Georgie to lie down beside him.

Immediately apprehensive, wondering if he'd taken a turn for the worse, she cautiously moved into the bed beside him. ''Now I can sleep,'' he whispered, touching her cheek with the back of his hand. ''Don't leave me.''

Don't leave *me*, she thought, frightened afresh by the touch of melancholy in his voice. Turning on her side, she lay awake all night, watching him: his breathing, the rise and fall of his chest, the color of his face and of his hands lying atop the covers, the depleted strength and great beauty of the man she loved. And if prayers would help, she prayed enough to help every soldier in the armies that had fought at Waterloo. But her special prayers were for one man in particular because she didn't know if she could live without him.

When morning came, Simon opened his eyes and, seeing her beside him, smiled as he had in the past, with joy and enticing warmth, with love. She felt as though her world had turned sunny and cloudless.

But his recuperation was slow: he'd lost a great deal of blood during the long day of battle and after. His strength was at low ebb for the first few days. Georgie sat with him, hid her fears when he seemed exhausted, never left him, hardly slept for five nights. When he wished to talk, she obliged, and when he didn't, she simply held his hand. He seemed stronger by the end of the week and even Morris's serious air lightened.

''I think we're free of infection now, my lady,'' he quietly said one morning as they arranged Simon's breakfast tray in the small adjacent parlor.

She softly exhaled, overcome with relief. "How wonderful. How very wonderful," she repeated, her smile dazzling.

"His lordship should be able to travel in perhaps another week."

"However long it takes, Morris. We mustn't rush his recovery. If we stay here a month it matters not at all, so long as my husband recovers his health."

But Simon had other plans, becoming weary of the enervating role of invalid. "Find us a carriage," he ordered the next day. "I wish to return to Brussels."

The journey passed in short stages, with frequent stops to ease Simon's discomfort, because the roads were in such disrepair after the passage of two armies.

On arriving in Brussels, they learned Napoleon had abdicated and the allied armies were marching on Paris.

"But you're staying here," Georgie ordered, when she saw Simon's eyes light up with interest.

He acquiesced, understanding the war was essentially over; the politicians would take charge now. With the tedious disputes of Vienna still fresh in his memory, his home in Yorkshire inspired a new and powerful attraction. "Would you mind repairing to Yorkshire for a month or so until France is once more free of marching armies?"

"If you think your family wouldn't mind."

"What does my family have to do with anything?"

"Well, then." She smiled. "Yorkshire sounds very lovely."

"Do you wish the baby to be born in Lyon?"

"I do, if the country is at peace. Our baby's birth would be a renewal of sorts for my family."

"We'll wait on events in Yorkshire and go south if possible."

"You're very accommodating."

"It gives me pleasure to accommodate you."

She recognized his tone. "Don't even think it. You're not fully recuperated yet."

"Let me be the judge of that," he pleasantly returned.

She gazed at him for a conditional moment. "I'm not sure you're prudent enough to judge such issues."

"If I'd been prudent, I'd never have met you."

"Nor I you."

"You see, then," he murmured, smiling. "There are merits in imprudence."

"And you should know."

"I've no complaints so far." His dark brows rose faintly in invitation. "Indulge me, darling. It's been a very long time."

"I know." She could already feel the enchanting warmth beginning to pulse inside her. "But, darling—really . . . are you strong enough?"

"If I faint, wake me with a kiss."

But he didn't faint. In fact, the marquis was deliciously healthy, although Georgie was near to fainting before long, from rapture and lust, from the intoxicating delirium of love.

When after a lengthy time, the marchioness was sated at last, the marquis rolled away, and sprawling on his back, turned to his wife. "You might want to look under your pillows."

Her lashes languidly rose, otherwise nothing moved on her supine form. "Later," she whispered.

"You'll like it."

"As much as I do you?" she murmured, turning her head to smile at him.

He grinned. "No, but you'll like it anyway."

With a muffled groan—physical exertion at the moment requiring energy she didn't have—she rolled over, slid her hand under the mass of pillows, and pulled out a slim green leather box. "You shouldn't have," she whispered.

He only smiled at the familiar female response.

"Simon!" she exclaimed a moment later, the opened box revealing a magnificent diamond necklace and earrings. "They're breathtaking."

"I promised you them in Vienna . . . I feel as though *I* won your wager."

"We both won."

"All three of us did," Simon added, reaching out to stroke the small rise in her tummy. "I'm the luckiest of men."

"Yes," she softly said, moving to lie beside him, thinking of all the random events that had brought them together, of the good fortune and guardian angels that had followed him that day at Waterloo. "Fate has been kind to us. We're going home."

"Now if fate would just take care of my loathsome relatives," he said with a grin.

"Would you like me to protect you?" Georgie facetiously inquired. "Morris, I think, will attest to my ruthlessness."

"Ah, a savior," Simon replied, amusement in his tone.

"You may feel secure, my lord, from this moment on," Georgie sportively pronounced.

He did, but not from fear, assured instead of a love he'd never suspected existed in this world. And for that he silently thanked whatever Gypsy gods or fate or mystical beings who might have had a hand in his good fortune. "Thank you, my darling Georgie," he playfully murmured. "To be under a lady's protection raises fascinating possibilities. Will you do everything for me?" he cheekily queried.

"Such insolence, Mar. You offend me." But she was smiling.

"How exactly would you like to be offended next, I wonder?" he whispered.

"Surprise me."

He smiled. Such largesse was his specialty. "First," he softly said, "we should put your new necklace and earrings on . . ."

Winner Take All

Adrianne Lee

To Larry, my own real life bad boy.

Special Thanks to:

Mary Shultz, aka Leandra Logan; Karen Solem of Writers House; Julie Morrison, The Missoulian; Sherrie Holmes; Ron Ring; Anne Martin, Kelly McKillip, and Gayle Webster.

Chapter One

Women liked Mitch Bohannah.

Mitch couldn't deny the phenomenon. In fact, he thanked God every day for it. He just didn't understand it. He wouldn't stop traffic with his good looks, not like Charlie. On the other hand, he wasn't coyote-ugly either. If pressed, he'd describe his face as more interesting than handsome. His strong features suggested a hint of Shoshone heritage, his black hair was a dead giveaway, but his Irish green eyes only confused matters.

His body wasn't anything special either. But he wasn't complaining. He was tall and lean, with enough muscle to perform whatever physical task presented itself at any given moment—from breaking a wild colt to pleasing a frisky lover.

Grinning at the thought, Mitch locked his car and strode up the walk to his office building in downtown Missoula, his boot heels clicking on the concrete. Now, his business partner was another matter. He'd have thought women would fall all over a man like Charlie—who belonged on a Calvin Klein billboard overlooking Times Square, who knew which wine went with which meat, who loved opera and ballet, or pretended to, and who never forgot an anniversary or birthday.

Mitch felt more at home on a horse than in his Lexus,

preferred Mindy McCready to Mozart, swilled beer with his burgers, and owned only one dress suit.

So what was the attraction? He didn't know. Maybe he never would. Or maybe women liked him because Mitch liked every damned woman he met.

He grinned recalling how much he'd liked the woman whose bed he'd just left.

He pushed through the double doors of B and B Enterprises and strode up to Wanda Crawford's desk. "Good morning, you sweet ray of sunshine."

Wanda, their receptionist and executive secretary, had skin the soft brown of sueded boots, and wore her hair in cornrow braids. The day she'd walked through their door seeking employment five years ago, Charlie and he had been taken aback by her sassy attitude and impressed by her self-confident manner. She'd been all of nineteen, and hiring her had been the smartest thing they'd ever done.

She glanced up from her computer and smiled at him with a row of even white teeth. "Thank you for the roses, Mitch. They're beautiful."

"Not as beautiful as you."

"But just as expensive," she sassed.

Worth every penny, he thought, from the joy in her big brown eyes. "They smell almost as good as you too."

"I'm gonna kill that son of a bitch!" The expletive came from the first office down the hall. Charlie's office.

Mitch made a face at Wanda and headed to see what the problem was. He peered around the doorway and cocked his head at his brother-in-law. "What s.o.b. would that be, Charlie?"

Charlie Barker's model-perfect face was an ugly shade of red that made his indigo eyes appear bloodshot. His wheat-colored hair stood on end as though he'd been jamming his hands through it. Mitch could almost see the steam coming out of his ears. He pointed a finger at Mitch. "You horny, worthless bastard! Why can't you think before unzipping your pants?"

"Hey, there's a lady out there. Watch your mouth." Mitch shut the door. Now he remembered why women didn't fall all over Charlie. He had the temperament of a mama grizzly. "What's got your cage rattled?"

"You. Where've you been all night?" There was a sudden calmness to his voice Mitch didn't like.

He lifted his brows and shook his head. "You know I never kiss and tell."

Charlie grinned without amusement, managing to look as if he'd swallowed something foul-tasting. "Your 'cohort' of the evening had no such qualms. She rushed right home and told her daddy."

Mitch's pulse kicked a beat higher. "JD called you?"

"Just got off the phone with him."

"From the look on your face, I don't suppose he was too happy." Mitch smirked, then shrugged. "But, hey, Sissy is over twenty-one."

"Tell that to JD. Far as he's concerned you raped his little girl."

"Raped?" Mitch's hackles rose. "Not only did Sissy participate, she reveled—"

"Spare me the details, and your justifications, Mitch. They won't bring back our biggest account."

Something dark and uneasy clawed Mitch's gut. "JD pulled his account?"

"Yep."

"Hell," Mitch swore. He reached for the phone. "I'll call and explain and—"

Charlie punched down the disconnect button. "JD doesn't want to hear from you. He wants your hide hanging on his office wall. Your balls served with gravy for his supper."

Mitch shook his head. "Aw, he's overreacting. Once I explain—"

"I might as well be talking to the wind." Charlie rose to his feet and planted his palms on his desk. "We've lost our biggest client."

There was no reasoning with Charlie when he was in this kind of mood. The best thing to do was apologize and let him cool down. Later, Mitch decided, would be time enough to soothe ruffled feathers, Charlie's and JD's. "Look, Charlie, I'm really sorry."

"Sorry doesn't cut it this time, pal. You and I are done. Finished. Either you buy me out or I'll buy you out."

A first wave of shock crashed through the shield of denial Mitch had held between his partner and himself. Charlie was serious, dead serious. "Ah, come on. This advertising business is the biggest little boomer to hit Montana in years. Since last year our client list has tripled. Our success is rising, not falling."

"*Was rising. Was*, pal. But your sex addiction is zapping our retro burn. We're falling like a meteor."

"Sex addiction?" Mitch laughed derisively; every inch of his skin burned with the insult. "I am *not* addicted to sex."

Charlie leveled his chilly eyes at Mitch. "You're so hooked you need help. Professional help. Aren't you worried about contracting something deadly?"

"I always use protection. And I'm clean. You want to see my latest lab report?" Fury licked through Mitch.

Charlie shook his head in disgust.

Mitch bit down the urge to hit something, preferably Charlie's pretty face. He couldn't believe this. Sure he loved women, but that didn't equate to a sex addiction. He didn't have to have sex on a daily basis. Just because he was lucky enough to have it that way didn't mean he *had* to.

His temper hitched higher. This conversation was nuts. Looney Tunes. "I resent your accusations, Charlie. If it weren't for Kimberlie, I'd put a dent or two in those pearly whites of yours."

"Kimmie happens to agree with me."

He might have slapped Mitch. Mitch scowled, but he supposed his sister would agree with Charlie; she thought the sun rose and set on her husband. What she saw beyond his looks was more than Mitch could fathom at the moment. But then, he'd spent the last hour ruminating about what made women like men and hadn't drawn a single, solid conclusion.

He pressed his palms to Charlie's desk. "Not that it's any of your business, but I could go cold turkey—stop sex completely for two months or more—without blinking."

"Hah!" Charlie's insulting, disbelieving chuckle grated Mitch's nerve endings.

Mitch bunched his muscles and leaned even closer to his partner. "Wanna bet?"

Charlie straightened, a thoughtful look on his face. "As a matter of fact I will bet you."

Mitch hadn't expected Charlie to take him up on this. At least not so quickly. But he'd be damned if he'd back down. "Good."

Again, Charlie chuckled. "You've lost before we've begun."

"Like hell. I'm so sure of winning, I'll bet my share of this business."

"What?"

The startled look on Charlie's face sent a spear of warm satisfaction through Mitch. "You heard me. If I lose, I walk away. You won't owe me a penny."

Charlie went still.

"If I win, you walk away." Mitch extended his hand for the shake. "Same deal."

Charlie was suddenly reluctant. "You'll never do it."

"What's the matter, *pal*? Afraid to put your money where your mouth is?"

Charlie's neck reddened. He didn't like being bested. He slapped his hand into Mitch's. "You're on. But I want Wanda in here. We're putting this in writing. You're not weaseling out of this bet."

* * *

Sex. All of her life that word had made Carroll Sydney blush. But no longer. She was through wondering about it, fantasizing about it, daydreaming about it. Armed with newly acquired knowledge—from such diverse sources as the *Kama Sutra* and her female coworkers—she was about to experience it.

The thought brought heat burning from her toes to her naturally strawberry-blond roots. Okay, so she was still a bit anxious. Given the craziness of this plan, who wouldn't be? But she'd always made up her mind quickly on most subjects. She just decided what she wanted, then went for it. As she was doing now.

As long as she had a plan, she could go forward. She was comfortable with plans. Hadn't her whole life been one big plan? Every day spent planning her future, her present consumed on the future, her past filled with the future?

And now she had no future beyond the next three months.

As she saw it, she had three choices: a) collapse in a puddle of self-pity, b) check herself into the nearest hospital and suffer being poked and prodded by nurses and doctors and visited and wept over by distraught relatives and friends, or c) cram as much living as she could manage into whatever time remained for as long as her stamina allowed.

The decision had been easier than the transformation.

She glanced at herself in the dressing-room mirror. The dark smudges under her eyes were hidden by the new makeup. In fact, she looked much better than she had the past few weeks. Even felt a little less tired.

But would she get used to her wildly curling hair flowing free down her back, loosened from its usual French braid? Or the short, short length of her skirt? She glanced at her dearest friend, Kelly-Anne Webster, reflected in the mirror. "Are you sure this isn't a bit over the top? I want to look sexy, not like a hooker."

Kelly-Anne tilted her pert face to one side and smiled, a devilish glint dancing in her soft brown eyes. "Well, that outfit would likely offend the sensibilities of most of our patrons at the library."

"Not to mention Quinn." Their boss. Carroll grinned. "But considering I won't be returning to work, what does his opinion matter?"

Kelly-Anne's mirth fled from her eyes and she glanced away, obviously gathering back her sorrow. Carroll wanted to reassure her, tell her not to be sad, but how could she? Nothing she said would ease what was to be. And they both knew it.

But she hadn't time for self-pity. "So, do you think I'll be irresistible to Mitch Bohannah and friends?"

Kelly-Anne glanced back at her. A wobbly breath left her slightly parted lips, but the smart-aleck glint Carroll loved about her friend filled her brown eyes. "I can't speak for Bohannah personally, or the others for that matter—not that I wouldn't like to—but if reputation is anything in this town, you've got the three best, er, ah, candidates for your purposes. You're going to knock their socks off, girlfriend. They'll be all over you like nuts on hot fudge sundaes."

The laughter that filled the dressing room sang of conspiratorial mirth.

Four hours later, the sound echoed in Carroll's mind as she drove along the shoreline of Flat Head Lake toward Kalispell. Her grapevine connections informed her that Mitch Bohannah was currently at his family's lakeside ranch. On leave from his advertising firm. Hopefully, he was alone. Or all would be for naught.

She contemplated what she was about to do, and bit down another annoying flush of embarrassment. More than anything, she wanted to give the appearance of sophistication. Turning bright pink at the thought of sex conveyed anything but savoir faire. The men on her list were masters of the art, used to women of the world, women of experience. Not naïve blush-puppies who'd learned the finer points of sex from gossipy gal pals and books.

She blew out a circumspect breath. On the upside, if

Mitch Bohannah lived up to his reputation, maybe he wouldn't notice her complete lack of finesse . . . and technique. In fact, maybe, just maybe, he'd teach her a few things, and by the time she moved on to Jimmy Jack Palmetto, the second Romeo on her list, she would be less of a blusher and more of a heart crusher.

Grinning at the possibilities facing her, she hit the accelerator and passed a slow-moving truck and horse trailer. At first, she'd been annoyed at the thought of driving all this way, but Northwestern Montana was a glorious vista of rolling countryside, rocky peaks, and endless blue sky.

She'd been so focused on the future most of her twenty-six years, she'd taken little notice of the natural beauty that surrounded her. This trip had given her the chance to enjoy her majestic state, to breathe in the delicious air, and really listen to the favorite CDs she'd brought along.

It felt like an adventure. Her first. And what a first. It wasn't every day a woman offered her virginity to a man she'd never met. Odd, that the prospect didn't immobilize her.

Carroll supposed nothing would do that again. Last month, she'd faced the worst thing life could offer. And it hadn't destroyed her . . . yet.

The top was down on her brand-new Mustang convertible and the hot August sun flowed over her. The heat should have warmed her through and through. It didn't. Tiredness and being constantly chilled were the only signs of her illness that she had thus encountered. As annoying as they were, they weren't debilitating. Nor would she allow them to slow her down.

She turned off the main highway and onto the last leg of her journey. In her rearview mirror, Flat Head Lake diminished to a bright spot of blue. The paved roadway wound through rolling farmlands to her left, and hilltop homesteads to her right, past a small grocery store that also served as post office and filling station.

Three miles later, the pavement ended abruptly at a cattle guard. Ahead the road was narrow, graveled, and meandered through a forest of tamarack and Douglas fir. She lifted a hand from the steering wheel and waved in farewell. "Good-bye, old uptight Carroll. Hello, brave new me."

She pressed the accelerator with confidence and determination. The giant trees blocked the sun and she was glad she'd worn the cardigan over the low-cut tank top. The road climbed and twisted through the redolent fir, on and on, then she rounded a bend and the road suddenly widened, the woods falling away like parting curtains. Before her lay rolling fields of fenced pastureland that dipped downward to a huge expanse of blue lake as wide and brilliant as the sky, rimmed with jagged mountains.

Her breath caught at the beauty. She stopped the convertible before a set of peeled log arches whose rough-hewn sign proclaimed she'd arrived at the Diamond B, the Bohannah family's secluded lake ranch.

It was the most romantic setting she'd ever seen. Embracing that thought, she stepped on the gas and pulled onto the dirt lane. The old Carroll would have turned around and headed back home; she'd said good-bye to that Carroll for good.

As she drove, she scanned the twenty or so acres of gently sloping ground. It was crisscrossed with fences, which she assumed kept the horses from running wild and likely kept wild animals from attacking the horses in the night. A large black stallion stirred as she passed.

The lane wound down to a wide-open stretch that circled in front of a majestic log building, a two-story lodge that hugged the edge of the lake. Praying Mitch Bohannah hadn't any company, she parked and stepped from her car. Her legs felt rubbery. She drew a bracing breath, the air pure and sweet in her nostrils, and headed to the door of the lodge. No one answered her knocks. She glanced toward the barn at the back of the property, a solid two-story structure painted red against the greenery. Would Mitch be there?

Before trudging the distance, she decided to try the other side of the house. On the lake side, she found a veranda that extended to the water. A lone man stood against the waist-high railing, his back to her. He had thick black hair and was tall and lean in faded blue jeans that gloved his narrow hips. A khaki T-shirt hugged his shoulders and back, accentuating the intriguingly muscled flesh beneath. He was watching a fishing boat as it chugged over the glassy surface, its motor a gentle whirr in the afternoon air.

Carroll gathered her nerve and softly climbed the log steps. "Hello."

The man started and spun around. He had the greenest eyes she'd ever seen, and as their gazes met, Carroll felt as though two electrical wires were jolting a sensuous charge through her. *So, this was sexual awareness.* Heat climbed from her toes to her roots. But strangely, it didn't feel like a blush of embarrassment, it felt good, it felt exciting. She prayed this guy was Mitch Bohannah.

Even though he seemed somewhat reticent. Oh, she could tell he wasn't repelled by her. Just the opposite. In fact, from the lustful gleam in his eyes, she couldn't figure out why he wasn't sweeping her up and carrying her inside to his bed. Maybe it was the cardigan. She began taking it off.

Her heart wobbled as she realized he also looked confused. Obviously, he was wondering what she, a complete stranger, was doing at his private domain. He lifted a brow. "Well, you can't be lost—"

"No . . ." Carroll tugged the sweater down her arms.

His gaze followed her action, then steadied on her ample cleavage, provided partly by nature and partly by her new Wonderbra. He seemed to have swallowed something too large for his throat. "The Diamond B is hardly on the beaten path to anywhere."

Her gaze flicked over him, steadying on his mouth, on lips as firm and roughly hewn as a whittled flute, meant to play, to give pleasure. His strong jaw needed shaving; the bristles conversely added to his appeal. Deep inside her something sweet and strange tingled. "The Diamond B was my destination . . . er, Mr. Bohannah?"

"You know damned good and well I'm Mitch Bohannah. And don't think I don't know what this is all about, or who sent you."

Relieved that she wouldn't have to actually tell him what she wanted, Carroll blew out a sharp breath and struck the pose she and Kelly-Anne had practiced in front of the mirror, with her hip jutted to one side. With all the bravado she could muster, she said, "Just think of me as a gift from God."

"Oh, you're an angel, all right, honey." His green eyes warmed with obvious appreciation as his gaze traveled the length of her in a slow, assessing motion that heated Carroll from the inside, chasing away the constant chill. He tilted his head sideways and his eyes hardened like chips of jade. "But no one's ever called Charlie 'God' before."

"Charlie?" she muttered, not understanding. Who was Charlie? Her mouth went dry. Apparently, she *would* have to tell him why she was here. She squared her shoulders, jutted her chin. "I drove all the way from Missoula for you to make love to me."

"Then you wasted your time." He shoved away from the railing, brushed past her, and headed into the house. "Enjoy the trip back."

"Wait!" She hurried after him. "Please, Mitch. Don't you find me attractive?"

He stopped and glanced over his shoulder, his dark brows dipped in a soft scowl. "Lookit, Ms. . . . ?"

"Sydney, Carroll Sydney." She took a step toward him. "Don't you want me?"

"Well, now, wanting you and having you are two different things. I've sworn off sex for the next three months."

"But you can't." Dismay brought her toe to toe with him. He smelled of soap and leather. She said breathily, "Let me change your mind."

He grinned, and shook his head. "Tell Charlie he's wasting his time. He can send as many *temptations* as he likes, I won't succumb."

"I don't know anyone named Charlie. And you have to make love to me. They all said you were the best. That's why you're at the top of my list."

Mitch's black brows rose. "Your list?"

Chapter Two

What list?'' Despite his intention of tossing this woman off the Diamond B, Mitch couldn't help being intrigued. Charlie had chosen his accomplice well. Carroll Sydney had all the right equipment to persuade any man into bed, just the right mix of innocence and sexiness to stir the coldest heart. Not that his heart was frozen.

In fact, his blood was heating and humming in all the required areas, and his hands itched to reach up and caress her face, her slender neck, her bare arms. But he didn't. He wouldn't. He wasn't addicted to sex. He could resist her lure, the enticing scent of her perfume, the sweet pull of her breath feathering his mouth.

Damn Charlie and damn the bet.

Carroll stepped back as though the nearness bothered her as much as it was bothering him. She glanced at her hands and an attractive pink painted her cheeks. If he didn't know better, he'd think she was actually embarrassed.

She gazed up with just the right touch of chagrin. ''My list of prospective lovers.''

Mitch frowned, amused. ''You have a list?''

''Yes.'' Her eyes were the color of aquamarine stones, with flecks of gold at the centers. ''My friends helped me compose it.''

He grinned at her, unable to resist flirting; he did so like women, especially attractive blushing women who looked good enough to eat—even if their motives were devious. "You sound as though I should be flattered to be on this list."

Her face went from pink to red, and his respect for her skipped upward a notch. He had to hand it to her, she was one hell of an actress.

"Well, yes." She nodded, setting her shimmery hair in motion, a wavy silken lure that had him longing to gather a handful and pull her lush body against his throbbing desire. He blew a breath through taut lips and stepped back.

Her hands landed on her inviting hips. "You *should* be flattered. You got the highest rating."

"The highest . . . ? Who exactly did this rating?" Mitch's grin slipped. It seemed his love life was the hottest topic in Missoula, and he didn't like that. "Charlie?"

God, his brother-in-law must believe he had an ego the size of the Continental Divide to think he'd fall for a wide-eyed sham like this.

She frowned. "Is Charlie a woman?"

"Hell, no."

"Then I wish you'd tell me who Charlie is—because I don't know anyone named Charlie."

"Charles T. Barker. Your employer."

She blinked and shook her head, her hair repeating its sensuous dance. He looked beyond her, at the lake, tracking the trolling fishing boat, but he didn't miss her huff of indignation.

"I've never heard of Charles T. Barker. And for your information, until last week, I was employed at the Mason County Library in Missoula. I worked there for five years. You can call Terry Quinn and confirm that if you like."

A librarian? He'd never come across a librarian who looked like Carroll Sydney. It was enough to rouse a man's interest in reading. He braced his backside against the railing. "What did Charlie offer you to woo you away from such secure employment? A position on staff at the agency once I'm gone?''

Her eyes flashed with anger. ''Are you always this hard to get through to?''

He ignored that. ''You have such an honest face, but I don't believe you. So, if that's all, you'd better be going.''

She sighed, tugging her cardigan back up her arms. His gaze followed, settling momentarily on her ripe, inviting cleavage and need flared hot through him. He gave himself a mental slap.

She buttoned the top of her sweater, and perversely, he found that more alluring. Challenging. Exactly what she counted on, no doubt.

''Okay,'' she said. ''Obviously, I've gotten some bad advice. Could we start again?''

''No, no.'' He pointed toward the steps, swallowing the desire that threatened to strip him of his resolve, that would cost him the bet, his pride, and his certainty that he was in control of when and with whom he had sex. ''You're leaving. Now.''

''Could we go inside, please? I'm getting kind of chilled out here.''

Mitch arched one brow as much at her audacity as at the request. He glanced at the thermometer hanging on the side of the veranda railing. ''Lady, it's ninety degrees.''

''Yes, I know. If we could go inside, I'll explain. Then maybe you'd reconsider.''

''I'm not going to reconsider.''

''Please don't send me straight back to Missoula in this heat without hearing me out. Or at least offering me some liquid refreshment to cool me off.''

Mitch felt like the ball in a tennis match being slammed this way and that. One minute she was cold, the next she was hot, boiling beneath the blazing sun. Deciding he would never figure out women and that that paradox was part of the attraction of women, he rubbed his bristled jaw.

"I suppose I can spare a glass of water. Then, you're on your way. Wait here and I'll get it."

He opened the French doors with a bang and strode across the hardwood planking, his bare feet making a soft slapping sound on the naked flooring.

Carroll followed him inside, shutting the door quietly. She was grateful he didn't have air conditioning. The lodge held a gentle warmth that settled about her like a comforting shawl, but did nothing to warm her cold fingers.

This room had a vaulted ceiling with a loft. It was the kind of place one would expect to find bearskin rugs and mounted wild animal heads. Instead the throw rugs were fake fur and the only wild animals gracing the walls were vivid oil painting depictions of grizzlies and elk in their natural habitats.

The furniture was rusty brown leather with burlwood arms and burlwood tables and lamps. A two-story rock fireplace dominated one side wall and what looked like a huge bar from some Old West saloon hugged the opposite wall and served as the kitchen.

Mitch pulled a glass from the cupboard, filled it with water and ice, then pivoted and froze. His cool green eyes widened, sending an unbidden but pleasant twinge to her toes. His brows lowered. "I asked you to wait outside."

"Yep. I'm trespassing." Carroll had led her life obeying rules. Laws. But now, she'd cast away all of her long-held ethics and morals. This small indiscretion felt incredible. Dangerous. Heady. She could only dream what being made love to would feel like—especially by this man.

Swallowing hard, she gazed past his annoyed expression to the wall behind him, to a group of framed pictures, photographs of Mitch at varying ages, on horseback, on water skis, on fishing trips. She murmured, "But there are so many other things I've never done."

"Pardon?" His growl sliced into her dour thoughts. She could tell he hadn't heard her.

"Oh, nothing. May I?" She reached for the glass. He

handed it to her. Their fingers bumped and he pulled back as though he were afraid of even that tiny contact. Was he afraid? Of her? Or of himself? This was not the Mitch Bohannah her friends had described—the fearless sexual animal with an erotic appetite in need of constant sating.

What had happened to him? Trying to figure that out, Carroll settled on his sofa, leaving plenty of room for Mitch to join her. He chose the chair opposite, motioning for her to drink up. His patience with her delaying tactics seemed stretched beyond good manners.

Well, he wasn't the only one who could be rude. The old Carroll would have been disinclined to pry into a man's private affairs. But the new Carroll had a schedule that disallowed the luxury of proprieties. Of good manners. Impudent, and knowing it, she asked, "Why aren't you having sex anymore? Have you contracted a disease? Become impotent?"

"What?" he barked. Outrage reddened his neck and he clasped the arms of his chair so hard his knuckles whitened. He had great hands, she noticed, long tapered fingers, the skin tanned, the nails short and clean—the kind of hands that would be gentle on a woman.

He leaned toward her. "Not that it's any business of yours, but, no—to both. And don't you go circulating lies like that throughout Missoula. I'm fine. Physically and otherwise. It's because—" He broke off and squared his shoulders. "I'm taking a sabbatical."

She'd been prepared for just about any answer but this. Carroll's eyebrows arched. "From sex?"

"Yeah." The word came out short, final. End of subject. He plowed his hand through his hair. His glare told her not to pursue the topic.

"I've never heard of such a thing," she said. She took a long sip of water. It sent a chill through her middle. Wondering why she hadn't asked for hot coffee when he'd offered water, she eyed Mitch Bohannah suspiciously, then glanced around the room again. "Is that why you're hiding out here?"

"I'm not hiding out," he growled indignantly.

Carroll decided he was protesting too loudly and too firmly. She'd hit the nail on the head—and that gave her hope that this self-imposed sabbatical could be breached. She just had to figure out how. But if she thought of a way, would she be staying long enough to put that plan into action? Too bad she didn't know what this Charlie had to do with it.

She sipped her water and considered her options. She could do as Mitch wished, just leave and drive back to Missoula. There were, after all, two more guys on her list. But something about Mitch Bohannah kept her riveted in place.

Was it the challenge?

Or the man?

Or both?

She studied him a long moment and realized she wanted to know him better, wanted that intriguing mouth to ravish her own, wanted to feel those strong hands on her in ways she couldn't even imagine.

But how could she convince him to let her stay?

If only she could go back and change the way she'd introduced herself. She'd made a mess of this. If only she'd come up with some lie or other instead of blurting out that she wanted him to make love to her. Embarrassment thickened her throat. She should never have listened to all of her girlfriends who'd told her to use the direct approach with this man. To a woman, they'd said, "You won't have to do a thing. One look at you and he'll be the aggressor."

Yeah, right. All that advice had gotten her was a fast shuffle back to her car. She had to change his mind. But how? Her gaze wandered the room again, coming to rest on the photos behind the bar. Did he have an inkling of how lucky he was? Taking for granted all the things his life offered while others had nothing more than unfulfilled dreams and desires? All of her life she'd wanted to do the things he was doing in those photographs . . .

Of course! She sat straighter on the sofa. "If I paid you, would you teach me to ride a horse?"

"What game are you playing? First sex, now horses." Mitch's eyes narrowed; he looked about to say "she's determined to ride something." Instead, he said, "Do I look like I need your money?"

"Well, no, but I wouldn't ask you to do it for free."

He waved his wonderful hands through the air. "Did you see any signs outside that said this was a dude ranch—with a riding instructor on call?"

She ignored his sarcasm. "I really do want to learn and you've obviously been riding since your teens. I'd like to try that big black stallion."

"Nightfire?" Mitch laughed. "He's not for beginners."

"Do you have a horse I could learn on?"

"Yes. No. I'm not going to teach you."

She lurched off the sofa, strode to the bar, set the glass on its polished surface, then turned to face him. If she didn't convince him now, she would be back in Missoula by suppertime. The only weapon left to her was honesty. She didn't like people doing things for her out of pity, but this time if it was the only way to get what she wanted, she'd use it.

"Last month I found out I have a rare form of leukemia. It's incurable. Fatal. The doctor says I'll be lucky to have three months before—" She broke off, fighting the urge to hug herself, feeling self-pity welling. Damn. One thing was certain; before she faced candidate number two, she was going to have a plan and a lie prepared. No more baring her soul.

"Anyway, I've decided I'd like to spend that time pursuing some lifelong dreams. Since I was a little girl I've wanted to have a pony. The closest I ever got was the Christmas Aunt Virginia bought me a giant plastic horse for my Barbie doll. I want to learn to ride."

Mitch had to give her credit for being creative. The direct approach hadn't worked, so now she was playing on his sympathy. But he didn't trust her. Didn't believe her. He shook his head.

As though she hadn't seen him, she gave a toss of her head, her lush reddish-blond hair swishing across her shoulders, the sound like silk through a man's hands, the scent as clean and fruity as a tree full of ripe apples, inviting him to touch, and taste. Desire pounded his veins.

She gave him a pleading look, saturated with vulnerability. It touched something deep inside him, something at the core of him, his decency, his basic humanity.

She sighed. "I'd like to learn to water-ski too. I'd like to wake up in this glorious lodge. I'd like some sweet memories to fill the not-so-sweet days I'm facing in the very near future."

God, what was the matter with him? He was allowing himself to be sucked into this grim, heart-wrenching fantasy. No. He wouldn't even wonder whether it was true. It wasn't. "That's probably the saddest story I've heard in ages, but I don't believe you."

Carroll's expression grew serious. Stony. "I wish I could share your denial. But I don't have the time to waste. What I do have are the lab reports, if you'd care to see them."

"Charlie has thought of everything."

"What is it with you and this Charlie?"

Mitch had had it. His patience snapped. "The bet! The bet!"

He said it as though she ought to know what he was talking about. Carroll stared at him for several seconds, her mind churning with a slew of disjointed information, everything she'd heard since meeting him, and suddenly she understood. Or could guess. "You made a bet with this Charlie that you wouldn't have sex for three months, and you think he sent me to make certain you'd lose."

He grinned, a satisfied-cat grin, a huge dangerous cat

with gleaming green eyes full of enough fire to melt the most resistant female. "I knew you knew."

Carroll returned his smile, feeling on solid ground for the first time today. This explained more to her than he suspected. And now she had leverage, something to barter with. His ego. His pride. "Let's just say 'Charlie' did send me. Are you saying I'm such a temptation to have around you wouldn't be able to stop yourself from ravishing me?"

He blanched. She'd struck home. She resisted an urge to smile. He blew out a noisy breath, causing his nostrils to flare, a look that spoke of a wild ancestry, a look that felt like a caress in the most private sensuous part of her.

He said, "Of course not."

"Really?" She sidled over to where he sat. His gaze traveled up her legs to the abbreviated skirt that barely covered that most private sensuous part of her. "Then why are you afraid to let me stay a few days?"

He lurched to his feet, seeming to feel more confident standing. "I'm not afraid."

She stepped closer to him. "Then I can stay?"

"No."

He grasped her gently by both upper arms, but he released her so quickly, and backed away with such speed, she knew she'd guessed right about him. He was afraid. What the hell had he wagered? No matter, she had the upper hand now, and she would play it for all it was worth. She advanced on him again.

"Why can't I stay?" As she moved closer, he retreated. She asked sweetly, "Are you expecting company?"

"No." He shoved his hand through his hair again.

"Then why not?" She unbuttoned her cardigan, began easing it down her arms.

"Because you weren't invited." His gaze fell to her bulging breasts, and she saw desire come alive in his eyes. "Because I don't even know you."

Carroll pulled the sweater off and trailed it to the floor the way Kelly-Anne had shown her, then spoke in the breathy voice her other friends had coached her to use. ''You could get to know me.''

Mitch laughed, as though at himself. ''I am not going to do this.''

''So, you really are afraid you can't keep the bet.''

''I could keep it with my hands tied.''

The image of him tied to a chair or bed and vulnerable to the wiles of a determined sexual partner made her grin.

''That's not what I meant,'' he said, as though reading her mind. He grinned at himself. ''I don't need to have sex. I am not going to lose this bet. I can be around a temptation . . . like you . . . and remain a gentleman.''

Carroll planted her hands on her hips, and ran her tongue slowly, purposefully, across her lips. ''I don't believe you.''

His gaze swept her anew. Determination rose from behind the lust in his eyes. ''It's true. Piece of cake.''

She puckered her lips as though to blow him a kiss. ''Prove it.''

Chapter Three

Prove it? Mitch choked on the suggestion. *Prove it to her?* Why should he? Her narrowed gaze bored into him, repeating the challenge. *Prove it to Charlie?* The hell with Charlie. But dismissing his brother-in-law only cleared the fog blocking the real test in her dare. *She was challenging him to prove it to himself.*

"Well . . . ?" she said.

"I'm thinking," he answered. But what was there to think about? Either he had a problem with sex or he didn't. And he didn't. So, if having a seductive woman—this seductive woman—staying in his house for a few days would prove it, why not?

He'd already gone four nights and three days without sex. Hadn't been much of a sacrifice. Easy as saddling Nightfire. The thought of how the stallion hated being saddled brought a disparaging grin to his lips. Easier. He would survive.

But what bothered him was that he felt cornered. Never mind that he'd brought this all on himself. He deserved to pay penance for bedding the daughter of their best client. It wasn't ethical. No matter that Sissy'd had the hots for him and was way too easy to please. He could have resisted her come-ons—if he hadn't had one beer beyond his rein-in point. But that no more made him an alcoholic than occasionally thinking with his pecker made him a sexaholic.

Hell, he was just a healthy male with a healthy appetite. Nothing wrong with that. He could resist ravishing Carroll's tantalizing body, no matter how much his own flesh ached for her. He could defy her provocative scent, no matter it seemed to have crept into every corner of his lake home. He could repress his inclination to bed her out of sympathy, no matter what sorry-assed tale she contrived. Pity-fucks weren't his style.

She tapped her foot. "What's the matter, Bohannah, aren't you gentleman enough to stand by your word?"

Yes, by God, I am. Mitch gave her a slow, self-assured grin. And he'd prove it to one and all. "All right. You can stay, for a couple of days. I'll even toss in a riding lesson. Two, if you survive the first."

She looked as hopeful as a child on Christmas Eve. "Water-skiing too?"

He nodded, though the thought of her in a bathing suit rattled him more than he'd acknowledge to himself. "But I'm not going to charge you anything. I don't need your money."

Winning the bet would be payment enough.

"I'm not going to need money soon either."

He eyed her with continuing suspicion. Had her sad tale of impending death actually been the truth? Was she as sick as she claimed? She looked damned healthy to him. He supposed if she had plenty of stamina for the rigorous lessons she wanted him to give, her lie would be exposed. "Then leave it to someone. Make a will."

"I made a will years ago." She hugged herself, rubbing her arms.

Years ago? Surprise darted through him. She had to be barely past twenty-five. He was pushing thirty and hadn't made a will yet. He'd never given his future much consideration. Nor his death. He suppressed a bark of derision. Devising a will meant one expected to die. Mitch expected to live, long and hard, until his breath deserted him. Had this woman always known she would die young? Or was she just anal?

"If you won't take money for the lessons, what about for my meals and board? It's not like I'm an *invited* guest."

Meals and board? Meals meant sitting across the table from her. Board meant sleeping down the hall from her. His mouth watered. Talk about temptation. This would be one hell of a test. Mitch glanced at the lake, then back at Carroll. "I don't have rooms to rent. And there's plenty of food. Fix whatever you like for yourself. I'm dining with friends in town and don't expect to be back until after midnight."

It was a lie. Out before he could stop himself. What was he doing . . . running away? He didn't need to hide from her, distance himself. What would that prove? No. He wouldn't question his reasoning. He'd lied, and now he was stuck with it. He grabbed his car keys and strode to the French doors.

"Aren't you going to wear shoes?"

He stopped cold and stared at his feet. Sure enough, he was barefoot. Heat edged up his neck. He shrugged and tossed his head, grinning at himself. "Left 'em near the other door."

Turning, he spun toward the hall that led to the front door. The boots he'd left in the foyer were his barn boots. His good boots were upstairs, in his closet. But he'd be damned if he was going to go get them, no matter how uncomfortable he'd be spending the next eight hours or so in his muck-shoveling boots.

"Before you go, could you show me my room?" she asked. "I'd like to bring in my bag and unpack, maybe take a nap before dinner."

"It's at the top of the stairs, second door to your right." He stopped again, and glanced over his shoulder. "Do you need help carrying the bag?"

"No. I can manage. But thanks for offering."

He nodded, unable to resist another blood-searing gaze

at her long, bare legs. "We'll have that riding lesson first thing in the morning. I hope you brought something appropriate to wear."

Mitch woke up hung over, his feet sore from the stable boots and his temper getting tighter and tighter. The only way he knew to improve his mood was not an option. Grumbling to himself, he took a long, cold shower, wrapped a towel around his waist, and lathered his face. The door to his private bathroom opened.

Carroll stood there, an angel with a halo of strawberry tresses, a gown as sheer as a gossamer veil, every curve and mound of her body revealed, a body to drive a man insane.

"Hi," she said, her voice raspy like pointed, polished fingernails grazing his nerve endings. Her intentions were as obvious and devious as the devil.

Need slammed through Mitch. He was powerless to stop his body's reaction, powerless to stop his gaze from raking hungrily over her. She moved toward him, the filmy fabric of her gown shifting, teasing, mesmerizing. She reached for his towel, the touch of her hand jolting him out of his stupor.

"Oh, no you don't." He caught hold of her hands and lifted them away from him.

She gazed down at him, then up at him, grinning. "But you want me."

There was no hiding *that* fact. "Maybe so, but I'm not going to have you. Go get dressed."

She reached up to undo the string at the neckline of her gown. "But I need a shower . . ."

He caught her gently, but firmly, by the shoulder and arm, spun her around and scooted her through his bedroom and out into the hallway. "That's what the guest bathroom is for. Use it."

He strode back into the master bedroom, banging the door and locking it as he went. He took another cold shower, longer this time, then shaved, dressed, and headed downstairs in a worse mood than he'd been in when he awoke.

The lingering scent of her teasing perfume in the hallway made him flinch, and skewed his temper a notch tighter. She'd beaten him downstairs, made coffee, and was out on the deck, a mug and a plate of half-eaten banana slices at her elbow.

"'Morning," he growled, sidling up to the picnic table, his own coffee mug full to the brim.

"Oh, good morning," she chirped, as though nothing had gone on earlier. She wore crisp new jeans that hugged her curves like a freshly tarred roadway, and a multitonal blue plaid flannel shirt that she had only half buttoned. A heaping mound of creamy cleavage, barely held in place by a wisp of aqua lace, taunted him.

His foul mood nose-dived.

"How'd you sleep?" she asked pleasantly.

"Fine," he snapped. He'd slept lousy. Too much beer and too many fantasies about her. Too much need, and no satisfaction. "How about you?"

"Better than I have in weeks. Must be the mountain air. The moment I got out of bed I knew today would be one of my good days."

So, she's going to keep up the charade about being at death's door. Mitch swallowed his disdain, and tried ignoring the eyeful of glorious bosom staring him in the face. Temptation was the name of the game and he was going to win it if it killed him. He tossed back a swig of hot coffee, burning his tongue and throat in the process. Nothing and no one would cause him to lose his bet. "Looks like it's gonna be another scorcher."

"Yes." She gazed at him from beneath heavily lashed lids, the look both innocent and seductive.

He grinned at her. "Hope you're wearing sunscreen, or you're gonna have a nasty burn on your chest."

She flinched as though he'd slapped her and her cheeks

grew pink, but she made no move to button the gaping shirtfront. He stared pointedly at her breasts, noting for the first time that her skin was mottled with goose bumps. How could she be cold with the sun beating down on her? He had on a lightweight blue cotton shirt and could already feel the heat.

Was she really ill? Really dying? He sat down beside her, contemplating how far she'd go to convince him. A trickle of sweat beaded his upper lip, but she had her hands curled around her coffee mug as if they were cold. Doubt flickered through his thoughts, and he decided he'd take her up on her offer to speak with Terry Quinn, her ex-employer at the Missoula library.

Bees buzzed around the honeysuckle blossoming beneath the veranda. Carroll glanced at him, the seductress momentarily under wraps, her face awash in wonderment. "Why did it take my impending death for me to realize what pleasure one can derive from a good cup of coffee, a fresh banana, the simple beauty of a mountain lake on a clear summer morning, the blue of the sky, the green of the water, the brown of trees?"

He had no answer. He also took these things for granted. Everybody did. Human nature. He drank another sip of coffee, making a point of tasting the rich bean flavor. He glanced at the sky and the lake, drinking in the glorious contrast of brilliant blue sweeping across the jade expanse. He settled more comfortably beside her, as though by sharing this appreciation they had somehow developed a bond. "I'd say life pretty much overwhelms most of us. Too much demand these days for a fast-paced existence that leaves little or no time for enjoying the beauties of nature. The precious bounty at our fingertips."

Carroll gazed down at his hands, at his fingers, as though contemplating the feel of them on her. She ran her tongue over her lips. His pulse beat a tad faster.

Across the lake a bird called, a loud piercing shriek. She lifted her brows toward Mitch.

"Osprey. Calling to her mate."

She nodded, but said nothing, and they sat in companionable silence, like old friends who know they have the next fifty years to share their thoughts and feelings and are taking this moment to contemplate and relax. Mitch never relaxed around women. Not like this. It felt strange. And nice.

Too nice.

He drained the rest of his coffee and stood. "If we're going to teach you how to ride, we'd better do it while your energy level is high."

Carroll rose, and watched his green eyes narrow as his gaze roamed over her in a look that screamed of sexual hunger and determined defiance. She shivered. Ignoring the inclination to hug herself, to button her shirt, she straightened her shoulders. She should never have waited so long to experience sex. She was way past ready to discover the joy of physical pleasure. "Like what you see?"

But he was no longer admiring her breasts. His gaze steadied on her feet. Mitch frowned. "Didn't you bring boots?"

"Well, no, I—" She hadn't expected to need many clothes. Just the basic seduction stuff: flimsy panties, cutaway bras, fishnet stockings, the white nightie, a lace-up teddy, a clingy slip dress. And what she had on. She pointed to her tennis shoes. "What's wrong with these?"

"No heels. Your feet won't stay in the stirrups. You'll have nothing to hang on with and you'll land on your tempting little tush."

"I didn't think you'd noticed," she teased.

"I'm not blind." He tilted his head to one side. "Just abstaining."

"Couldn't you make an exception . . . just this once?" She stepped toward him. "You could go back to abstaining in a day or two."

"No." He moved back. His frown returned, deeper than before. "Do you have any shoes with heels?"

She doubted the five-inch red pumps in her closet were what he had in mind.

"Nope." She shook her head. "I suppose I could pick some up in Kalispell, or Polson."

"What size do you wear?"

"Seven, why?"

"There are some boots in the front coat closet. I think one of them might fit. Try them, then meet me at the barn. I'll go saddle your horse. And button that shirt. I wouldn't want my stable hands attacking you."

Ten minutes later she wore a stiff pair of size seven royal blue Tony Lamas. She wondered which of his many women had left them here expecting to return on another day and wear them again. Not that it mattered. She wasn't jealous. She was grateful.

Mitch stood at a small corral next to the barn. Tall and lean and commanding in the gentle way he spoke to the brown horse tied at the railing. In faded, body-gloving jeans, dusty cowboy boots, and a worn black Stetson, he might have stepped from a Louis L'Amour novel. Her heart skipped a beat.

"This is ole Padre." Mitch introduced her to the horse. "He's a gelding. A real gentle fella. Come stroke his forelock. Let him get used to your touch, your scent, your voice."

Wedged between Mitch and the horse, Carroll again experienced that incredible sense of delight. Joy, such a huge and all-consuming pleasure, came packaged in the mundane, the simple. She'd never consciously paid attention to that fact, but it was hitting her like a tidal wave at the moment.

The horse nudged Carroll and pushed her back against Mitch. The contact sent a zap of desire through her. She laughed, self-conscious and tickled at the same time. Mitch righted her, then stepped back. She grinned up at him.

The awe in her eyes stoked something deep inside Mitch. She was finding pleasure from something he'd taken for granted his whole life. In being with the horse, in the magnificent surroundings. Her awareness roused appreciation in him, while also begging him to review his own outlook on life. He hadn't realized how lucky he was, just to be alive, just to be doing this. Every minute counted. Her delight heightened his own. She was a special woman. In that instant, he realized that if Carroll Sydney really was dying, he would miss her.

"How do I get on?" she asked.

"From the left side, always. And it's called 'mounting.' "

"My left or the horse's left?"

"You face the front of the horse and put your left foot in the stirrup."

It took two tries before she lifted her foot high enough to slide it into the stirrup. She felt as though she were stepping onto a kitchen counter. Muscles along her inner thigh and buttocks screamed a silent protest, made worse by the tightness of her jeans.

Mitch said, "Hold both reins in your left hand, and use that same left hand to hold on to the horse's neck. Grab on to the saddle horn with your right hand."

He guided her as he spoke, his big warm hands engulfing her small cold ones, chasing off the chill, stirring sensuous tingles inside her.

If he felt the same, he didn't show it. "There you go. Now, you sort of bounce up, swing your right leg over the horse's back, and sit in the saddle."

Carroll held the reins loosely in one hand, and placed that same hand on the horse's neck. Grabbing tightly to the saddle horn, she started to mount. Padre began walking. Carroll hopped. "No! Stop, horsey!"

"Tighten your hold on the reins," Mitch said.

She tried. But the horse kept moving. Carroll kept hopping. "Stop, horsey! Stop!"

Mitch caught up with them. He grasped her hands on the reins. "It's 'whoa,' not 'stop.' Whoa, Padre."

Her cheeks burned, and she was certain her leg had been wrenched from its socket, all ligaments and muscles ripped.

"Okay, try the mount again." There was laughter in his voice. She shot him a dirty look.

The smile reached into his eyes. "Remember, keep the reins taut."

She drew in a deep breath, recited the steps in her head, reins, neck, saddle horn, then started again.

"Now, bounce."

She did, lifting as she went, but for all her effort, she might be an elephant attempting this maneuever. She hadn't strength or momentum enough to lift herself. As frustration stabbed through her, solid hands cupped her bottom, boosting her. Instead of helping, it startled Carroll. She let out a yelp and released reins and saddle horn, and landed in Mitch's arms.

Mitch held her against him. She weighed next to nothing, but there was nothing like an armful of woman to stir a man's juices and his bubbled to boiling in an instant. Damn, but he wanted her. Without a thought beyond that, he found his mouth covering hers, his tongue stroking her lips, opening them, and he was inside, tasting her, enjoying her.

Carroll's mouth felt seared, invaded, violated, and she wanted more. This had to be but the tip of the iceberg, and yet, it was like the tip of the devil's fiery pitchfork. Something so hot and promising her bones were melting.

Mitch held her to him, a compliant, eager woman, something he'd experienced often enough, yet there was something different, something sensational, something right and good, something he couldn't define, couldn't identify. But he wanted more. Wanted more so bad he ached with the need. Throbbed.

No. Damn it. No. He set her to her feet and backed away from her. His lungs heaved, hard and fast. "That—" He bent over to catch his breath, gasping. "That—"

He was trying to say, "That won't happen again." In

the end, he gave up. "That's enough for today."

"No." She looked stricken. "I really want to ride. Please."

"No more games?"

"I promise."

"Okay."

Carroll, weak with desire, could barely command her leg to rise into the stirrup. This time when she felt the hands on her bottom, she had to shut her eyes, force her concentration on mounting the horse. This time, the boost helped. She rose up, swung her leg over the saddle, and sat with such a hard thwack, she was sure she'd bruised every inch of her bottom.

"Put your other foot into the stirrup and stand," Mitch commanded. She did and he adjusted the fit of the stirrups.

"Is it supposed to feel as though you're doing the splits?"

Mitch laughed. "Yep. Anytime you can't take it anymore, just say the word. We'll stop."

But Carroll wasn't ready to quit. Her nerves danced with excitement, her muscles ached, but not in a bad way. Every cell in her body felt alive, every sense of her being incredibly in touch with the moment.

"I'm going to lead you around the corral and let you get the feel of the horse beneath you. Hold on to the saddle horn."

Carroll gripped it with both hands. As the horse moved, she jarred from side to side. A smile rose from deep within her. Soon she was holding the reins and, with Mitch's guidance, commanding the horse on her own.

But when he helped her down from Padre, she thought her legs would buckle. "I may never walk correctly again."

"Best thing for that is a good roll in the sac—" Mitch broke off, abashed that the suggestion had even popped out of his mouth. "The hot tub should help ease those sore spots."

"Will you join me?" She obviously hadn't missed his

slip of the tongue, obviously intended to take advantage of it.

He grinned and shook his head. "I've got a phone call to make."

Chapter Four

It was true. She was dying. Cold black despair coiled in Mitch's gut. Numbly, he stared at the phone, then glanced out to the deck where Carroll lounged in the hot tub, her arms spread along the rim of the pool, her head tossed back, her eyes closed as though in pleasure.

Death. In his carefree existence, Mitch had given it little consideration. He didn't want to consider it now. But he felt the Grim Reaper standing at his shoulder, touching his heart with a gelid hand.

His chest squeezed. This vital, brave woman, whom he'd known less than two days, had somehow gotten inside him and made him care. He felt as though he were losing someone he'd known his whole life. A beloved relative. A treasured friend. It was crazy. But real.

Shit! He wanted to slam his fist through something. Wanted to sweep her up and carry her off somewhere beyond the cancer.

But how could he be less brave than she? How dare he dishonor her courage by pitying her? She'd weighed her options and had decided to enjoy to the fullest whatever time she had left. In good conscience, he couldn't take that from her.

He strode to the French doors, his gaze riveted on her as his hand jammed through his hair. In that moment he knew he would do whatever he could to heighten her joy in the few days she would be at the Diamond B. But how?

The image of her in the gauzy nightie filled his mind, fresh and graphic and crystal clear. A pulse thudded against his temples, and hot, heavy blood stirred through his belly. How easy for him to just give her what she wanted.

He considered the ramifications. The bet. Charlie and his pompous, lame accusations. If he was addicted to sex, he wouldn't have lasted this long without taking Carroll up on her erotic offers. But if he took her up on them now, he'd lose everything . . . if Charlie found out. In the face of death, losing what amounted to a pile of money didn't seem so all fired important.

Then what was important? He nodded to himself. His word. Charlie might not ever know, but he would never forget he'd broken his oath. And thereafter his word wouldn't be worth the breath he used to give it. He couldn't seduce her. Wouldn't bed her. He pushed air through his nostrils. But he could take her dancing.

And he did.

Carroll wore a skimpy red dress with high-heeled red shoes that made her incredible legs look even longer. All evening, he felt driven to distraction. All evening, he struggled to remain a gentleman, to keep his mood upbeat. She rewarded him by being excellent company, by laughing unexpectedly from deep inside herself, the joy burbling, glistening in her aqua eyes.

Ever conscious of her weakened state of health, he taught her the Montana Boot Scoot, treated her to the best steak the OutLaw Inn offered, shared two carafes of dry red wine bottled in the Flat Head Valley, and fought the urge to kiss her again.

Carroll paid him back by showing him her list of prospective lovers. Mitch was appalled. *He* was the only decent guy on that list, and he spent the entire drive back to the lodge making sure she knew it.

Carroll teetered in his arms, tipsy, giggling, her body

pliant and inviting as he gingerly struggled to get her upstairs. Desire wore at the reins of his resistance, but he forbore giving in to the ache coursing through his body. He helped her disrobe, and nearly lost the battle of abstinence. The little red dress dropped to the floor and his need shot through the roof.

On a hasty "good night," he retreated to his own room, his self-respect intact, his head pounding, desire heavy in his blood. He dropped into bed, exhausted from putting up a front, from laughing and joking when he wanted to rage, from denying to them both his attraction and hunger for her, from tuning out this nightmare he could neither face and deal with, nor conquer. Sleep took hold of him the second his head hit the pillow.

In his dream she came to him, sweet and naked, slipping beneath his covers, cooing in his ear. Her touch gentled across his belly, an erotic caress that shivered his flesh, lifting goose bumps of need. Mitch moaned, giving in to the sensations, knowing there was no harm in this, an innocent sleep-illusion.

His pulse began a mounting thrum, a gentle beat against his temples as he sank deeper into the pleasure, imagining this was really happening, imagining the angel whose hands were stirring such life in him was Carroll. He swore he could even smell her apple-scented hair.

He felt himself growing rock hard, felt her fingertips hesitantly creeping lower on his belly, the innocence of her touch intensifying his abandon, increasing his delight. The warmth of her hand encountered his engorged penis and a gentle massage ensued, feminine fingers slipping up and down his erection in a teasing exploitation Mitch approved and cherished and welcomed.

His heart hammered against his chest and his breath came quicker, the sensuous stroking sending him to erotic heaven. He could swear she was curled beside him, snuggled into him, and he nuzzled her in return. To his surprise, he confronted warm female flesh, breasts as full and sweet as ripe peaches, nipples as hard as pebbles, damp curls of silk between velvet thighs, curves as real as any he'd ever embraced.

Mitch wrenched his eyes open. Carroll was there in all her naked splendor, touching him, tasting him, driving him beyond the point of retreat. He made one feeble attempt at protest, but she silenced him with her tongue, wickedly stroking to the tip of his erection, the erotic, mind-dizzying caress robbing the last of his resistance, vanquishing all memory of the bet, melting the importance of his word in a lava-hot pool of need.

He pulled her to him, pushed to the edge, ready to explode. His mouth found hers, and he tasted the salty sweetness that belonged to them both. Blood roared in his ears, throbbed in his groin. He twisted her beneath him, felt her spreading her legs, and he thrust into her. The resistance he encountered didn't register.

Not then.

At the moment of connection, Mitch's and Carroll's eyes met, and he saw a touch of pain in hers, and something more, a wisdom as deep as the ages, a knowledge as old as time. It was as if she finally knew what it meant to be a woman. He hesitated, slowing the second thrust, careful with her, gentle, as gentle as his own urgency allowed. He saw himself reflected in her eyes, saw a look of awe on his mirrored image and knew it matched the wonder within him. He felt as though he were discovering for the first time what it meant to be a man.

This was beyond sex, beyond physical pleasure, as though Carroll had reached into his mind, into his heart, into every fiber of his body, every molecule of his spirit, as if their souls had melded into one.

The charge rushing through him was as electrifying as a lightning strike, lifting him out of himself, the pleasure so boundless he seemed to spin round and round, faster and faster as though inside a tornado of ecstacy.

She arched upward, lifted her hips to meet his thrusts as

though from years of experience, and yet her sweet exclamations—"Oh, oh, my"—sounded to him as if she were a novice, encountering this rapture for the first time. That innocence drove him wild, made him want to prolong her bliss as well as his own, but when he felt her body tighten around him, his own release came, hot and exquisite, and somehow purifying. He cried out Carroll's name, then lowered his weight gently onto her.

With his breath ragged, his heart zinging a happy beat, Mitch considered his new realization that sex could be more than a linking of bodies for instantaneous pleasure, that it could be a connecting of minds and souls for a lifetime of gladness, and he concluded that from this moment on, he could settle for nothing less, would settle for nothing less.

Thinking he might be crushing her, he lifted onto his forearms and gazed down at the woman beneath him, still joined, in no hurry to end this coupling that felt so right to him. She was flushed, her eyes wide with awe, her smile sated. She said, "I had no idea."

Her words took a moment to register, and then he remembered the resistance he'd encountered on entering her for the first time. Recalled all the times that he'd thought her innocence was an act. Dear God, what had he done? "You're a virgin?"

She grinned. "Not any more."

Chapter Five

Carroll's head throbbed as if tiny little men thumped tiny little hammers at her temples, her calves ached as if the spikes of those five-inch-high red pumps jabbed the most sensitive muscles, her thighs hurt as if she still straddled the horse, her bottom smarted as if the saddle bruises might never heal, and a new, wondrous ache throbbed at the core of her legs and actually made her smile.

And blush.

She could hardly lift her head from the pillow, but she felt goose bumps raised on her flesh, and for once they weren't caused by being cold. Just the opposite. Inside her, a warm glow burned like the flame of an incandescent candle, the heat as strong and sure as Mitch's hands on her body.

If anyone had told her a year ago she would willingly seduce the king of one-night stands, then repeat the act twice more during the night with more abandon than a ten-dollar hooker, she'd have declared them insane. She stretched and reached across the bed for him; he was gone. The shower running in the bathroom registered in her tender brain, and she smiled, envisioning Mitch naked beneath the fingers of water, wishing it were her fingers on his bare flesh, kneading and rousing him to play again.

There was a lot to be said for having one's first forays

into sex with a man of experience, a man who knew and appreciated the female anatomy. But more than that, Mitch had touched places on her body she hadn't thought of as sensuous, filled places in her heart and mind she'd never known were empty.

She tried sitting up and winced as her various pains slammed together and crescendoed inside her skull. Apparently wine should be taken in small doses. She'd never imbibed with the gusto she'd shown last night. This was her first hangover. Once was enough. She didn't care to ever repeat this.

But it was the only thing about last night she didn't want to do again. She shoved her tangled hair away from her face and stared at the bathroom door in anticipation.

She'd planned on waiting until she was married to sleep with a man. She'd planned a lot of things, all to commence when she had that ring on her finger, that certificate in her purse. But what if she'd never met Mr. Right? Never married? Never spent a night of lovemaking like last night? That would have been the biggest shame.

She ran her tongue along her lips. Even they felt bruised. Gingerly, she touched her mouth and sighed happily. She might be late coming to the realization, but she understood now that even the best-laid plans did not always come true. Sad, really, that this wonderful feeling enveloping her would end soon. Too soon. But she had savored every caress, every taste, every sensation, searing them into her memory banks like archived data to recall on those days ahead when she felt less well than today, when the illness raged.

The bathroom door banged open and Mitch stood there, towel around his waist. Her heart hitched, and she sat up in bed, letting the sheet fall, ignoring the thumping in her brain, all the various aches and pains forgotten in the possibilities that his smile stirred.

She eased from his oversized, rustic pine bed, blushing slightly at her nudity, but only slightly. Last week she'd have died from embarrassment at the thought of parading naked before a man who was not her husband. But sometime during the night, she'd lost that inhibition . . . at least before this man.

"I need a shower too." She strode past him sassily, but stopped short at his indrawn breath.

She spun around. He was scowling, his gaze sweeping over her. "Did I do that?"

She glanced down at her body, spotted the bruising that concerned him on her legs, on her arms. She wanted to hide them like an ugly deformity, but her nakedness rendered her helpless to do anything except shake her head, and offer a look of assurance. "This isn't your fault. My illness causes me to bruise easily. Almost anything will do it."

Sadness shimmered in his eyes, turning them a mossy shade, the color cool and grief-stricken and lonely.

Her heart contracted. She didn't want to see loneliness and regret in his eyes. She swallowed over the lump growing in her throat and strove for an upbeat tone. "I'll be ready to hit the skis right after breakfast."

She said this with more enthusiasm than she felt. Her head throbbed worse now that she was on her feet, and the thought of trying to hold her own on water skis held no appeal.

"I don't know about you," Mitch interjected, a slow, crooked, engaging grin robbing his eyes of melancholy. "But I've had all the physical activity I can handle for a few hours. What if we go fishing instead?"

"Fishing?" Carroll knew darn good and well he wasn't too worn out to water-ski. It was her he was worried about. Something sweet and wonderful scattered through her like a handful of tossed confetti. "I've never been fishing."

"Never?"

"Nope. My dad was an avid fisherman, but he thought only my brothers should share that sacred male ritual."

Mitch shook his head, his expression implying that her

dad was some kind of old-fashioned chauvinist, a feeling Carroll secretly shared. He said, ''You're in for a treat, then.''

Sun glistened off the water, skipped like twinkle lights across Carroll's hair, and rose high and quick into the sky, threatening to scorch everything within its reach. Mitch insisted she borrow a baseball cap, and slather on sunscreen before boarding the sixteen-foot Glasply, the boat he used for both skiing and fishing.

''Belonged to my dad,'' he told her, shouting to be heard above the roar of the motor as they cut through the waves at top speed.

''Are your folks still living?''

''Yep. Spend their summers traveling in their motor home.'' He steered the boat into a favorite fishing spot and anchored. ''And their winters in Arizona.''

He offered to bait her hook, but she insisted on learning how and shortly mastered the art of cojoining a chuck of fresh crawdad meat and a kernel of corn into place.

''Okay, what now?'' Her face was lit as though from some internal lamp, her expression as eager as a child's.

Mitch smiled inwardly. ''Release the bail—that knob on the reel—and keep your thumb on the line so that it doesn't unwind too fast. There you go. When the line goes slack, the hook is on the bottom. Turn the pole over and reel up four cranks.''

''Okay.'' She glanced at him for confirmation that she'd done it all correctly. ''Now, what?''

He grinned, eased himself down on his seat, tugging his cap lower and crossing his long legs at the ankle. ''Now, we watch the tip of the pole and wait.''

''Did you grow up on this lake or in Missoula?'' She stared at the pole. ''Tell me about yourself.''

The request took Mitch by surprise. He didn't like talking about himself, but the gentle slap of the water, the fierce concentration on her pretty face, and the warm feeling between them conspired to free his tongue.

Between pulling cutthroat aboard and releasing the illegal small ones, he spoke of his family, his sister, his brother-in-law, his business. The afternoon passed in relaxed enjoyment. They ate the picnic lunch they'd brought, chatting like old friends, discovering they had a lot in common given the different paths their lives had taken.

Watching Carroll catch her first fish, listening to her describe her brothers and her nieces and nephews, Mitch felt as though he'd known her forever. Instead of a woman dying, he beheld a flower blooming, as though they were inside an insulated bubble that the world could not penetrate, where nothing and no one could reach in and bring them harm. He wanted the sensation to continue endlessly, wanted this newfound contentment to grow and prosper.

Wanted to spend forever with Carroll.

The realization startled him. How could he have met this woman three days ago and fallen so completely, connected so perfectly, that he didn't want another woman in his life? How was that possible? He felt a fish strike his line and began reeling, pondering his feelings with every twist of his wrist. But like so many other of his questions about women, he couldn't explain this one either. It felt as if they were family, the two of them.

Was this love at first sight?

He didn't know, nor did he know what to do about it.

Not then anyway.

Hours later, he made the most important phone call of his life. It was private and irrevocable and he didn't regret it for a second.

Laughing, Carroll and he fried the three "keepers" they'd caught for supper, and afterward did the dishes like a couple used to sharing this menial task. Then Mitch pulled her to him and kissed her long and hard as he'd been wanting to do all day. The explosion of feelings sweeping him confirmed how serious he was about this woman, how right his earlier actions had been.

"Come on. I have a great idea." He gathered towels, padded cushions from the outdoor loungers, an open bottle of brandy, and two plastic glasses. "I'll bet you've never been skinny-dipping in the middle of a lake on a moonlit night."

Carroll's brows arched as though the idea intrigued her, and a devilish gleam of delight shone in her eyes. "I've never been skinny-dipping anywhere."

The night air retained the warmth of the day, making jackets unnecessary and lending appeal to a swim. As soon as Mitch stopped the boat, she asked, "Do you want to undress me?"

He laughed, and kissed her neck, then her mouth, and immediately felt himself growing hard. He pulled back, and grinned down at her. "If I undress you, we won't make it into the water."

"Then I'd better do it myself." She stood up and began peeling off her skimpy shorts.

Mitch stripped and dove in, the cool water enveloping, rushing black and quiet over him, lowering his arousal to a manageable state. He popped to the surface and called to her, "Hey, slowpoke, hurry up."

Carroll moved to the side of the boat, her hair fanned out like angel wings, her body aglow with moonlight, pale and dark curves that caused his breath to catch, his blood to thicken and heat anew. She started down the ladder, then cried out in alarm as her toes touched the water. "Ooh, it's cold."

"Not really." He reached up, caught her ankles and pulled her in.

Her shocked yelp and accompanying reprimand resounded across the lake. The splash sent water exploding skyward. But she surfaced, sputtering and laughing, and swam in small circles. ''Wow, this feels so strange, so free.''

''That's the appeal of it.'' He swam to her side. They raced three laps around the boat, then rested, clutching one another, catching their breaths, laughing softly. Their eyes met and held.

She kissed him on the cheek. ''Thank you for this . . . and for everything else.''

''My pleasure, ma'am.'' Mitch pulled her close, relishing the feel of her against him, capturing her mouth with his, and in that instant, even the cooling water couldn't salve his arousal. Only Carroll could do that.

He helped her back into the boat, laid her down on the lounge cushions, dried her hair and then her body, using the towel gingerly so as not to hurt her. He poured brandy into one of the plastic glasses and each of them took a sip.

With only the man in the moon as witness, Mitch made love to Carroll with deliberate slowness, savoring each moment, searing this beauty, this joy, this taking and giving with her into his mind as permanently as a brand of ownership. Afterward, he cradled her in his arms and whispered, ''Marry me.''

The words startled him as much as they seemed to startle her, but as he heard himself say them, he knew he meant them. He knew what he felt for Carroll was true and real and would never again be matched for another.

Carroll shoved up and out of his arms, her face—completely visible in the moonlight—contorted with disbelief and incredulity. ''What?''

''I know it's impetuous.'' He brushed a damp curl from her cheek. ''But it feels right. It *is* right. *We* are right.''

''Mitch, are you nuts? I don't have a life to make with anyone.''

''Bull. Life hasn't any guarantees. I might be trampled by Nightfire tomorrow. You've made me realize I should make each moment count. That life is about giving and sharing love. Whatever time we have, Carroll, I want us to spend together."

Tears burned the backs of Carroll's eyes, and her heart swelled in her chest. With a trembling hand, she touched his face, a face that had grown way too precious to her in the last three days. That he could even feel remotely the same staggered her. Alarmed her. "Oh, Mitch, if I had a future, I'd want to spend it with you. But I won't ask you to stay with me while I grow sicker and sicker."

"You aren't asking." He took hold of her hands. "I'm offering."

"And I adore you for the thought." But the thought also broke her heart. She choked back the tears. "I can't accept. Call me selfish, but I couldn't bear to deal with your pity. Your eventual disgust. Your sorrow."

"No. I don't pity you. I won't be disgusted." He sucked in a noisy breath. "I'll only be sad because I love you."

Carroll gathered a snuffly breath. Two wayward tears escaped the corners of her eyes, burning hot trails down her cheeks. Love? *What would Kelly-Anne say if she heard this? I not only slept with the baddest bad boy in Missoula, I made him fall in love with me.* She licked her lips. Was it true? If it was, then God help him. She couldn't bring misery on this wonderful guy who'd given her such joy.

She pulled her hands free and lifted her wet hair from her bare shoulders. Goose bumps covered her. She had to make Mitch understand that she wouldn't go along with him. She should leave, drive out of his life tonight before he was seriously, permanently, emotionally injured.

But she heard herself say, "It's getting chilly. Let's go back. I want to sleep on this. I'll give you my answer in the morning."

Mitch complied, steering the boat into the dock and securing it. But once in the house, he swept her up and carried her to his bed, laying her gently on the downy covers. Sleep was the last thing on his mind. She reached for him eagerly.

"Just so you'll know," he said, gathering her to him,

and nibbling sense-robbing kisses down her neck. "I'm not going to take no for an answer."

His mouth found her sensitized nipples, and Carroll let all else fall from her mind, giving her full attention to the moment and the man. But this time, she wanted to pleasure him as he'd been pleasuring her, wanted to give him something back, and this was all she had to offer that he would accept.

She caught his head in both of her hands and gently pulled him to her, then kissed him with all the new expertise she'd learned the past days, twining her tongue with his, cherishing every delicious tingle this produced within her. Sighing, she forced him slowly onto his back, his head nestled on his pillow, his green eyes glazing, darkening with passion. She kissed his neck, his shoulders, his chest. She suckled his nipples as he'd done to hers and smiled to herself as he emitted a honeyed moan.

His breath came quicker, and she stroked her tongue over his flat belly, following the thin trail of raven hair toward the copse of dense black curls. She coiled her fingers around his engorged flesh, treasuring the rigid silken feel of his penis against her palm, remembering the ecstacy of having him between her legs.

Her own breath raced faster, and she flicked her tongue, gathering the salty droplet on the tip of his erection as though imbibing some forbidden nectar, then she filled her mouth with him. He groaned, the sound deep in his throat, a sound rife with abandon, and Carroll felt her own body casting off its restraints, giving way to a melting liquid desire that only this man could quench.

She rose and straddled him, leaned toward him until their lips met again, then she lifted her hips and lowered herself onto him. The joining drove a shaft of heat through her belly, the friction sweet and welcome, every rise and downward thrust sending her up a ridge of euphoria, higher and higher, faster and faster. The explosion struck her like a volcanic eruption, cresting through her again and again, hot and wet and shattering.

She slumped, dropping gently onto him, cradling her face in his neck. Exhausted. Happy. Sated. Eventually, she slipped to his side, but curled against him, spooning, she knew it was called. As sleep reached for her, Carroll felt that sense of rightness he'd mentioned, cocooning her.

"In the morning," he whispered.

But in the morning all he found on Carroll's pillow was a note.

Mitch, don't worry about your bet. No one will ever learn from me about our days of passion. Sorry to run out on you like this, but your proposal wasn't part of the deal. You knew what I wanted from the start. No commitments. Just some good loving. You surpassed my expectations. Thank you for everything. But I've got places to go and people to see and time is running out.

Cold anger flushed Mitch. His brain screamed. His gut twisted. People to see? Had she headed back to Missoula to look up candidate number two on her list? Icy fingers wrapped his heart. How could she do that after last night? After his proposal? After she'd made love to him?

"No, no, no." His throat constricted and realization slammed through his pain. He read her note again, and knew he was right. She was doing something he'd done dozens of times in the past. He'd convinced himself he was being kind, letting down disappointed lovers—who'd expected more of a relationship than he'd wanted—as easily as possible. God, what a heel he'd been. He deserved this hurt a hundred times over.

He leaped from the bed, tossed on jeans, and scrambled downstairs. Her shiny new convertible was gone, but another car was pulling into its former parking place. He scowled as his brother-in-law climbed out of his car.

"What the hell are you doing here?" Mitch growled.

"Come to gloat? Well, tough, I don't have time for you. I've got to get to Missoula."

He tore back upstairs with Charlie on his heels. He slammed into the bathroom and showered and shaved in less than three minutes. When he came out, Charlie was sitting on the unmade bed.

Mitch scowled at him again. "I was hoping you'd be gone. What are you doing here, anyway?"

"I heard you were entertaining a lovely redhead. But I said, no way. Mitch wouldn't go back on his word. He wouldn't risk losing our bet. But my source swore it was true, so I came to see for myself." Charlie lifted his hand. A pair of Carroll's flimsy panties dangled from his finger. "Seems the report was correct."

Mitch snatched the panties from him, nearly ripping Charlie's finger from its socket. "Don't touch."

He pulled on fresh jeans, and a white shirt. He had to reach Carroll and talk her out of her foolish plans, convince her that they belonged together. No matter how short that time might be. "You know, Charlie, if you'd have retrieved your telephone messages, you'd have saved yourself the trip up here. I conceded the bet last night. The company is yours. Lock, stock, and barrel. Wanda knows too."

Charlie's mouth dropped open. "But, but, I didn't really expect you to back out of B and B Advertising. You know damned good and well you're the best ad man this side of the Mississippi. I can't replace you. Damn it, Mitch! I just wanted you to get some professional help for your problem."

"The only problem I have right now is you holding me up. I have to get to Missoula and convince a very stubborn redhead that she and I need to elope."

"Need to elope?" Charlie's tanned face flushed crimson. "Good God, man, have you gotten someone pregnant?"

Mitch curled his fists at his sides, resisting the urge to level the ignorant idiot. He huffed in disgust and stormed out of his bedroom, thundering down the stairs with all the fury and purpose racing through his veins. But as he drove the Lexus beneath the archway of the Diamond B, Mitch pondered Charlie's outrageous suggestion, and muttered, "Sweet Jesus, don't let it be true."

He wasn't worried about diseases. Carroll was a virgin and he'd just gotten a clean bill of health from the lab. But they hadn't used any protection. Not once. It hadn't even occurred to him. Was he nuts? So what if they were safe? She could easily have gotten pregnant. His heart constricted and he closed his eyes against this new pain. He couldn't bear losing Carroll *and* their child.

What faced him in Missoula was worse than he expected. The breaking scandal would alter his life forever.

Carroll hadn't gone back to Missoula. She'd set out for Glacier National Park. She didn't want another man. She'd torn up the list. She knew instinctively nothing could be better than those three days with Mitch had been. She wouldn't risk filling her last days with anything she'd regret.

The warm, precious memories Mitch Bohannah had given her wrapped her heart like colorful threads of yarn, knitted into a protective quilt staving off the chills. Her biggest worry was that Mitch might not accept her decision and would do something rash—like run back to Missoula and stop her from meeting up with Jimmy Jack Palmetto.

Then again, the idea of a man as self-contained as Mitch acting so quixotically amused her. He was not Don Quixote. Slowing as she crossed into the city limits of Kalispell, she drew in a melancholy breath. Why had she and Mitch found each other when it was too late for any extended happiness between them? She supposed she'd never know, but that they'd found even this brief time was a blessing and she wasn't going to regret a second of it. Over the long miles of her drive, she retraced the wondrous moments one after the other.

Carroll spent the next week and a half on the road, stopping at points of interest, visiting all manner of roadside tourist traps, and generally filling her hours with nonsense, all in an effort to forget about Mitch. But the places she went, the things she saw, the people she encountered only confirmed how alone she was. How lonely she was without Mitch.

She'd left her heart in a lodge on a lake in northwestern Montana. It took her ten days to face the fact that without her heart, without Mitch, she might as well be dead *now*. She should have listened to him. Should have taken him up on his offer of marriage, grabbed the brass ring and held on tight while she could.

She turned around and headed back for the Diamond B.

On the drive, her thoughts so full of him she felt her head might explode, she was struck with an epiphany, the realization jabbing her like a cold, accusatory hand. *His bet!* Dear God, what had she done to him? She had been so grateful for all that he'd given her, she hadn't even considered what breaking his word had meant to him.

The Mitch Bohannah she'd come to know and respect and, yes, love would be the one who told on himself. He didn't give his word and break it. Not lightly. And not without consequences. Even self-imposed ones. She had no doubt her selfishness had cost him his job, his business. He might hate her. Might not want to see her at all. Imagining the state of his distress made her more determined. Somehow, she had to right the mess she'd created. Even if it meant going to ''Charlie'' herself.

Determined to reach Mitch as soon as possible, she ignored her weariness, drove on through the night, her foot recklessly heavy on the gas. She was so wrapped up in worry, in her anxiety to get back and square things with him, she didn't see the deer until it was directly in her headlights. Frozen on the white line of the road.

She swerved and collided with a tree.

Chapter Six

Carroll awoke three days later in the Kalispell Medical Center.

"You've been a sick young woman." A bald man, tall, with a runner's agile body, coarse, scruffy gray brows, and buttery hazel eyes, peered down his long nose at her. He wore a lab coat, a stethoscope poking from one pocket, and a name tag. Dr. J. B. Stephens. "But you're going to be okay now."

Okay? Carroll cursed to herself, joggled upward, then grabbed her throbbing head in both hands. "I'm dying and I've lost God knows how much of what precious little time I have left. That is not okay with me."

"Dying?" The doctor's voice was as soothing as velveteen mittens. "You aren't going to die from your head injury."

Carroll frowned, her hands braced on both sides of her thumping skull. "Not my head, my leukemia."

"Leukemia?" Dr. Stephens blinked as though she'd spoken in a language he didn't understand. He picked up her chart and studied it. "What makes you think you have cancer?"

"My doctor told me."

"Well, I don't see any evidence of that in your blood

work.'' He stared at the chart again. ''A severe anemia, but we're treating that.''

She gaped at the doctor, feeling as if she'd stepped into an episode of *The Twilight Zone*. He'd made a mistake. Or was playing a cruel joke on her. Heat suffused into her face. This wasn't funny. ''The lab reported—''

''What lab?'' His unruly brows knitted together. ''Not our lab?''

She tried to swallow, but her mouth was unusually dry. ''The Big Forks County Lab, in Missoula.''

''Oh, my.'' A look of pity clouded his yellowy eyes. ''You're one of the victims of *that fiasco*.''

She shoved herself gingerly up on her elbows. ''What fiasco?''

''The Big Forks County Lab. A shameful example of my profession at its worst. This kind of thing throws a bad light on the whole medical community. Old equipment, mishandled samples, and an overworked, drug-addicted lab technician.''

''What?'' Her lungs deflated. Carroll couldn't pull in any air.

The doctor seemed not to notice. ''Mounds of erroneous diagnoses and false data were released with dire results, lives ruined or otherwise altered. Some irrevocably.''

''Like mine.'' She gasped, sucking in at last. Her chest heaved, ached, her head spun. She sank back against the pillows, trying to process this unbelievable news, still not certain that it wasn't some horrendous mistake, unable to grasp the concept that she might be going to live after weeks of believing her days were numbered.

''The story hit newspapers across the country, made CNN and *Dateline*.'' Dr. Stephens poked a light into her eyes, then wrote on her chart. ''I'm surprised you didn't hear about it.''

''No.'' Carroll shook her head, immediately regretting it as a sharp ache *ping*ed from temple to temple. She'd avoided the news, most of it negative, and none of it related to anything in her life. Or so she'd believed. "But the bruising . . . the chills?"

"Symptomatic of the anemia. That will ease when your iron deficiency is corrected."

"But my doctor said I had three months—"

"A diagnosis based on the facts at hand, but your doctor's facts were flawed. Can't fault him for that," Dr. Stephens assured Carroll. But he seemed to realize she wasn't assured. "If it will ease your mind, we could run your blood work again."

"Oh, please, Dr. Stephens, would you?" Fear and a desperate hope threatened to strangle her.

The doctor patted her wrist. "I'll even request it be rushed. No guarantees, but I'll do my best."

Carroll feared if the leukemia didn't kill her, waiting for the new lab results would. Seconds passed like minutes. Minutes passed like hours. Hours passed like days. Why, she wondered, had time flown by when she'd thought she had so little of it left? And now, when everything depended on one little test, why couldn't the lab tech be in as big a hurry for the answer as she?

She wanted to scream. Her nerves felt raw, sliced open, exposed and bleeding. She couldn't eat, couldn't sleep. With her aching head and her depleted strength, she couldn't even burn off some of her anxiety by pacing. She yearned to call her mother and Kelly-Anne. She dared not. Not from a hospital bed. Not until—unless—she could tell them something positive.

Mostly, she ached to call Mitch. To hear his voice, warm and reassuring in her ear. Every half hour, she reached for the phone. Every time she did, she stopped herself. She needed to see him in person. Whatever the lab results, she still had to talk to him face-to-face.

In the late afternoon, the doctor came to tell her. "The second set of tests show the same results as the first. No leukemia. You've a severe case of anemia, a treatable condition."

She reeled at the news, her whole body shuddering as though from a horrendous scare, as though she could finally breathe after being buried in an avalanche. "I'm not dying?"

"Nope."

"I'm not dying," she said with growing conviction, needing to hear the words out loud, allowing herself to finally start believing them. "I'm not dying."

"Nope. You're likely to live to a ripe old age." Dr. Stephens grinned. "As long as you avoid running into any more trees."

The day she'd accepted her impending death, Carroll had seen the world through more vivid eyes. This afternoon her vision seemed even keener. On the drive to the lake, she promised herself she'd quit traveling through life in a windowless tunnel that led only to the future. She'd never take the beauty and joy that was all around her for granted again.

The Diamond B looked much the same as the day she'd driven out through the welcoming arch two weeks earlier. Even Nightfire glanced up as she passed, but it was a different Carroll in a different convertible arriving now. The car, no longer shiny and flawless, had a crumpled right fender, two weeks' worth of road dust, and a clunking sound that would have to be seen to.

She had a new outlook, her third in the last few months, and a new anxiety about facing Mitch. Had he meant what he'd said? Did he love her? Would he want her once he knew the commitment would be longer than he'd planned, like forty or fifty years longer?

And what about his own life? His own worries? Did he blame her for losing the bet and his advertising firm? How could he not? She blamed herself. She parked her car beside his Lexus and another car she didn't recognize. He wasn't alone. She hesitated, but only for a moment. She couldn't let his having company stop her. She had to talk to Mitch. Her good news couldn't wait; neither could her apology.

On wobbly legs, she knocked on the door. Loud music played inside. She knocked harder, but no one answered. She strode around to the veranda. The music, a lively Alan Jackson tune, was more deafening with the French doors hanging open. The aroma of sizzling steaks floated on the air.

Carroll stepped through the door. "Mitch?"

A woman popped up from behind the bar. She had short blond hair cut close to her head, eyes as blue as faded denim, and a complexion as smooth as a model's. She wore a silk halter dress that clung to her ample curves, and she wielded a long cooking fork with the ease of someone used to this kitchen.

She grinned at Carroll. "Well, hi, there."

As she neared, Carroll recognized the woman. Sissy Tayback, the rich, spoiled daughter of one of Missoula's wealthiest families. Her photograph often appeared in the society section of *The Missoulian.*

Though her mind scrambled to explain Sissy's presence, Carroll cautioned herself against jumping to conclusions. "Is Mitch here?"

"Yep." Sissy poked the fork toward the ceiling and turned the stereo down to background level. "Showering."

Carroll's thoughts skidded sideways. What was going on here? She glanced toward the dining table, noticing belatedly that it was set for two, with flowers and candles, and an open bottle of wine breathing on the counter. An intimate dinner?

Her throat closed, and all of her good feelings shattered, slicing through her like icy spears of glass. She didn't want to believe it. Wanted Mitch to tell her himself. The thought made her laugh inwardly. God, how naïve could she be? She'd actually believed he'd loved her. That he'd meant his proposal.

"Could I give Mitch a message for you?"

"A message?" Carroll choked at the dismissal.

"Yes. As you can see, your timing could be better."

"What's going on?"

"We're celebrating. Had quite a scare after that lab business, you know? But today we both got a clean bill of health. And Mitch just talked my daddy into going back with his advertising agency."

"B and B Advertising?"

"That's the one."

Carroll frowned, the realization that she'd overestimated Mitch's decency and honor ripping through her head as well as her heart. He hadn't told on himself. He wasn't the man she thought he was. Maybe there wasn't any bet. No brother-in-law named Charlie. Maybe he'd made a complete fool of her.

Sissy smirked and leaned toward Carroll conspiratorially. "Between you and me, the only reason Daddy gave his business back to B and B is because Mitch asked him for my hand. We're getting engaged tonight."

"Engaged?" Carroll reeled back and caught the door frame for support. "You and Mitch?"

The shower upstairs cut off.

Sissy's face grew wary. "Yes. Look, I'd invite you to stick around, but it's a private celebration, you know?"

All Carroll could do was nod. She stumbled backward onto the veranda, somehow managing to keep on her feet.

Sissy followed her. "I'll tell Mitch you stopped by, er, I'm sorry, I don't think I caught your name."

"No. Don't bother. He and I don't have any more business."

Numbly, Carroll staggered to her car. How could she have so misjudged Mitch? Fallen for the knight-in-shining-armor bit? She'd known who and what he was before she ever met him. She was an idiot to have been sucked into his lies.

He hadn't meant one word he'd said to her. She blushed from her toes to her ear tips, a furious, humiliated heat that sickened her. She wondered if she should have told Sissy what a cad she was marrying.

But she hadn't the strength to go back. For a woman who was going to live, she felt near death, worse than when she'd found out she had only three months. Then she'd wanted desperately to live. Now that years stretched out before her, she had nothing to live for.

Without Mitch, the Mitch she'd shared those three wondrous days with, what was the point? She climbed into her car, feeling as battered as it looked. She cried all the way back to Missoula, all the self-pity she'd held at bay bursting free like water through a cracked dam. The car could be repaired. Nothing could fix what ailed her.

''He was back chasing skirts the second I left the lodge,'' Carroll told Kelly-Anne, her voice just above a whisper. They were at the library, shelving returned books. Quinn had rehired Carroll the second day she was back in town.

Kelly-Anne nodded. ''I swear men like that can't help themselves.''

''I don't know how I could have believed for a second that Mitch Bohannah was capable of making a commitment. I doubt he can even spell the word. I'm lucky to have escaped with only a battered ego.''

The look of pity in her best friend's eyes inched Carroll's distress a notch higher. Kelly-Anne tilted her head to one side. ''I'm sorry you were hurt so badly by him.''

''Hurt? No.'' Carroll laughed derisively. ''It could have been worse. I could have married him, then imagine how fast he'd have run when I started getting really sick.''

Kelly-Anne blinked. ''You wouldn't have gotten really sick.''

''Well, I . . .'' The idiocy of her argument infuriated Carroll even more. ''Well, that's not the point.''

Kelly-Anne hugged Carroll. ''No. The point is the man's a cad. And a liar. I mean, I really believed he was concerned about you. He kept bugging your mother, and me and everyone at the library. He seemed frantic to find you. I just don't understand how he could turn around and get engaged to Sissy Tayback."

"Easy. His business means everything to him. If you want to feel sorry for someone, save your pity for Sissy. Mitch won't be faithful to her. He's incapable of keeping his pants zipped."

"I guess I just don't understand men." Kelly-Anne sighed and shook her head. "If he loves Sissy, then why was he trying so hard to find you?"

"I can think of three reasons. One, he felt guilty. He was worried he might have inflicted some sexual disease on me or gotten me pregnant. Two, he was furious that I'd walked out on him. And three, his ego couldn't stand the thought that I might have found Jimmy Jack Palmetto was a better lover."

Kelly-Anne pressed her lips together, her eyes squinting as though she were recalling something. "You didn't see his face. He didn't look angry, but frantic and heartsick."

Carroll shook her head. None of this mattered. Mitch was engaged to someone else. And as much as she wanted to get past this heartache, her misery continued to the point that she feared she was distressing everyone who loved her. They'd wanted to celebrate when they found out she wasn't dying. She'd refused their party plans. But that wasn't fair to them. She had to find a way through this and put her life back together. "I don't want to talk about Mitch Bohannah anymore. Promise me here and now you won't mention his name to me again."

"I promise." Kelly-Anne pushed her book cart farther down the aisle. "I see you're still wearing your hair loose. I like it."

"I can't go back to the braid. Not yet. I'm not that Carroll anymore. In fact, some days, I'm not sure who I am anymore."

"You've changed some," Kelly-Anne concurred. "But mostly for the better, I think."

Except for the constant ache in her heart, a dull pain that wouldn't ease. Time, she supposed, would take care of that. "Maybe getting my own apartment will help me find myself. Trouble is, I'll have to stay at Mom's until I can save enough for first and last months' rents."

"Back to making plans, huh?"

"No. I can't go back to the old Carroll. She's gone forever. I won't be as free as I was the past two months, either, but I'll never again be Ms. Conservative."

"What?" Kelly-Anne teased. "No more planning for the future?"

"No. I think I'll live my life as it comes and try and make the best of what it hands me."

"Sounds like a great idea." Mitch's voice came from somewhere behind her and sent a cascade of shivers through Carroll. She felt her face begin to flame, the blush sweeping up her neck, past her jaw, and straight into her cheeks. She wanted the floor to open and swallow her.

God grant me the strength not to make a fool of myself, she prayed, slowly pivoting. He looked glorious. His raven hair spilled across his forehead, his emerald eyes burned into her. Her heart squeezed and her throat clogged.

"What happened to your head?" He leaned close to her and his aftershave roused memories that curled her toes.

She licked her dry lips, her hand going automatically to the inch-long bandage on her forehead. "An accident. I'm fine."

Concern tugged his ebony brows low, drew her attention to his eyes, where blazed a lusty fire she'd seen too often. "Are you sure?"

"Yes." She turned away from him, forcing her mind back to her job. Her hand trembled as she plucked a book from the rack.

Mitch circled her until he stood in front of her. "Can we go somewhere private and talk?"

Aware that Kelly-Anne was gawking at them, Carroll whispered, "I don't have anything to say to you."

He looked like he didn't believe her. He stepped toward her, capturing her with his scent, his gaze, and something indefinable, a magnetic pull she couldn't name, couldn't resist. He spoke in a normal voice. "I have something to tell you."

No, no. She couldn't take hearing about his engagement. Not from him. "You don't have anything to tell me that I don't already know."

His brows arched and a devilish smile tugged at the corners of his mouth, that mouth that held the key to her fantasies, that knew all the ways to drive her wild. He swept a strand of her hair from her cheek, his touch weakening her knees.

He said, "Is that so?"

"Shh." She stiffened, and leaned out of his reach. "This is a library. Please lower your voice."

"If you won't talk to me in private." He said each word louder than the previous one, unnerving her, she could tell, on purpose. "Then I'll do this here."

She cringed. Kelly-Anne scooted away, abandoning her book cart and leaving them alone in the aisle. Carroll backed into the bookcase.

Mitch reached out, but stopped short of grasping her arm. "Please, come outside with me? To the park."

Against her better judgment, she led him out and into the block-long park across the street. The weather was balmy, summer lingering into September. She hugged herself, rubbing her arms. She chilled less quickly every day, thanks to her medicine, but somehow being near Mitch had gooseflesh filming her skin.

Mitch draped his jacket across her shoulders. It held his heat, which seemed to hug her. Pain slashed her heart. She didn't want to feel as warm and protected as she did in his coat, didn't want to be reminded of how she'd felt in his arms, and yet she couldn't bring herself to remove the jacket.

He motioned to a park bench. She sat. He sat beside her,

facing her. Before he could say anything, she blurted, "I'm not pregnant."

Something like relief flashed through his eyes. Relief or regret or confusion. She couldn't be sure. She blew out a huge breath. "And I'm not dying. So, if that's all . . ."

She started to stand, but he pulled her back down. "I know. I spoke to your mother earlier today."

"What? Dear God, you didn't tell my mother I could be pregnant?"

He arched an eyebrow as though he were offended at the thought. "Of course not. I don't kiss and tell."

No, you kiss and dump. Just how is Sissy? She drew a ragged breath, and bit back the tears burning her eyes. This was not the way she wanted to part from him. She'd always prided herself on being a good loser. She'd never lost anything she loved more than Mitch, but she wouldn't survive this if she surrendered her dignity. If it killed her, she would maintain a modicum of class.

She should congratulate him on his engagement. That would be classy.

"I—" She broke off. She couldn't congratulate him. Couldn't even mention his engagement. "I—I don't kiss and tell either. If you're worried I'll go back on my word to keep mum about the bet, I won't. Your secret is safe with me."

"You can tell anyone you like." He grinned, leaning closer.

She didn't understand. "But if Charlie finds out—"

"He already knows. I told him the afternoon we came in from fishing."

"What?" Carroll's mouth dropped open. He'd already conceded the bet before she left? The knot in her chest loosened. She hadn't been totally wrong about the man Mitch was. Somehow, that made her feel better. But it left her with more questions than ever. "Why are you still working for B and B?"

"It seems Charlie was just trying to prove a point with

the bet. He doesn't want to run the agency alone. I told him the only way I'd stay his partner was if I could get our biggest client back. That wasn't easy. JD Tayback wanted to feed selected parts of my anatomy to his hogs."

She smiled and glanced up at Mitch. "I know the feeling."

"Ouch." Mitch grinned. "His terms for returning included my staying the hell away from his daughter."

Carroll turned fully toward him at that. "Isn't that going to be a little difficult, since you're marrying Sissy?"

"Marrying Sissy? I'm not marrying Sissy. Did you forget I proposed to you?"

"Well, no, but—"

"But nothing. I've never proposed to anyone else. I never will. I love you, Carroll."

She struggled to pull air into her lungs. "But Sissy was at the Diamond B, fixing an engagement dinner for two."

"You were there?"

"Yes, and she said—"

"Damn." Mitch's neck reddened. "Sissy likes to eavesdrop. She heard just enough of my conversation with her father to put her own spin on it. She showed up at the lodge with expectations that I couldn't fulfill."

"None of her expectations?"

"Not a one. I swear."

She believed him. He reached for her hands, and she let him take them into his large warm grasp. "But I ran out on you. On us."

"Yeah," he said, kissing her hands. "When I woke up that morning and you were gone and I read that note you'd left, I wanted to hunt you down and wring your pretty neck. I was pissed and hurt and feeling used. I was so certain you and I were special. That we'd shared something incredible, a once-in-a-lifetime love. How could you have lied to me? How could I have been so wrong about how you felt about me? Then I realized what you were doing."

"What was I doing?" She stared at their intertwined

hands, awed by the love that she felt in his gentle grip, that she saw in his incredible eyes, that was filling her empty heart.

"Giving me an easy way out."

She touched his face and he nuzzled her hand. Her pulse skipped joyfully. "I thought I was dying."

"I didn't care." He traced a finger along her jaw. "I knew we belonged together."

"Yes, but now I'm going to live and live and get really old with you."

"Yeah." He laughed happily, then pulled her into his arms and kissed her. "We can't lose for winning."

Strangers in the Night

Leandra Logan

Chapter One

Jack Taylor watched a flame strike the fresh cigarette in his mouth, bringing it to a swift and fragrant burn. Mildly sedated from a few scotch and waters, he inhaled in contemplation, wondering who would bother to light his fire in a strange hotel lounge, well past the social hour on a Sunday night. Ever so slowly he turned on his bar stool, blinking in a haze of his own smoke.

It was the exquisite woman from the plane. Leaning into the brass rail of the bar, holding the tiny burning match between their faces.

Her eyes danced mischievously behind the narrow lick of fire. Puckering painted lips, she snuffed it. "Noticed you needed a light . . . about twenty minutes ago. You must be the forgetful kind."

Jack shrugged with an easy smile. "Forgetful on purpose. I'm trying to kick the habit."

"Ah, I see." She stood poised in thought. "Guess we're all entitled to our bad habits. But I'd hate to be your corruptive influence so soon."

"How disappointing."

She tossed the matchbook aside, reaching for his cigarette with an unexpected southpaw hook. "Better give it to me."

He gently caught her wrist in midair, his strong thumb

pressing into tender skin, delicate bone. Her pulse was surprisingly . . . jumpy. "That's a nice pitch you have, Lefty, but leave it be. We could do with a little corruption around here."

She laughed, pulling back. "I suppose that's true."

Jack pushed his glass of scotch aside to tap some ash into a tin tray, his hand brushing hers on the bar. Her proximity was disturbing enough to raise the fine hairs on his neck, a sure sign that he was already enjoying this tango a bit too much. But what red-blooded male wouldn't allow his imagination to run wild with such a husky and teasing come-on, a scent so heady and sweet?

She blended well with his forbidden nicotine rush.

Suddenly he could think of a dozen more bad habits she might help him break.

Her right hand touched the sleeve of his tweed sports jacket just then, putting the pear-shaped diamond on her right ring finger on glittering display. Jack tried not to gape, but it was . . . big. Not quite the size of a marble, but probably worth more than his Los Angeles bungalow.

Jack had long ago discovered that left-handed women could be tricky, often wearing watches, even rings, differently than their counterparts, putting the moves on you from unexpected angles. Their eyes all glittered the same, though, just before the thrust forward. Like hers right now.

"I'm Andrea Doanes."

His mouth quirked slightly. "Jack Taylor."

"Emergency layovers like this are so frustrating, Jack. Holed up in a strange hotel, your plans messed up."

"Sometimes you have to make the best of things, Andrea." He pointed to the adjoining bar stool with the two fingers bracing his smoke. "Join me?"

"All right." The skirt of her aqua linen suit slipped higher up her silken thigh as she hoisted herself onto the high seat. The move was rather awkward, suggesting she was unaccustomed to bar perching. She hailed the bartender with more confidence, though, ordering Jack another round and a white wine for herself.

She gestured to a booth in the darkest corner of the lounge, presently filling up with a cluster of boisterous males in business suits. "I was sitting over there."

"I know."

"Really."

Jack shrugged under her curious stare. "I'm the observant kind."

As it was, a legally blind man with any kind of libido could've hardly missed her chic figure among the weary travelers and rowdy salesmen. Polished onyx hair, knotted up neatly for travel. Eyes the shape and color of almonds, roasted warm. High cheekbones that would take a blush with drama. Small breasts, plump enough to squeeze. A tight round rump that when in motion could make the walk sign blink a little longer on your average street corner.

Such a view sure beat the hell out of staring at his own reflection in the mirrored wall behind the beer taps.

The bartender, a small Hispanic man dressed in a crisp white shirt and pressed dark slacks, set the drinks down before them. His gaze lingered admiringly on the lady, then settled upon Jack, expectantly. Jack gave his head the slightest shake. As much as he would've preferred to put both drinks on his running tab, he sensed he'd offend Andrea Doanes. Even as he made the judgment call, she was hastily digging some bills from her small black handbag.

Once the transaction was settled, he lifted the fresh drink in an appreciative toast. "Thanks. It's just my size and color."

"Well . . ." She smiled, suddenly shy. "You were so kind on the plane. Rushing up to remove that rude jerk from my lap."

Jack's heavy brown brows jumped. What an understatement. The "rude jerk" was high on complimentary cocktails, all over her like a slobbering octopus. Jack had all but heard suction cups pop as he'd peeled him off her and into the aisle.

"What goes on in the first class section these days, with all the upgrades and frequent flyer miles doled out to everyone." She seemed disgusted and dazed all at once. "Three males within reach and you had to march up from coach. Such a shame the world's chock full of opportunists and cowards."

The march was hardly the longest mile to Jack, but he realized that to someone as well put out as Ms. Doanes, it might seem so. He blew smoke through his nostrils, mildly amused. "Aw, kicking down that curtain was nothin'."

"Don't be so modest. The pilot might have had a real situation if you hadn't intervened."

"Well . . ." He matched her warm inflection. "We can figure he had enough responsibilities."

The pilot, a silver-haired gent named Harlan, had come out in the midst of the ruckus to make sure Jack and the attendants had the drunk secured in his seat for the duration of the flight; but he'd had a bigger worry just then, namely the unexpected lightning storm hitting the West Coast. It screwed up their time of arrival at LAX, ultimately curtailing it completely, setting them in San Francisco on a wing and a prayer, then in this mid-priced airport hotel, the Baron, for the night.

Andrea swallowed some wine, leisurely surveying him over the rim of her glass. In a few minutes' time he went through the motions of touching his strong jawline, rolling his shoulders, and raking a hand through his chestnut hair. She sensed his new and sudden self-awareness concerning his whisker growth, worn clothes, and corner barber's trim. He didn't necessarily seem uneasy about his appearance, perhaps just baffled by her interest.

She felt no such confusion concerning his appeal. Jack Taylor was her knight in shining armor. A most unlikely hero at first glance. A far cry from the Hollywood handsome she was accustomed to, with hard blue eyes, a nose set slightly crooked from a break, and that sports jacket nearly as shiny as armor. Even his large mouth had a sullen quality to it. But it was a very attractive mouth. Surely he'd apply hard pressure to a kiss. Urgent, masterful pressure. The image brought an unusual heat to her belly. Left her anxious for a taste of his strength.

Amusement crinkled his facial lines as he tried to read her thoughts. It was as though she'd temporarily gone blank. "Didn't your mama tell you it's impolite to stare?"

She brightened and retorted saucily, "Women stare at you often, I expect."

"Few go the distance, though."

And no wonder, with the wolfish grin he was suddenly brandishing. It made her wonder if she was in over her head, if this follow-up was a mistake. She shifted uncomfortably on the stool, her voice growing stilted. "I just came over to let you know your heroics were appreciated."

His eyes crinkled with new sincerity, suggesting he'd been teasing her with that flash of bare teeth. "My pleasure. Really. You're bound to be fine now, with that louse in police custody. He won't be back tonight, or on our flight in the morning, for that matter."

She relaxed again. "If you like, I could arrange to get you first-class seating for the morning flight. How does that sound, both of us up front with all the perks."

"Nice thought. Still . . ." Wincing, he trailed off.

"Not your style?"

"Not really. I'm afraid I'm a coach kind of guy. Ample leg room makes me nervous. When things pinch me a little, I know I'm alive." As it happened, Jack was beginning to pinch in one of his favorite places below the belt and dream of bad habits sure to make her blush.

"You're a unique guy, Jack," she marveled. "Tough and funny. Bitter and sweet."

He snapped his fingers. "Hey, that's exactly what they said about me in my high school yearbook!"

They chuckled over the absurdity, a companionable

quiet falling between them then. Andrea toyed with the Baron matchbook she'd used to light up Jack's single cigarette. Jack was smoking that cigarette for all it was worth, right down to the filter stub. He had the strange desire to check her pulse again, feel that flutter of nerves in direct counterpoint to her cool sophisticated shell. She was positively electric, sending crazy mixed signals into the air.

It absolutely made no sense that she lingered here beside him. The amenities taken care of, room keys long ago secured at the front desk, Jack knew full well that she could at any time slip back into her first-class frame of mind and shimmy off. The waiting and uncertainty made him itchy, anxious. Crazy. If only she'd leave and put him out of his misery.

"So, Jack, you travel a lot?"

She would throw the conversation a life preserver. To his own frustration, he felt nothing but sheer relief. "A fair amount," he admitted. "I run a small business out of a small office in L.A."

"What kind of work do you do?"

"Marketing research. I come up with strategies to entice people to spend more money than they should. I was up in Seattle testing out a credit card for a department store chain. It's an elaborate system that offers points for every dollar spent. In turn, the points are worth free gifts."

"Is it successful?"

"Only time will tell." He puffed his cigarette. "So what's your story?"

"I live in Los Angeles too."

"Visiting relatives in Seattle?"

She toyed with a cocktail napkin, rubbing her lips together. "No. Just went to the mountains for a little retreat. To get away. Think."

As Jack's eyes strayed to the pear-shaped diamond, she self-consciously realized she'd probably been twisting it around way too much again. "You know anything about diamonds, Jack?"

"A little. I might be fooled by glass, but not by the real thing." It was clear by his meaningful expression that he knew what she wore was genuine.

Impatience marred her smooth forehead. "No, no, do you know what it means when the ring is on the right hand rather than the left?"

"What are you trying to tell me, Andrea?"

She pinkened. "That I have every right to flirt with you, I guess."

"But out of practice, maybe," he suggested mildly.

Her color deepened, her raven lashes swept low. "It shows that much?"

"I'm the observant type, remember?"

She lifted her chin with effort, as if it weighed a ton. "Well, in any case, you're right. I have been out of circulation for a few years, convincing myself that my marriage was something great. I was rarely tempted to stray and never did."

"So what happened to spoil your illusions?"

"Let's just say that my husband gave in to all sorts of temptation."

"Ah."

"Finally, catching him in the act, I could no longer deny his indiscretions. Nor could I pretend that hard work could bring any relationship around."

"So you're separated?"

"Yes. I moved to Glendale a month ago. Have a small apartment there in a nice neighborhood."

"And the retreat?"

"Was at Corbin's request. He wanted me to go away, reconsider our breakup."

Jack grimaced in disapproval. "Mighty accommodating of you to do it."

"My husband can be a very persuasive man. I thought if I humored him one last time, he might not make things so tough in the end."

Every muscle in his body tensed, down to the hands that

threatened to snap his glass to bits. "How tough does Corbin get?"

She regarded him with sympathy and wonder. "Oh, Jack. The look on your face. Surely you can't hope to save me from all the world in one single day."

That very thought had occurred to him and apparently it showed. For a man who considered his face an inscrutable canvas, his heart a steel fist, this kind of unmasking was disturbing. But something had locked in place between them the instant they'd made eye contact on the flight. As Jack faced those huge eyes, liquid with fear and hope, he was sure he could've flown without wings, landed without a parachute. Sending a drunken maniac sailing across the aisle had been a mere trifle under the circumstances. *Just as neutralizing a husband would be if it came to that.*

Was he going mad with chivalry? It was crystal clear that pound for pound, this lady carried more emotional baggage than the cargo hold of their plane. Certainly his cue for a prompt and curt good-bye. If only his tongue would form the words.

"We are strangers," she proposed softly, as though sensing his hesitation. "You shouldn't concern yourself."

Her protest was halfhearted at best, Jack realized. She wanted him to care, at least a little bit. "So, did you manage to get anything out of that retreat of yours?" he asked.

"More than you can imagine," she said with feeling. "I've come back with an unexpected dose of courage. There's no reason why one of the old dreams can't be chased. I can go back to college, or start my own business, do whatever I please."

"Not what this Corbin hoped for, though."

"Nope." Andrea ordered another round of drinks and Jack promptly put them on his tab. "He prefers me cooperative."

"You seem young to be in this sad mess," he observed.

She twirled the stem of her fresh glass. "Twenty-five. I was a twenty-one-year-old student when Corbin first took an interest me. He'd showed up on campus, scouting locations for his latest film.'' She shook her head wistfully. ''I was too young to know.''

Jack made thoughtful sounds. ''Andrea Doanes . . . Corbin Doanes. He produces those blockbuster movies, doesn't he?''

''Yes. I figured you instantly made the connection.''

''I'm not much for fiction.''

She pushed wisps of black hair from her forehead, visibly pleased. ''It's so refreshing to talk to someone who doesn't automatically worship him, define me merely as 'the wife.' ''

''Especially as being 'the wife' has made you so unhappy.''

She bit her lip. ''It would've been a fine label had I been appreciated. I've been a great asset to Corbin always, acting as his production coordinator, his right hand—or left in my case,'' she joked. ''But he's never acknowledged any of this. He's taken all my help and insisted upon perceiving me as the shallow trophy wife. With time, it's all gotten way out of hand, the power, the cocaine, the lovers.''

He couldn't keep a trace of disgust out of his voice. ''Why'd you stick with him so long, Andrea?''

''Because I thought he would come to see the truth. If I worked hard enough— If he kicked the coke habit—'' She broke off helplessly.

''Everyone in Hollywood divorces. Strange he can't be a good sport about it.''

''No, Corbin doesn't like to lose—ever. People just don't quit him. He buys them like possessions and expects lifelong loyalty.'' Her voice cracked. ''Hey, I know I sound stupid for falling for a fairy-tale illusion, but he talked a good game. And it was all quite nice in the beginning . . .''

Jack grew grim. ''That type of predator can be very convincing, smooth, earnest, drawing people in without giving away his sickness.'' Jack generally saw through them himself, but not always. It was only human to be fooled once in a while.

The hour was growing late, the lounge about to close. Andrea took the initiative, making motions to leave. He didn't stop her.

"Thanks for listening, Jack. Thanks for everything." She slipped off the stool, drawing a hesitant breath. "Would it be all right if I called you sometime?"

Dead certain that he was far too forgettable for her league of play, he went along with the game. Reaching for the hotel matchbook she'd tossed aside earlier, Jack scribbled his private office number inside.

She tucked the matchbook in her handbag. "I'll give a shout next time I need a hero."

He swiveled on his seat, and grazed her downy cheek. "One long bicycle ride and you'll be fine. Guaranteed."

"What do you mean?"

He winked. "You'll figure it out, when you're ready."

A trifle wary, she adjusted the strap on her shoulder bag and buttoned her aqua jacket. "Good night, then."

Jack watched Andrea glide out the glass door leading to the lobby, all at once regretting a lost conquest, and the release of his private number. He should've cut her loose an hour ago, before her story could rock him.

Chapter Two

Jack closed down the bar, then headed for his room for a relaxing hot shower. He was standing under the jet spray when the telephone began to ring. Dripping with suds, he charged out into the bedroom. The phone sat on a night-stand, along with a clock radio that read one thirty-five. He lunged for the receiver, stubbing his toe in the process. "Yes!"

The feminine voice on the line was in direct counter-point to his bark. "Jack, I get the message."

"What are you talking about?"

There was a hesitant breath. "They say when you fall off a bicycle, the best thing to do is dust off your seat and climb back on."

He chuckled then, recognizing the caller. "Yeah, Lefty, that's about it. None too quick, though, are you?"

"Smart ass. As it happens, I figured out the puzzle a long while ago."

"That should've given you the peace of mind to sleep like a baby."

"Tell that to my body. I can't simmer down, Jack, hard as I've tried."

Running a towel through his soppy hair, he shifted from one leg to another, wired with expectancy. "Sounds like you're blaming me."

She made a husky hooting sound. "Of course I am! I want that ride you described, Jack. A whole new ride on a different style of bike."

Jack caught a glimpse of himself in the full-length mirror on the closet door, the bare and rigid giant, a warrior full of battle scars inside and out. It was a reality check. At thirty-six he was beyond this kind of spontaneous encounter. The risks were generally a mile high, everything from fetishes, to kinks, to cons. He'd long ago stopped sending out indiscriminate mating signals to every willing bit of fluff.

But this lady was an exception, a goddess, a dream. The refined kind who initiated eye contact on a street corner, only to scurry away on fancy high heels because he appeared a little too rough, a little too knowing, a little too frightening.

Under other circumstances, Andrea probably would have been skittering too. But he'd rescued her, so she had confidence in him. A confidence that would probably evaporate in the heat of the morning sun, like the fog on San Francisco Bay. Could he endure it?

"Jack," she prodded over the line. "Do you understand what I'm saying? I want you to be the one to saddle me up."

"Oh, honey . . ."

"Was it all just so much talk?"

"I was trying to help you sort it out, but I didn't mean me." The protest was forced, painful, regrettable. "I meant men in general. Sex in general."

"But I want *you.*"

He released a taut breath. "That's very flattering, but I suspect you're seeing me through tired and lonely eyes."

"I've never been more awake in my life!"

"You know what I'm getting at," he replied, as cross as she. "Illusions have gotten you into trouble before, even with your eyes wide open."

"You're very real, Jack." She grew sultry. "Built to last, for hours, I bet."

He shuddered, blood rushing to his groin. "Morning always comes, though, and you'd find me no prize in the harsh light of day."

"Who can ever tell?"

"I've been down the road time and again. I know."

"Is something wrong with me, Jack? Corbin's always inferred I have certain . . . failings."

"He's a lying bastard. It's all part of the mind-control game. A classic ploy."

"I'd like to believe that."

Jack crunched his eyes shut. "You've led me right into this."

"Yeah, sure. Tell me you haven't been thinking about us rolling around naked and I'll say good-bye."

"Okay, honey. I'm in eight-zero-nine. Or do you want me to—" Jack broke off as he heard a dial tone in his ear. So she was determined to provide the room service. Seemed only neighborly to unlatch the door.

Andrea knew she was out of her mind, about to give herself to a stranger. But Jack seemed so very right for her just now. Edgy, reckless, and exciting. Better yet, he still knew the difference between right and wrong and put up some struggle to stand for something. A struggle Corbin gave up on long ago.

She knocked once on Jack's door, then twisted the knob to find it unlocked. She quickly slipped inside and closed herself in. Sliding the security bolt in place she turned to take in her surroundings. The room was set in a dull glow from the two wall-mounted lamps flanking the bed and a wedge of light pouring from the half-closed bathroom door. The decor in her room was the same, gold spread and carpeting, a low dresser holding a television set. King-size bed.

The hiss of running water was the only sound.

Andrea was set for easy unwrapping, her clothing and

hair loose. Kicking off her slip-on sandals, she began to move in her bare feet toward the wedge of bathroom light. With every step she peeled off clothing, her simple cotton wraparound dress, her bra, her panties, dropping them in her wake.

With the keen instincts of a tiger, Jack stood in the tub, tracking her progress in the next room. Agonizing seconds later the connecting door opened all the way. Through the filmy white shower curtain he caught sight of her curvy, flesh-toned silhouette. There was no hesitation; she immediately curled her scarlet-tipped fingers around the front edge of the curtain and drew it back.

He was prepared for her nudity, but hardly the perfection of her body. Full high breasts and heart-shaped buttocks, so very firm. Smooth skin baked to a new copper-penny finish, every inch of her done evenly, right down to the downy triangle between her thighs.

Ever so daintily she stepped inside the enclosure and gave a little shiver as the prickly jet spray hit her chest. The circulation of cool air and warm water caused her nipples to quickly harden to small tight buds.

The tantalizing sight brought Jack to full erection. He couldn't wait to touch her. With a low growl he caught her by the shoulders with his huge hands, lifting her on tiptoes. Hauling her close, he crushed her breasts against his chest, rubbing those tight buds into his mat of coarse hair. His voice was a hot gust against her lush mane of hair. "Let me know if it hurts."

"Hurts so good, darling." Andrea curled her arms around his neck, lavishing in the burning friction between their bodies. Her only true ache centered lower, a moist heaviness that had settled between her legs.

She gave a small cry as the hands that were roving her back fixed in the small of her spine and dipped her beneath the jet spray.

"I want you wet, Lefty."

"I came wet."

With a low, achy groan he initiated a deep kiss. Andrea responded in kind, melting her mouth to his, sucking his tongue, tasting his unique flavor with a dose of sluicing water.

Moans echoed off the tiled walls as they clung to one another, roiling in sensation.

Without warning, he clamped his hands on her round little bottom and hoisted her up on his hipbones. Hanging tight around his neck, she wrapped her legs around his middle, pressing her petals of flesh against his rigid sex.

He stared down at her then, his blue eyes gleaming like the flame that had lit his single cigarette. Andrea met his gaze steadily with a husky command. "Move me."

Balancing her cheeks in his palms, he slid her labia up and down the length of his swollen penis, causing hot delicious sensations to spread through them like liquid butter.

Teased to the brink, Andrea braced her hands on his collarbone, and took him inside her.

Caught in a slick velvet tunnel of ecstacy, Jack leaned against the tub enclosure as she hugged his shoulders, put the squeeze on him with tight internal muscle. Then he began to move her over his shaft, in a pumping motion. Seconds slipped to minutes. And then it was over. A shuddering climax that carried them to the depths of the tub. They lay together in a spent heap, the water lightly washing them.

Jack was the first to rise and exit, giving Andrea some downtime to get herself together. She emerged from the bathroom some minutes later to find him half lounging in a chair near the closet, one leg raised over the arm, dressed in a white terry robe courtesy of the hotel.

She focused on a length of exposed masculine thigh. "You're overdressed, Jack."

"I was a little chilly. Picked up your clothes, too, draped them on the dresser."

"I'm plenty warm in my skin." She sauntered closer with a feline hip sway. "Care to find my hottest spot?"

He regarded her cautiously, through hooded eyes. Warning bells clanged madly in his head. This woman was entangled in a very complicated fix. And things were going to get a lot worse before they got better. "Andrea, I think we're in deep enough as it is."

"I like it better when you call me Lefty." She knelt down before him on the worn gold carpet, driving a hand up beneath his tented robe, over smooth hairy muscle.

He quickly caught her wrist as he had in the lounge, gratified to find her pulse hammering off the scale under his thumb. How much he wanted her again. But it was crazy, foolish, and too much fun not to have consequences.

She tipped her gaze to his, puzzled by his hesitation. "This is uncomplicated sex, Jack. That's all."

His smiled tightly. "There is no such thing."

"We make the rules, no one else."

"Oh, Lefty, when you talk like that, you give me all sorts of selfish ideas." He reached down and stroked her cheek. She closed her eyes, resting her face in his palm, burrowing into his touch. He wondered how long it had been since she'd been touched with any tenderness.

In the end, he lost the struggle for any above-the-belt reasoning. The surrender coincided with her fingers loosening the sash of his robe, parting the terry fabric from his damp and chilled skin. He sank back in the chair, blissfully adrift in a mindless sea of sensation as she came down on him.

Nobody used her tongue more cleverly than a left-handed woman. Or maybe he just had a particular weakness for them. At the moment, it didn't particularly matter . . .

The best-laid plans . . . The innocuous saying took on sweet erotic meaning to Jack as he slowly stirred to life the following morning. He stretched his strong bare limbs on the cushy motel mattress, feeling every pull of muscle, every achy spot; reminders that he'd been thoroughly laid indeed.

Instinctively, longingly, he reached out for Andrea.

Finding only empty space to the touch, his eyes flew open and he jerked into a seated position.

"Lefty?" he called out thickly, staring at the open bathroom door.

He needn't have bothered and he knew it. Clearly, he was alone. The room held an unmistakable hollowness.

But Andrea Doanes hadn't been a dream. Dreamy, yes, but real flesh and all woman. The scent of sex, the damp white sheets, went far to support the reality. As did something else. His large mouth crooked slightly as he pulled a long black strand of hair from the empty pillow beside his.

If only she'd stayed.

Thankfully she hadn't.

In any case he'd have to get by with his naughty memories of last night. Just pick up and carry on. He'd ignore her on the last leg of their journey if she wanted it that way.

The flight to LAX! Suddenly he realized that the sliver of light streaming in between the gold drapes seemed rather bright. He snatched up his wristwatch from the nightstand to find that it read 9:30. The dawn was history—along with his scheduled flight! He generally woke up early automatically, but the night of exhausting play had no doubt confused his body clock. By contrast, she probably hadn't slept a wink, her adrenaline on intravenous feed as she mused whether he'd been a mistake. The last thing he recalled as he drifted off was her deepening grimace; to his experienced eye that suggested uncertainty, emotional retreat.

She'd probably tiptoed out of the room with deliberate stealth, hoping to leave without further contact. A dirty trick to play on a marketing consultant who, for all she knew, might have had several appointments waiting for him down in Los Angeles.

But he was a big boy now, not above stacking the deck with a few tricks of his own from time to time. It was probably all for the best.

If ever there was a woman who should remain a lovely

and enchanting one-night stand, it was Andrea Lefty Doanes.

Andrea was at that moment already back in her Glendale apartment, trying not to think about Jack. Still dressed in the yellow sundress she'd worn on the flight from San Francisco, she opened windows, then dug into the refrigerator to take inventory of its contents. The half-dozen cartons of yogurt wedged in the fridge door were expired. She turned each carton over to confirm the date before pitching it in the stainless steel trash bin beside the stove. The cherry vanillas were the oldest. Perhaps even outdated when she'd purchased them.

Andrea huffed in frustration. She had to stop walking around like a zombie and pay attention to life's smallest details. Start to really live again.

But she'd begun that process yesterday, hadn't she? An affirmative smile lifted the corners of her mouth as she remembered the night's uninhibited passion. Jack Taylor had tapped into long-buried energies and revitalized her. Given her hope and confidence.

So how could she ever justify giving him the slip the way she had? Creeping out of his room like a prowler in the wee hours, intent on putting space between them.

Jack had to be awake by now, furious to discover he'd missed their flight. Maybe she should've left a parting note of some kind. But how could she have possibly put her feelings into words?

Dearest Jack: Sorry I had to cut loose so abruptly, but you're heaven and hell to me all at once. I'm so very grateful for your attention, but hate the idea of ever being completely possessed by a man again. And you have that power to possess a woman. At least this woman . . .

Andrea gave the fridge door a frustrated shove into place. Space wasn't proving much comfort, she realized. He'd rocked her world so completely that she still felt vulnerable to his charm miles down the coast.

The ring of the telephone startled her, breaking the spell. Since her return she'd been pointedly ignoring the four messages waiting in her answering machine. Most of her Hollywood friends sensed that something was wrong in her marriage and were trying to probe for details. But she'd agreed with Corbin that they would keep a lid on their troubles until the last possible minute.

Odds were it was Corbin himself on the line, wondering if she'd come to her senses about the divorce. She had, of course, but not in a way Corbin would like. In the span of a few hours Jack Taylor had rescued her from a masher with a heavy hand, brought her to climax with a slow one, and somewhere in between managed to rekindle her spirit with a dose of common sense.

Corbin's retreat plan had backfired on him big-time.

The answering machine picked up the call on the seventh ring. To Andrea's surprise, it was Corbin's sister's voice she heard.

"Andie? This is Lynn again. Hate to be a pest—"

Andrea picked up the receiver and shut down the machine. "Hey, I'm here."

"You're finally back! I was worried."

"There was a delay in San Francisco last night."

"Heard about the storm on the radio. You okay?"

"Perfect. Is there something you need, Lynn?"

"Can you stop by the house today, Andie? You have some mail here, and I have more questions about this job-from-hell you've passed on to me."

"You should be firmer with your brother. Tell him to hire more office help."

Lynn gave a soft hoot. "Then Corbin would have to admit that you were doing the job of three people, and he isn't going to do that."

"So true. When do you want me to come?"

"Now would be best."

Andrea detected trouble in her sister-in-law's tone, but

didn't call her on it. With the promise to be right over, she hung up.

Poor Lynn. At this point she was still desperately trying to keep a foot planted in both camps, caring both for her brother and sister-in-law. Andrea could hardly believe she and Corbin shared the same gene pool.

Chapter Three

The Doanes estate cut an impressive swath on Beverly Hills's Banyon Drive. Beyond the high-security fencing, sprawling lawns fronted a giant stone and glass mansion that served as both a home and production offices. Built in the thirties, it had been added to several times until it now resembled a castlelike fortress.

There'd been a time when Andrea had indeed believed the property was straight out of a fairy tale, along with Corbin himself. Now as she eased her sleek red Corvette to a stop at the gates, she felt nothing but a wave of claustrophobia. It was a strain to smile into the camera for the sake of the security guard on duty, wait unreasonably long for the gates to yawn open for access. He was checking with Lynn, no doubt, to make sure she was welcome. The entire staff housed in the mansion had grown cold toward her after her departure from the residence. Considering how kind she'd always been to them, it hurt.

She took the driveway with more show than necessary, stepping hard on the accelerator to squeal along the winding strip of blacktop.

Let them all know she was here. Damn them.

Pulling the sports car to an aburpt halt under the sheltered entrance, she clattered up the stone steps in white sandals, the skirt of her yellow sundress aflutter.

Was Corbin home? If not, he would hear that she'd been carefree today. Hear it over and over again from all his resident spies. Andrea Doanes was on the way out, making room for the original Andrea Kramer, an older, wiser version of herself. There were battle scars to deal with, but Corbin's diminishing tutelage hadn't knocked her completely out of the ring.

Jack Taylor had come along at just the right time, giving her morale a boost, reaffirming her worth. Images of their lovemaking sprang to mind. What a glorious way to kick off her liberation.

How furious Corbin would be if he learned of her encounter with Jack. Notorious for adhering to a double standard, Corbin would find a way to strike back, punish her. As tempting as it would be to throw her encounter in his face, she would wisely remain silent on the subject.

"Andie!" Just as Andrea was about to ring the bell, the varnished front door swung wide. Lynn Doanes herself stood on the threshold rather than the expected maid. Like her brother, Lynn was a stunning blonde, with small even features and a smile that could dazzle a crowd. But in constrast to Corbin, Lynn's green eyes held genuine depth and vulnerability.

"Hello, Lynn." Andrea gave her sister-in-law a brief squeeze, then complimented her on her smart cream suit.

Lynn led Andrea through the spacious foyer and into the wing housing the production offices. "The suit's skirt is tighter than I like, but Corbin's hoping to pitch a concept to some investors this afternoon, so I'm on call to be especially posh and obliging."

Andrea had been on just such a call many times over and didn't miss dealing with the rich, arrogant financial backers who treated her like window dressing. It was a direct insult considering how important she was in the operation of Corbin's office.

As usual, Andrea found the plush gray and plum office humming with activity. Corbin believed in a communal existence—except for himself and a few cherished employees—so dividers were all that separated workers from each other. An ideal setup for keeping his staff on their toes. Any misstep would undoubtedly be reported by someone in the ranks hoping to rise a notch.

Andrea's former desk was right out in the line of fire. She was relieved that Lynn was now the one obligated to occupy the modern glass and chrome piece, sit in the sentinel position.

"Now, about that mail, Andie."

Andrea stood by, toying with the leather strap of her shoulder bag as Lynn nervously dug into a drawer for Andrea's correspondence. *What was the matter with her?* Perhaps it simply was the obvious, Andrea's marital dissatisfaction, Corbin's constant demands, the feeling of being watched by the employees.

"Is Corbin here?" Andrea whispered, gazing over the sea of faces hustling between cubicles.

Lynn's voice lowered to match hers in volume. "Yes, sorry. Barged out to poolside with some reporter from *Movieland Magazine* and Mindi Fellowes. You know Mindi, she's starring in his current film."

Andrea knew the ambitious actress right down to the skin. It was Mindi that Andrea caught in bed with Corbin. Finally, Andrea had been confronted with the physical proof of Corbin's infidelity. It wasn't a vague party rumor that he could sweet-talk away or some tabloid innuendo that he could laugh off. Of course he'd tried to force his double standard on her, had expressed outrage that she dared voice an objection. He was *the* Corbin Doanes, after all, and had appetites she could never hope to satisfy or understand. He even claimed to be protecting her with his secrets!

"Here we are." Rather than simply hand Andrea some letters as expected, Lynn carefully set some file folders and smaller envelopes on a stack of files already positioned on the desktop. With two hands she pushed everything across the desk. "May want to sit down," Lynn suggested brightly, her intense green eyes sending her a darker, subtler message.

Andrea wrinkled her nose in confusion, but pulled a guest chair up to the desk and began to slit open envelopes addressed to her. She tried not to scowl as she realized several were already slit open.

"Ms. Doanes?" Both ladies turned to the open doorway to find a frazzled main-floor maid in a starched gray uniform. "There is someone at the gate causing a ruckus."

Lynn reluctantly rose to the call. "I'll be back, Andie. *Keep reading*."

Andrea waded through flyers and magazines, then opened the top folders to find more flyers. Why were they stuffed in folders? she wondered. Something was up here. Lynn was putting up a decent front for the ranks, but she was troubled, trying to send a message.

Certain she was on display, Andrea kept a placid expression as she hauled the weightier folder into her lap. Her features froze as she stared down at the top sheet inside. The head of the page was stamped "Confidential," a deterent that was to be obeyed immediately by the staff, one that could get any snoop on the premises fired on the spot.

Andrea found the papers to be most confidential indeed.

They were surveillance reports on *her*.

One by one she thumbed through the four identical folders holding the reports. Each folder held a week's worth, dating back a month to the day when she'd moved out of the mansion to Glendale.

The bastard had been spying on her throughout their separation!

And what dull reading; all the inconsequential details of her movements were painstakingly reported. Corbin had been smug, no doubt, monitoring her simple lifestyle. To him her existence probably seemed like hell. Mundane, predictable, safe.

It had been all those things—until Jack. Andrea lurched forward in the deep leather chair, causing thick loose black hair to curtain her face. She hid behind the shield for a long quaking moment, absorbing the shock, considering the implications. If Corbin didn't know about Jack yet, he would be finding out in short order. And how it would enrage him, make the divorce terms so much tougher to hammer out. Corbin would be even less inclined to give her the settlement she deserved.

To think she thought she could control her secret encounter by keeping her mouth shut. It never occurred to her that Corbin would have his ways . . .

Quickly she sifted through the last file for the final installment. The reports ended in Seattle, shortly before the flight out.

"Andie?"

Lynn's prompt jogged Andrea back to life.

"Just an irate actor at the gate," she announced with a huff, sliding back into her chair.

"Oh." Andrea's voice was small and distant.

Lynn leaned forward on the desk between them to speak in a compassionate hush. "I planned to prepare you. I'm so sorry."

"I should've known something was up," she murmured tightly. "He was giving me so much freedom."

"Corbin predicted you'd quickly grow bored away from the action, eventually come crawling back for a second chance. I just didn't know why he was so confident, or that he was keeping such close tabs on you. Anyway, the retreat to Seattle was supposed to be the last straw in your exile."

"The arrogance."

Lynn entwined her fingers on the desk. "You aren't open to talk of a reconciliation, are you?"

There was a detectable note of hope in Lynn's voice and it tore at Andrea's heart. "Not a chance," she gently admitted. "I won't make a public spectacle out of the divorce, but I do want it, and my share of community property. After all, I have been an enormous help to Corbin these past four years."

"You've been such a good friend too, Andie. I'm going to miss you."

Andrea's heart sank further; she realized that Lynn would have to choose between her and Corbin soon, and the only practical choice was Corbin. Lynn couldn't give up the family fortunes by openly siding with her former sister-in-law. Lynn would only resent her in the end if she did.

Andrea separated her mail from the reports and pushed the folders back across the desk. "Thanks for showing me these. It was risky."

Lynn calmly but methodically put the files back in her bottom drawer. "I could never remove them from the house, of course, so this setup seemed the only way."

Andrea was grim. "Soon enough I won't even be allowed back in here for my mail."

Lynn regarded her in concern. "Does it give you a creepy feeling, knowing someone's been watching you?"

"It's still sinking in, I suppose. What was the name on the letterhead? Cal-Sun Investigations?"

Lynn nodded. "Never heard of them."

"Odd that Corbin wouldn't use someone from his usual agency, the place he has on retainer." Andrea curled her fist. "How I'd like to catch him—or her—in the act!"

"Well, be on the lookout for a familiar male face. One of the reports had a note scribbled in the margin, something about getting him a ticket. Must've been to Seattle and back. Ooo, I knew my brother was a sneak, but I can't believe to what extent."

"I can't believe he's gone this far."

Lynn shrugged. "Corbin was controlling even as a child. And hot tempered . . . At least you didn't get involved with some other guy. That would really set him off. Make all our lives even more miserable."

Andrea felt her throat tighten as she envisioned the upcoming installment covering Jack. "When is the next report due?"

"Any time now." Lynn tugged at her suit jacket sleeve to check the time on her diamond-studded Cartier watch. "In fact the messenger is late. Why?"

"I would like to see it. First, I mean."

Lynn hesitated. "That might be a little tricky. Corbin left directions from the outset that the daily delivery be placed on his desk unopened. Since I open all his business mail, the strange request was what aroused my suspicions in the first place."

"But he is preoccupied today, isn't he? Mindi is always a distraction and he loves showing off for the press."

"Point taken. He wouldn't interrupt a precious interview in progress just to make sure the report arrived."

"How much longer should the interview last?"

Lynn was thoughtful. "On the outside, I figure we have perhaps another thirty minutes. But is it so important, Andie, when all the reports so far have been innocuous? Wouldn't it be better to just take the information you have and go?"

"I would like to see it, Lynn. For my own peace of mind."

Raw fear sprang into Lynn's bright green eyes, then her lovely face settled into a deep frown. Andrea was sure Lynn was absorbing the implications of such a request, beginning to wonder if this friendly gesture was going to backfire on her somehow.

Andrea decided to placate her with a half-truth. "It's probably nothing, but I got kind of chummy with the passengers on my flight. You can understand how it happened, lonely souls stranded in a hotel bar. I spoke to men. They spoke to me."

"Very understandable," Lynn agreed with relief. "That would happen on a layover. And you are a knockout." She relaxed in her chair. "Hopefully this private eye is good, smart enough to judge the situation for what it was."

Lord, how Andrea hoped he wasn't that good.

Chapter Four

Planning to intercept the courier at the front door, Lynn brought Andrea back out to the foyer on the pretext of examining a new abstract print on the wall. Andrea was wired from head to toe, waiting for the doorbell to ring, keeping an eye on the corridor leading to the lavish outdoor pool area. It was a race against time: prompt delivery of the goods, versus Corbin's exercise in self-importance.

Finally, the doorbell rang. It took all of Andrea's willpower not to play lady of the manor once again and lunge forward. Instead she hovered out of sight near a Chinese floor vase as Lynn accepted the large red and white envelope.

"You look like you could kill the messenger today," the uniformed man joked, handing Lynn a clipboard for her signature.

Lynn smiled tartly as she signed off on the top sheet. "That will depend upon your message. See you tomorrow."

The courier looked a trifle surprised by the comeback as he wheeled round for a hasty departure.

Andrea's gaze strayed to the corridor as Lynn closed the front door. "Where can we look at this, I wonder?"

Lynn gestured to the formal powder room just off the living room. "Let's slip in there."

They locked themselves into the plush blue and white lavatory with gold-plated fixtures and gleaming triple-sink vanity. Andrea turned the envelope over in her hands with a thoughtful expression. "We have to open this without leaving a mark on it."

"I know." Lynn frowned, then moved over to the walnut vanity and opened a top drawer to extract a silver-tonged hair pick. "Maybe if we run this along a seam." She set the envelope on the marble sink and with a gentle hand slowly slit open the bottom edge. Standing back with a shaky sigh, she allowed Andrea to remove the papers inside.

Andrea's fingers shook as she paged through the update on her. It was a strange feeling, to see your life spelled out in black-and-white for another person's benefit.

Lynn paced around anxiously, peering over her sister-in-law's shoulder. "So, anything?"

"Well, no." Stunned, Andrea checked and rechecked the time line of her movements. "There isn't a suggestive word about me. Nothing revealing at all."

"Wonderful!" Lynn rejoiced. "So this private eye has some sense of fairness, just as I hoped, and realized you were socializing harmlessly."

Andrea didn't buy in to the fact that a spy in Corbin's employ would make such a merciful judgment call. All the other aspects of this report, save the hazy gap of time during the flight and layover, were like the previous ones, detailed, methodical, detached. So why omit the sexy paydirt her husband could use to diminish her reputation, destroy her credibility?

Not wishing to burden Lynn with further confidences or questions, Andrea silently handed over the papers to her. Lynn returned to the vanity to edge them back into the envelope.

"I am so relieved for you, Andie." Rummaging around in the ornate medicine cabinet, Lynn discovered some clear nail polish. Ever so gently she brushed a beading of the sticky sealant along the bottom flap of the envelope to close it up like new.

Andrea sighed. ''Guess I'll be going, now.''

Lynn whirled around just as Andrea was grasping the doorknob. ''Be prepared to hear from Corbin today.''

Andrea's fingers tightened on the glass knob. ''I know. He'll be waiting for the good news that I'm a mess on my own, that I'm coming back to stay.''

''You'll be careful when you turn him down, won't you?''

''Oh, Lynn, he'll never hear that you showed me those reports, I promise you.''

''The going will get tough . . .''

''I know. But I would never jeopardize your position here, I promise.''

Lynn scooted up to give her a big hug. ''Do me one last favor. Stay put here while I deliver the report to Corbin's desk.'' She waved the envelope. ''Wouldn't want anyone catching you in the vicinity of this thing.''

Andrea stepped away from the door, readjusting her shoulder bag. ''Okay. I'll count to twenty slowly. Then I'm outta here.''

When Andrea did eventually make for a break across the foyer, it was too late for a clean one. There were footsteps and conversation echoing from the personal quarters on the right side of the house.

Her heart sank as Corbin emerged from the patio with Mindi Fellowes and the man presumably from *Movieland Magazine*. As they approached, she felt she had no choice but to stop and play the beguiling Mrs. Doanes.

''Ah, darling. Welcome home.'' Squeezing her upper arms, Corbin leaned close to kiss Andrea's cheek and make introductions. ''You know Mindi, of course, and this is a *reporter*, Lance Green.'' There was warning in his tone and painful pressure in his fingertips. ''I wasn't expecting you back yet. How unfortunate that you just missed my chat with Lance.''

Andrea understood. Corbin was in the process of hustling the newsman on his way with a favorable story and did not want his flimflam tampered with.

"Perhaps we could chat for a moment, Mrs. Doanes," Lance Green suggested. "Add the spouse angle to my article."

She begged off wearily. "Another time."

"I explained to Lance that you were in Seattle, darling, scouting a location for a film in the works."

Andrea didn't skip a beat. "Yes. And there was a mixup with my return flight, Mr. Green. I'm afraid I'm exhausted. You know how it is."

Corbin was actually beaming with approval as he released her. Never giving her credit for any acting skills, he assumed she was back in the saddle again, and damn glad for it.

"Another time, then, Green," Corbin was saying as he clapped a hand to Lance's shoulder, skillfully guiding him to the front door. "Thanks so much for the visit."

Andrea watched their exchange. It was easier to distance herself emotionally from Corbin now and she could see more objectively how his good looks and charisma took people in. A tall, elegant figure in his late forties, dressed to perfection, he was magic to the public, the fair-haired boy spinning family-themed yarns for the big screen. No wonder his fans adored him.

When Corbin turned back to the women he was still smiling. "So, Andrea. Shall we talk?"

"Later would be better." She patted her large shoulder bag. "Just came for my mail. And you are busy. With Mindi . . ."

He grew patronizing. "Don't mind Mindi. She knows all about the trouble."

"She should," Andrea retorted, "she's part of the trouble!"

"But she's been trying to be most supportive in your absence."

Andrea folded her arms across the bodice of her yellow sundress, regarding them coolly. "Supportive from the missionary position I caught you in or one of your other more inventive positions?"

Corbin's gruff laughter echoed off the high plaster ceiling. "That's a rather sharp joke coming from you."

"A sad joke is more like it." She glanced at Mindi and was taken aback by the disturbing gleam in her eye.

"Oh, lighten up," Corbin scoffed. "We know you're back where you belong. Let's talk it through."

Andrea squared her shoulders. "All right, Corbin, let's lay it on the line. I'm leaving you for good, that's all there is to it."

He remained remarkably cool and confident. "Now that is a sad joke."

"Believe it."

He pressed his fingertips to his mouth, as if in contemplation. "At least hear me out. I've thought over your complaints and realize that I have probably neglected you. Being married was a new experience for me. I'm accustomed to tuning people out at times, expecially those closest to me."

Andrea shook her head, baffled. "I don't see . . ."

"I believe I've found a way to involve you all the deeper in my life, darling. Give you the closeness you desire. Share as we never have before."

Mindi sidled closer to Andrea, murmuring into the curve of her ear. "It would be a very workable arrangement for all."

"All?" Andrea glared at one, then the other. "Where, exactly, does Mindi fit in, Corbin?"

Mindi chuckled, tracing her finger along Andrea's bare shoulder blade. "It would be the three of us from now on, see?"

Andrea shoved Mindi away with a cry. "Not a chance!"

Corbin seemed genuinely perplexed. "Think about it, Andrea. A communal arrangement would add excitement, variety."

"For you!"

"Yes, of course," he admitted, matter-of-fact. "But it follows that if I'm happy, I will be around more for you."

Andrea absorbed the latest blow, amazed that they just kept coming. Finally, she found her voice again. "Any third party in a marriage is unthinkable to me and you should know better than to even suggest it," she said scathingly.

"I told you she was too provincial to even consider a change," Mindi mocked.

"You think you can keep him any better than I have, Mindi?" Andrea challenged. "He'll tire of you too. Guaranteed."

Mindi gasped in affront, appealing to Corbin. Corbin didn't even acknowledge the actress. He had eyes only for his wife, the one who was getting away. "I haven't tired of you, Andrea," he stated softly. "That is why I am trying to renegotiate."

Andrea was way beyond listening to his pitch. But she did consider trying to shame Mindi into using some common sense. She was on the crude side, but at twenty, hardly old enough to know better. In his bid for total control, Corbin would see her confidence and creativity stripped away in no time. Then wearying of Mindi, Corbin would select another partner and another.

Sadly, Andrea could think of no words persuasive enough to convince Mindi of her fate as she stood by so cockily, dead-bang sure she would be the next Mrs. Corbin Doanes if she hung tough. Hell, maybe Mindi even deserved to wear the title. Perhaps the punishment fit the crime.

Corbin's patronizing veneer was thinning by the second. "Think this through more carefully, Andie. You'd miss the power, the glamour, the wealth. You'd miss me."

Andrea took a deep breath. "My favorite times of our marriage were the early months when you were exclusively my own, Corbin, before the rumors started, before I was forced into a fog of denial and excuses.''

''We are worth another chance. Take my offer.''

''No, I believe marriages are built for two and no more.''

''I can't believe that after all the time spent under my tutalege, you still think so narrowly.'' His tanned shoulders lifted under his filmy gauze shirt. ''This is not a bad deal, Andrea.''

''Isn't it?''

''Consider the alternative,'' he suggested, ''running off penniless, with your reputation destroyed.''

Andrea's mouth dropped. ''You wouldn't go that far.''

''Oh, I will follow through on both counts. Wait and see.''

His twisted expression confirmed as much. Her heart about to explode, she stumbled for the front door. He reached out for her one last time.

''Don't make me hurt you.''

''Oh, let her go, sweetie,'' Mindi snapped.

Andrea met her husband's lethal gaze with her last ounce of savvy. ''Take the bimbo's advice, Corbin. It's undoubtedly the best thing to ever fall out of her mouth.'' With that she flung open the door and left.

Corbin stood in the door frame as she took the fieldstone steps to the sweeping driveway. Though not a giant man by any means, his raw energy had slamming force. ''You will not do me in this way.''

She paused by her Corvette, a trembling hand on the door handle. ''Consider it done.'' Wasting not a motion, she slipped behind the wheel and sped away.

Andrea was several blocks from the estate's gates when the tears began to flow. How much was a woman on her own supposed to handle? When did a woman call in a hero?

Suddenly Jack's image floated into her misty vision. Maybe she'd abandoned him too soon. And maybe he hadn't liked it. In either case, there was only one way to find out.

Chapter Five

"Jack Taylor, you look like the proverbial cat with a canary between his teeth."

"Lovin' life is why, Glory." Jack had sauntered into his downtown L.A. office Monday with a mile-wide grin that put his only employee on instant alert.

Glory Kane shifted her bulky form in the creaky desk chair, her pudgy face alive with curiosity. Jack met her bold gaze with tolerance. No question, his gal Friday was far too nosy and not very congenial with demanding clients. But the stocky senior citizen could manage the paperwork, take messages down accurately, and never met a bill collector she couldn't muscle or stall.

All in all, not a bad employee profile.

Jack originally had taken a chance on Glory because she'd once taken a chance on him, back in their East Los Angeles neighborhood where he was a cocky street tough in training. Glory had spied him in the company of some older toughs, pilfering candy from her small mom-and-pop grocery. Since he was the only one dumb enough to get caught, and still held a trace of fear in his clear blue eyes, she figured he still had potential to grow up straight. She gave him a severe dressing-down, then offered him a job as stockboy to earn his way.

The kind gesture proved his salvation. He came by some

honest loose change and the sort of discipline so badly lacking in his manic-depressive mother's care. So when Glory's back and legs began to give out in her sixtieth year due to years of standing and lifting, Jack helped her sell the store and hired her on to assist him.

Wedging a hip on the gray steel reception desk, Jack picked up the stack of mail that had accumulated over the course of the past several days. He knew his silence would annoy Glory and with amusement he watched her launch into a time-worn routine for attention.

Glory made some humming sounds, moved around a few pens, and adjusted the collar of her jersey print dress. When those ploys failed to distract Jack, she took a deep breath and launched into blunt interrogation. "Expected to see you in here the first thing this morning. And it's way past noon."

Jack peered into one slitted envelope, then another. "I missed the connecting flight out of San Francisco. Overslept."

"That's not like you. Have a restless night?"

"Sure did." Jack paused to fondly relive the highlights of the previous night's lovemaking. Andrea Doanes's toned body, ever so silky on the surface, crawling all over him.

"You sounded kind of strange when you called in from your hotel room. That's why I suggested a nice hot shower."

"I followed that advice."

"And it didn't soothe you?"

"Let's just say it wasn't my last act of the night."

Glory snorted. "Leave it to you, Jack, to find sex on a stormy night in a strange city."

Jack tossed most of the mail into a nearby trash can, then leaned over the desktop to filch some of Glory's jelly beans from a jar beside the phone. The phone began to ring just as Glory was trying to twist Jack's wrist, force the beans from his fingers. She reluctantly released him.

"That's my private line," he said, popping the colorful candy into his mouth.

She scooped up the receiver with a glare, cupping the mouthpiece. "You're still a petty thief at heart!" Her snarl settled into a matronly salutation as she did her duty. "Good afternoon, Glory speaking. Oh, yes, I remember you. No, he still isn't in, but I do expect him shortly. Yes, I'm sure this time. Heard it right from the horse's mouth. Good-bye."

Jack swallowed the sugary candy. "So who's calling me a horse?"

Glory's chubby fingers jammed the receiver back in its cradle. "Me."

"Glory . . ."

Her eyes glittered with mischief. "Look, this lady is way too polite to call you anything like a horse."

"Was she polite enough to leave her name?"

"It doesn't suit her, but she calls herself Lefty."

"Really . . ." Jack slid off the desk, landing on his feet.

Glory snapped her fingers. "Why, she's the one, ain't she?"

Jack gave her a blank look. "Excuse me?"

"The one you screwed. You look about to melt into a heap of molten flesh."

"Have I told you lately you're every guy's dream of a mother figure?" he mocked.

She patted her gray curls, overlooking his sarcasm. "I'm not near as sharp as a good mother should be. Why, it never even occurred to me that this lady who's been callin' would rent a video with you, much less indulge in the mattress rumba. She oozes class, that one."

His lack of class was an obvious inference. Jack stared down at his faded olive green T-shirt and worn jeans, his blind enthusiasm waning. What could Andrea Doanes possibly want of him now, hours after giving him the slip?

He'd be wise beyond his years not to care what she wanted.

He pretended not to care for five full seconds. ''She leave a number?''

Glory peeled the top sheet off her pink message pad. ''Want me to get her on the line?''

''No, thanks. I'll handle it in my office.'' Jack sauntered toward the inner door, turning back stiffly. ''Say, she didn't ask you anything about me, did she?''

''Nope.''

''You volunteer anything?''

''Sweetie, she already spent the night with you. What the hell could I tell her that she don't already know?'' With a deep coarse laugh, Glory jammed some jelly beans into her mouth.

Jack closed the rickety door between them with a pensive sigh. There were things about him that Glory could have told Andrea Doanes, things not to be discovered between the sheets. But it had been an insult to Glory's intelligence to ask and they both knew it. Per his direction, she never led with the chatter, on either his business or private line.

Not that it hadn't been tough in the beginning to curb her tongue. Predictably, blabby Glory had done it differently in the grocery store, belting out everything from her bra size to the store's audit figures. Claimed it was the way to build up goodwill, keep the customers coming back.

Jack, on the other hand, had few repeat customers to woo. After all, how much market research did one client expect to need?

His mouth quirked as he sank into his chair and pulled the phone close and began to punch in Andrea's number. It only rang twice.

''Jack here.''

''Thank God it's you.''

''Hey, simmer down.''

''I can't.''

There was a distinct catch in her voice. It lodged in Jack's heart like a fishhook in a trout. He was almost tempted to overlook how she'd rejected him after their night together. After all, his rough appearance and manner were acquired tastes. If only the encounter hadn't been magical. The sting wouldn't be so deep.

"Jack, you there?"

Tilting back in his chair with a heavy sigh, he asked the big question. "So what's the matter, Lefty?"

"Everything."

His brows gathered sharply. "You hurt?"

"Not physically. I've just been back to the house though—"

"That wasn't smart."

"I had to face him sometime."

"Yeah, I guess." He rubbed his whiskered jawline, absently wishing he'd shaved.

"Things are worse than ever, Jack."

"Look, it's clear you're in a jam with that husband of yours, but how a big a jam is up to you. I had *plenty* of extra time to sleep on it, and my advice is to move forward quickly, file for divorce—"

"I will. I plan to. But he's serious about keeping me under his thumb."

"It's one last stall," he reasoned. "Quite frankly, in his place, I wouldn't want to lose you either."

"You don't understand. It's more than making a financial settlement now, winning a court case. Either I stay with Corbin on his terms or he's going to destroy me."

His own wife. The great Corbin Doanes had threatened his own wife. Jack's initial dislike was quickly evolving to intense hatred. "Where does your lawyer stand on all this?"

"My lawyer performs well in the courtroom, but as for standing up to Corbin's dirtiest tricks, I can predict her caving in quickly. Oh, Jack, people just don't know. Once a man flirted with me at a charity ball, and he was roughed up hours later by a quote mugger unquote. And that is just one example of timely misfortune dished out Corbin

Doanes style. There is an inner Hollywood circle that does not cross Corbin, that numbly supports the respectable-producer myth."

Jack tipped forward in his hard wooden chair. "This is a tight spot, honey. Seems damned if you do or you don't."

"There isn't another soul in town I can trust. Will you meet me, talk things over?"

She dumped you on the spot. She's out of your league. In spite of these reality checks, he released a surrendering sigh. "Where are you?"

"In a taxi, on the way to my hairdresser on Wilshire Boulevard. Can you meet me there?"

"At your hairdresser's?"

"Don't sound so murderous. It's the best place I can think of."

"Anyplace would be better."

"No," she insisted firmly. "It's the perfect cover for a rendevzous."

"Why do we suddenly need a cover?"

"Just found out Corbin's having me followed."

"You sure?"

"Saw the reports myself."

"Who's doing it?"

"Some man from Cal-Sun Investigations. And I must say, this detective is very good at his job. That's why I took the taxi, to throw him off if possible, at least for the afternoon."

"But a salon . . ."

"We don't have to stay there."

"What's the name of this place?"

"The Mop Shop."

"Seriously?"

"Yes! It's a unisex place, so you won't be conspicuous. Hurry."

Jack's office was downtown too, but it took him some time to get his old cumbersome Chevy out of the city lot, fight the clogged streets, and find a parking spot off Wilshire.

The Mop Shop. Jack paused on the sidewalk near the entrance, confirming that, as the name suggested, the salon was a bit off the beaten path. It was definitely not a place that would appeal to the glitzy Rodeo Drive crowd. If she was already easing into a more simple lifestyle, Jack was primed to be impressed. He also approved of her decision to limit her trust in her Hollywood pals. Most likely they were the fair-weather type, who would favor the powerful movie mogul once the marriage woes became apparent.

Heads turned as he made the doorbell jingle. Jack took in the admiring female eyes full of curiosity. He was a striking figure in his snug faded clothes, muscular, suntanned. However, when he peeled off his wraparound sunglasses to reveal his cool, hard blue eyes, the women shyly avoided direct contact.

Accustomed to that response, Jack concentrated on his surroundings. The place was full of mirrors, done up in glossy black and silver. The front area boasted a check-in counter, a waiting area with chairs and magazines, and two manicure stations. There were dividers behind the front counter, but it was still possible to glimpse styling stations on the left and sinks on the right.

A girl of eighteen or so with a bleached wedge of hair hanging longer over one ear appeared behind the desk. She wore a baggy black smock with "Jude" embroidered on it. "Haircut?"

Jack ruffled his chestnut hair, appreciating its slightly shaggy length. "No, thanks. Still breaking in this one."

She matched his streetwise look, tapping a pencil on the appointment book. "Then what can I do for you?"

"I'm looking for Andrea. She's a customer."

Jude's heavily shadowed eyes dropped to the open page. "Oh, yeah, the two o'clock. She's just finishing up a shampoo and trim. Won't be long."

"I'll wait." He gestured to the plastic chairs. "Maybe read a magazine."

"You don't have to. I mean . . ." She slanted her eyes toward the manicurist's table.

Jack raised his palms. "Oh, no."

She snatched a hand for a look. "You're a real mess."

"You been talking to my friends and neighbors?"

"Seriously, I could do wonders for your rough cuticles, not to mention these hacksaw nails."

"No, thanks."

"C'mon," she whispered. "I have a hungry kid to feed."

"Well . . ."

"And if you expect to impress a lady like Andrea Kramer, you'd better try a little harder."

Jack shrugged. "Okay, kid. Have at it." Jude steered him over to her table, and set his fingers in some moisturizing solution. So Andrea was calling herself Kramer now. Probably her maiden name. Despite the fact that he hardly had a claim on her, Jack viewed the change as progress, a symbol of the growing space between Andrea and her soon-to-be-ex. In fact, he sank into a long daydream on just that subject.

"See you made it."

Jack snapped out of his reverie sometime later to find Andrea standing over the manicurist's table. He approved of her casual white slacks and clingy pink top, and was relieved that her shimmery black hair still had a swinging fullness to it, the trim barely noticeable. Also barely noticeable was the tremble in the hand she placed on his shoulder, the quaver in her chin.

Her eyes proved her most revealing feature, highly charged with stress and arousal. Jack understood the basis of her fears, the helpless feeling of being stalked. As for the arousal . . . The lingering smolder between them was harder to believe. They were no longer suspended in space and time in a dark, smoky bar. Jack was no longer the hero, having just rescued her from a drunken jerk.

On this bright day in the big city, Andrea Kramer Doanes had all the options in the world. Her pick of any number of heroes. So why pick him all over again?

This mystery fascinated Jack and he wanted to explore it. He stood up and reached into his pants pocket. Producing a money clip, he peeled off a twenty. "Keep the change, kid."

Jude stared up at him piteously. "There isn't any. You owe me another sixty-three cents."

With a rueful look, he peeled off another dollar bill. Then he took Andrea by the elbow. She resisted his push to the entrance. "Let's leave by the back."

"Good idea." On impulse Jack peeled a third bill—another twenty—from his clip and gave it to Jude. "If anybody comes in here looking for the lady, say she mentioned a shopping spree around town."

Jude winked and pocketed the cash. "It's a deal."

They hustled out the service entrance into the bright sunshine, dodging a small delivery truck. Jack still had a tight hold on Andrea's arm. "The things I do for you," he growled, holding up his index finger. "Jude is a hatchetman. I'll never crook this with any authority again."

Andrea planted a kiss on the finger, her voice dropping provocatively. "That would be a rotten shame for the female population."

He traced her mouth with his thumb. "This one hurts too."

She brushed his hand aside with a gentle scoff. "You're nothing but a con."

"And you are an enchanting witch. Especially when you smile."

She grew more serious again, training a suspicious eye on the passing delivery trucks. "Can you think of anyplace to take me, Jack?"

His eyes glittered wolfishly. "Certainly . . ."

"Somewhere safe," she clarified.

"You're always safe with me, Lefty."

"I wish you wouldn't be so flippant about all this."

"Don't look so scared and I won't have to try so hard to be charming."

"But—"

"I handled things yesterday with the drunk on the plane, didn't I?"

Andrea nodded.

"I'll do it again. Promise."

She hesitated. "I wouldn't mind going to your place."

He looked vaguely apologetic. "You wouldn't find it very tidy, or appealing. How about yours?"

She gazed up at him, exasperated. "Oh, Jack, *my* apartment would be too risky. The worst choice."

"Why?"

"Because when the detective does realize he lost me, he'll head there. More than likely end up spotting us together."

Jack just couldn't stop imagining her bed, nice fresh sheets, fragrant with her scent. "Does all this cloak-and-dagger really matter, Andrea? If your tail is that good, our friendship has already been logged in."

"Amazingly, he somehow overlooked our little indiscretion. There was a black hole in the last report, starting with the flight, carrying through to my return home. As if my spy were sleepwalking through it."

"Hmm. This snoop doesn't sound very good to me."

"But he has been until now. Very professional and thorough."

"So how do you explain—"

"Oh, Jack, you can figure it out."

"Me?"

"Sure. Who was acting out of turn last night?"

Me. "Guess I don't follow."

She looked skyward. "I'm beginning to think you'd make the worst kind of detective."

"I'm glad you don't sound too broken up about it. Stay put while I get my car. It's parked a couple blocks over on a side street."

Chapter Six

When Jack pulled his old black Chevy around the block to pick up Andrea, she was wearing some chic oval Audrey Hepburn–style sunglasses. They had driven along for several miles before he realized she'd dozed off behind them. The seats were that comfortable, even if the twenty-year-old car's current sticker price probably closely matched that of the Hepburn shades.

She slept all the way to Santa Monica. Even then he had to give her a gentle shake. "Hey, Lefty. Wake up."

Andrea stirred, sitting straighter on the passenger seat. She was sheepish once she realized she'd lost track of time, that they had parked someplace. "I didn't mean to—"

"No problem."

"Where are we?"

"Santa Moncia Pier."

She stifled a yawn, gazing out at the churning Pacific across the street. "Hmm, didn't realize I was so tired."

"Understandable, after having hot sex through most of the night."

"Yeah . . ." She peered at him over the tops of her black plastic frames, melting a little in husky reminiscence.

"And then skipping out on me at dawn," he added flatly. "That had to be especially tiring. All that tiptoeing . . ."

She peeled the glasses off her face now, looking particularly vulnerable and wounded. Her voice was small. "Thought maybe we wouldn't have to go there."

"Didn't expect it to stick to my ribs so long, but it's just one of those nagging things that seems worth mentioning."

"I didn't take off to upset you. Just wasn't sure what we'd talk about on the flight home. Figured you'd understand how I felt about the whole thing, needing comfort, a fresh start."

He sighed deeply. "I understand. You didn't expect to see me again."

"I'm not exactly on the dating circuit right now. It was nothing personal."

He raised his hands in surrender. "Okay, okay. Just couldn't resist filing a complaint."

She watched him intently. "Was I wrong to call you?"

"No, I want to help if I can."

"I really appreciate it. This problem has grown disgusting; it's more than I can handle."

He gently took the glasses from her lap and set them back on her nose. "C'mon, let's go for a disgusting walk and talk it through."

"So there you have it," she said some fifteen minutes later. "Corbin will use any means possible to get me back, and hopes to keep control of me with the dirt his private eye digs up."

Jack had been keeping his strides short to stay in line with hers. They were barefoot in the damp sand at ocean's edge, their pant legs rolled up, allowing the frothy water to chase at their ankles.

He congratulated himself on picking this setting for their chat. It seemed the perfect tonic for Andrea. From behind his own dark lenses he surveyed her wind-tossed hair, her sun-kissed complexion, and her steady carriage. She was now the picture of southern California vitality, even lovelier than she'd been last night in the dim lounge.

Jack had listened carefully to her story, and was especially stunned by Corbin's proposal for a three-way-style marriage. Andrea was certainly more than enough woman for any man! It seemed to have been the last straw for Andrea. Jack couldn't blame her.

"So give me your theory on the detective," he urged at long last. "Who do you think he is and why didn't he pick up on our friendly games last night?"

"The answer is obvious. He's my masher from the plane and he was in no condition to do his job at that time."

"Oh, I see." Jack rubbed a hand over his mouth, thoughtfully amused. "You're telling me that obnoxious bungler who pawed you like an ape is capable of surveillence worthy of Sherlock Holmes?"

"It does seem strange, but it makes perfect sense. Once he started drinking on the plane, he lost his composure. Then he spent the night in jail rather than at the hotel. Once he came to his senses again he realized Corbin would expect his quality rundown, so he pieced events together the best he could, figuring he was safe because I'd never fallen out of line before."

"You know what I think, honey?"

"What, Jack?"

"That you owe every hardworking gumshoe in the state of California an apology for adding that bozo to their ranks."

"I'm right about this guy," she insisted. "And it's hard to believe you didn't eventually figure it out yourself."

"I'm just a simple market research man, remember?"

She chuckled. "As simple as the sphinx."

"But younger and healthier."

"Hmm, and sexier."

Jack slowed her down, encircling her in his arms. She tilted her chin in anticipation as he dipped his mouth to hers. Andrea clung to him, her body small and fragile against his. Last night's fire quicky ignited again as they explored one another, reveling in the familiar taste and sensation. For a brief moment they were alone with their desires, the waves crashing around their mythical deserted island.

This is crazy. Reason began to gnaw through Andrea's hazy senses. She barely knew this man. What if they'd been followed after all? It was foolish to keep on kissing him this way. She would put a stop to it. Soon . . .

"I want to help you through this, Lefty," he rasped, tracing her jawline. "Would you like that?"

"It would probably be selfish of me to draw you in any further. I got the moral support I came for. Just hearing a rational human being outside of the Hollywood scene agree that Corbin's a monster has been a relief."

"Kisses and conversation aren't going to solve anything."

"Well, what do you think I should do next?"

He considered it. "Get a new lawyer. Somebody tough and expensive."

"I don't have a lot of spare cash."

"Some of them will probably be willing to wait for a percentage of your settlement. It won't be cheap, but it'll be worth it."

"Anything else?"

"Trust no one. Especially in that house."

Andrea balked. "But I don't want to hurt Lynn—"

"You said yourself she has divided loyalties, which are only going to cut deeper when the war heats up."

"I can't bear the idea that Corbin might turn her completely against me."

"If it's any consolation, I think she'll try very hard to stay out of it. She already crossed the battle lines once to show you those reports. That kindness has made her vulnerable to Corbin's wrath."

"I would never use that secret against her."

"But if she's smart she'll worry a bit, and be careful not to upset you."

"This whole thing will be fueled on paranoia before we're through!"

He tapped her nose. "And I wish you the most severe case. It may save your skin."

Her brown eyes sparkled with a hint of mischief. "If I take your advice, I shouldn't even be talking to you."

He was pleased. "Now you're getting the idea."

"Jack," she murmured thoughtfully. "I wonder if I should try and speak to that private detective from Cal-Sun."

"For what reason?"

She shifted uncomfortably on the sand. "To . . . make sure he doesn't have a line on you."

He placed a hand on his chest, openly baffled. "Me?"

"Yeah. I'm worried. If Corbin were to eventually find out about our night together, he'd deliver some punishment."

"But the San Francisco report is in; it said nothing."

"What if that detective begins to feel pressured by Corbin to deliver? What if he decides to interview some of the sober passengers on the plane to make sure the time is covered?"

"Please don't track that snoop on my account, honey. Those guys are usually tough and pretty fast talkers. You're bound to reveal more than you learn. And what's to stop him from going on to betray you to Corbin, letting Corbin know that you're on to the surveillance?"

"A slice of my settlement would stop him, I bet."

"You can't rely on it. Besides, splitting with the lawyer will be bad enough."

"At least be wary of Corbin, give me one less worry."

"Your concern is flattering, but he doesn't scare me."

"You're already planning to do something on your own, aren't you?"

"Don't worry about it."

"At least promise me you won't dive in as impulsively as you did on the plane."

"I won't do anything foolish."

Andrea tipped her head against his chest. "All things considered, Jack, I'd say you can't seem to stop."

"Where'd you say you're goin'?"

Jack checked his reflection in the wall mirror, then turned to Glory, standing at the door connecting their offices. "I didn't."

"C'mon, c'mon, I don't have all day. Where can I reach you in an emergency?"

He sighed resignedly. "The Sterling Athletic Club."

"In Beverly Hills? That's very swank, I hear."

"Your point?"

She gestured to his clothing. "Well, look at you."

Jack glanced down at his slightly rumpled white cotton shirt and khaki slacks. "People golf and exercise there. It isn't the spot for a fancy suit."

"Good thing, as you don't own one."

"Glory, lay off."

She pressed her chubby fingers to the bodice of her tight candy-striped shift. "Forgive me for trying to ease into the godawful truth, but you could very well be mistaken for a waiter or something if you don't spruce up. Now wouldn't that be embarrassing!"

Jack gritted his teeth, knowing what was coming.

"C'mon. Strip."

"I'm late," he sqawked.

"And I have letters to type."

Jack reluctantly obliged, peeling off his shirt.

"Don't look so hangdog. Drop those pants too." In the meantime, she began to clear off the front part of his massive wooden desk. "There now, I'll be right back."

Left standing in his socks and briefs, he watched her disappear into his closet. "Hope no clients stop by."

Glory returned moments later with a steam iron in her hand. "The extra pay I deserve for TLC is a cryin' shame." She plugged the iron in near the desk and spread the slacks on top. With practiced strokes, she pressed one wrinkled leg, then the other. A fond look of exasperation settled upon her chubby features. "Remember when I used to do this for you in the back of the grocery store, before big dates?"

"Sure, Glory." With a vague smile he swiped the pants back and slipped them on. They were toasty against his skin.

She laid his shirt out for pressing, making a wistful sound. "I'd sit behind the register for the rest of the night, wondering if you were tussling with the neighborhood cops, or enraging some girl's daddy."

"Ah, sweet memories." He snatched the shirt back. "A shame I had to grow up."

Glory shook her head, yanking the iron's plug free of the wall socket. "When other boys were bringing home frogs and candy wrappers, you'd return with a black eye or a broken nose."

Jack sat down to slip his loafers back on, keeping his voice even. "I was a hotheaded kid back then, always having to battle my way free of tight corners. I admit it. But that's history."

"Really? Yesterday you were tangling with the damsel in distress. Today, it's the husband. Offhand, I can't think of a tighter squeeze."

Apparently Glory had been eavesdropping as he tried to track down Corbin Doanes with a series of telephone calls. It would be a waste of energy to fume over it. Glory was incorrigible about such things. He stood up and patted her crown of gray curls, a habit of his that she didn't like. "Don't fret. I'm sure they don't allow fistfights at that club."

"Say, does Andrea Doanes have any idea what you're up to?"

"Nope." Jack moved to his desk and picked up his wallet. Stuffing it in his back pocket, he shot her a warning look. "And we'll keep it that way."

"Sure, sure, I know my place. Sitting in the background with the bottle of iodine."

He winked on his way out.

It was one o'clock on that Tuesday when Jack made his way into the athletic club's pro shop. Scouting for Doanes among the upper-class patrons, he busily checked out the price of a leather golf bag.

"Can I help you, sir?"

A young male dressed in a white uniform of shirt and shorts was posing the question to Jack. His badge introduced him as Ted. Jack gestured to the bag. "This costs enough to feed an impoverished country for a week."

The clerk smirked. "Or a party of two in our dining room."

"I'm looking for Corbin Doanes."

"He expecting you?"

"Yes."

Ted seemed unsure. Jack didn't break eye contact once. "He's out on the driving range." He pointed to some glass doors. "But he doesn't have much time. He's teeing off in thirty minutes."

"How like old Corbin, practicing to keep that winning edge." Jack strolled outside to the range. There was a row of men and women taking swings at tiny white balls, walloping them out over the plush green landscape.

Corbin was in a center spot, dressed in pale blue linen, setting a ball on a tee. Hands in pockets, Jack sidled up behind him. "Gee, I haven't seen this much excitement since my kick-the-can days."

Doanes turned, expression guarded. "Who the hell are you?"

"Jack Taylor."

"I heard you were calling around to track me down."

"Wasn't too tough a job."

"Really? I was beginning to think you couldn't find your way out of a shoe box with a flashlight."

"Gee whiz, you're going to hurt my feelings."

"Is that right." Doanes picked up the steel-headed driver he'd left leaning against his golf bag, and caressed its graphite shaft. "Judging by the slackass job you've done following my wife so far, I feel justified in giving you some shit."

Chapter Seven

I'm a capable private detective, Doanes, and I resent the implication that I'm not!''

''Keep it down, Taylor.'' Corbin looked around at the other golfers. Judging some growing interest among them, he shoved his club in his bag. Tipping his hand cart up on its wheels, he directed Jack to follow him.

They started down a narrow blacktopped path canopied by palm trees. ''This is sort of a nature trail for walkers. At this time of the day most members are inside for lunch.''

''You have a problem being seen with me?''

''Naturally! Do you think I want someone seeing us together, then spotting you near my wife someplace?''

Jack remained cool, taking in the manicured grounds. ''Nobody's caught on to me, yet.''

''Well, it was stupid to come here.''

''We've only spoken on the phone once, and I think it's about time to reevaluate the situation.''

''You do, eh? Let me tell you something. I pay people well to do as I tell them. I expected you to wait for my next move.''

''It's about time you face it,'' Jack said evenly. ''Your wife isn't about to cheat on you. I'm not going to catch her in the act at anything.''

Corbin raked a hand through his silvered blond hair, clearly on the fence. "Maybe not."

"You sound disappointed."

"I was gratified over her modest lifestyle until she turned down my reconcilation offer."

Jack drilled him with cold stone eyes. *Ah, yes, with the nimble and willing Mindi Fellowes thrown into the marriage bed. How could a girl refuse?* "In any case, I've come to quit."

"But you can't!"

"I don't believe for a minute that you respect my professional opinion, Doanes, but for what it's worth, continuing your surveillance on Mrs. Doanes would be a waste of my time and your money."

"Well, I don't value your *opinion* much."

Jack lifted his broad shoulders nonchalantly. "C'mon, give it to me straight, then. Why did you hire me in the first place?"

"Because my people said you were competent enough to spy on someone, that you were reasonably good-looking in an animal way, and that you were cynical enough to have a price for any chore."

"What people are we talking about?"

"The private investigation agency I have on retainer."

"Why didn't you have them tail your wife?"

"Because they would be too reputable to follow through—in the worst-case scenario. Which, Taylor, this has finally come down to."

Jack's blood dropped to a chilly below-zero. "What do you have in mind?"

"To make Andrea sorry. You see, Taylor, no one quits me without suffering the consequences. My child bride came to the marriage with nothing and she is going to leave with nothing, save for a harsh lesson from the Doanes school of business."

"Where do I fit in?"

Corbin Doanes smiled for the first time. "Per my direction, you will be dealing her that lesson."

"Jeez, you startled me!"

Andrea jumped at the gravelly exclamation, her pulse zinging into orbit. She'd just stepped into the dimly lit office of Cal-Sun Investigations and hadn't had a chance to take in her surroundings. She squinted at the sturdy woman seated behind the gray steel desk, half dozing in her chair, listening to a baseball game on the radio. "Is this Cal-Sun?"

"Yeah, but it's nearly seven. We're closed."

Andrea scooted closer, hovering over the desk. The woman was wearing a hidious red and white candy-striped dress. "You a detective?"

"No, I ain't."

"Is there an investigator here that I can talk to?"

"There's one in all and he's been gone for hours."

Andrea watched the woman yawn hugely, loudly, like a disgruntled bear in the wild. It was puzzling that Corbin would do business down in this seedy section of town. But he had to have a reason, one she probably wouldn't like. "Do you expect your man back tonight?"

"He better show his sorry ass back here tonight. I'm worried sick about him."

"Sorry to hear that."

"You in trouble, dear?"

Andrea nodded slowly, sensing she was missing something here. "You know, you seem familiar to me."

A pudgy hand landed on an ample candy-striped bosom. "Huh? Naw . . ."

Despite the denial, Andrea was sure there was a sudden flicker of recognition in the old woman's eyes. She began to pace on the hard flooring, looking for anything that might enlighten her. There was little on the walls, a couple of cheap dime-store prints, a coat rack with four hooks. Nothing important.

An odd shiver raced down her spine as she stared out the second-floor window into the dark menacing street. She didn't frequent downtown Los Angeles at night and badly wanted to return to her safe Glendale apartment.

But along with that sense of safety came a feeling of helplessness. Sitting pretty in Glendale wouldn't get her anywhere. She couldn't stop Corbin from mistreating her, and she couldn't stop fearing that the detective on her tail would somehow find out about Jack.

Sweet, overprotective Jack. He'd be furious when he found out she'd come here alone. His fault for dismissing this private eye as inconsequential. Personally, she couldn't rest until she found out for certain why there had been that black hole in the last surveillance report. It was bound to be a tense showdown though, and she was beginning to hope she was wrong about the identity of the detective. But that drunk on the plane sure did seem an ideal soul mate for the crass woman here tonight, who was now coaxing jelly beans from a jar with some choice language.

"Thought I'd stick around for a while," Andrea announced. Making herself at home, she whisked off her mint green cardigan sweater, revealing a sexy white strapless dress.

"A fancy girl like you, wasting your time around here? Leave a message. I'll see that one of our operatives gets it."

Andrea draped the sweater and her purse on an old chair opposite the desk. "You said there was only one operative."

The beady old eyes shined guilelessly. "You like baseball? This is a humdinger of a game. The first of a doubleheader between the Angels and the Red Sox."

"Yeah, right." Andrea wandered over to the window again.

Suddenly the phone rang. Andrea froze near the pane, nervous and intent as the woman picked up the receiver. That was when paydirt hit.

"Hello, this is—"

"Glory!" Andrea shouted in recollection. "You are Glory, Jack's receptionist."

"Oops." Glory listened to the caller briefly and promised to call back.

In the meantime, Andrea charged the desk. "If you're here, then he's—" She gasped in outrage.

"Take it easy, dear. Jack's—"

"He's a liar."

"Yes—"

"A cheat—"

"S'pose."

"A lowdown rat."

Glory placed her palms on the desk and hoisted herself up. "But he's a decent boy underneath."

"What!"

"No sense screamin' like that. Sit down."

Andrea remained standing, her body pencil brittle. "I won't."

Glory rounded the desk and shoved her into the chair, knocking her purse and sweater to the floor. A heavy hand on her shoulder kept Andrea there. "You gotta listen to me. Jack gets in deeper than he means to sometimes. But he does try to do the right thing—unless he's crossed first."

A squeal of fury rose from Andrea's throat. "Do you know what he did to me?"

"I think you did it to him first, didn't ya?"

"Well . . ." Andrea averted her gaze. "He lied the whole time. Even went along with my plan to ditch my snoop."

"It took me a few tries to get the whole story out of him, but it appears this all started when he rescued you on that plane, when he should've kept his crooked nose out of it."

"But that wouldn't have been right," Andrea scoffed.

Glory poked a finger in her face. "See, you still expect

Jack to do the right thing. It's automatic once you know him."

"Oh, I don't know what to think—beyond wanting a piece of him this minute."

"Look, dear. Why don't you go home and sleep on it? I'd like to leave now myself—"

"You're a liar too! You intend to stay here and wait for him."

Glory sniffed haughtily, the queen of her rundown castle. "Ain't none of your business what I intend to do. I have every right to ask you to beat it."

Andrea thought fast. "I'll give you fifty dollars if you're the one who goes."

"Hmm . . . Let's see the fifty." Glory opened her hand and wiggled her fingers.

Andrea dug into her handbag, produced her wallet, and thumbed through the bills. There were some fives and tens, a twenty. She was deflated. When would she ever get used to her new status, remember first thing that she didn't have Corbin's money to burn? Naturally there wasn't a fifty in here anymore! Feeling rather self-conscious in her expensive Chanel dress, she began to count off the paltry bills in Glory's palm. "Twenty, twenty-five, six, seven."

When she got to thirty-three, even Glory was embarrassed enough to stop her. "That's enough. You can owe me the rest."

"Gee, thanks."

Glory folded the bills and stuffed them into her bra. "Never know what kind of con you're going to meet out on the streets."

"I'll say not," Andrea replied.

Jack wandered into his office about eleven o'clock that night. He'd had his key in hand, but it wasn't necessary. The front door was unlocked.

"Glory? You know this place should be sealed up at this hour."

There was no bellowing reply.

Suddenly Jack felt skittish. Everything looked right, the radio was droning the logistics of a ball game, Glory's nap lamp was glowing on her desk, and the jelly-bean jar was picked clean.

But the big woman's chair was empty.

Where was she?

The connecting door to his office was open a crack, but there was no light on inside. He moved stealthily up to the door and eased it open with his shoulder.

A shaft of moonlight spilled through the window, illuminating his giant wooden desk. His chair was turned, facing the window. And someone was seated in it. Glory liked his more comfortable chair, sometimes fell asleep in it. With a lightning motion he grabbed an armrest and spun the chair around.

It was Andrea seated there, her stony eyes wide open, amber gems of fury.

Stunned, he could only manage a soft, "I'll be damned."

"If there's a God you will."

Chapter Eight

Andrea . . .'' Jack stumbled back a step, uncharacteristically at a loss for words. But it had been one of those grueling days at the athletic club.

Andrea slowly rose from his creaky old chair. The room was quiet, save for the traffic sounds coming from the street below, the muffled radio playing in the next room. Jack stood rigidly, expectantly, almost paralyzed by the intense energy swirling around them.

She found him out.

It was bound to happen.

He had been meaning to tell her.

She moved in close. Real close, until her heavy expensive perfume filled his nostrils. His heart slammed in his chest as he braced for her reaction. Then it happened. Her left hand snaked up, slapping him soundly across the face. It jarred him more than she expected.

''You actually look surprised, Jack.''

''Got me off guard. I instinctively brace for the right swing.''

She fumed under his calm rigid stand. ''I wanted so desperately to believe in you.''

''I know,'' he said quietly.

''You encouraged it.''

''Only to a point. Told you to trust no one.''

"How was I to know that included you!"

"It does and it doesn't. I—"

"Stop the doubletalk!" She prowled around the office, her long body undulating under her strapless white dress, her glossy black hair shimmering around her bare shoulders. "You're finished making a fool of me."

Such a motive was the furthest thing from his mind. Simply *making* her better described his intentions. And his desire to do so had never been more intense. He could taste her raw energy in the air he breathed, feel his flesh expanding in his pants. He desperately wanted to drive himself inside her again. Under the awkward circumstances, the weakness made him angry, his tone harsh. "You shouldn't have come here."

She whirled on him, full of venom. "Wrecked your little game, didn't I, you lowdown bastard. All this time you were the one invading my privacy, reporting my moves in detailed reports—for money."

"It's how I make my living. The market research stuff is just a cover I use when I'm close to getting caught."

"You were my hero, Jack," she cried out in anguish. "You were supposed to be protecting me!"

A dangerous blue light dancing in his eyes, he advanced on her. "I told you what to do about Corbin and you didn't listen."

Andrea quickly found herself pushed up against the desk. Stuck between solid flesh and mighty oak. She was too upset to be afraid. "You were full of great advice, bigshot. 'Don't confront the private eye' will go down as my favorite."

"So what's up here? With this scrap of a dress?" He thrust his hand down the sweetheart neckline, between her soft pushed-up breasts. Crumpling the soft fabric in his fingers, he tugged her flush against him. "Did you dress this way knowing you were coming to see me in particular?"

Her chin wobbled as she raised it. "No."

"Then what did you mean to accomplish?"

"Figure it out, *Mr. Market Research.* Why would I bother?"

He crunched more dress, burying his knuckles deeper in cushy flesh. "What if I had been the drunk from the plane? What do you think *he* would've done to you in this high-priced hanky?"

"Grabbed me the way you have, maybe?"

He slowly shook his head, chestnut hair falling across his forehead, a tolerant smile curving his large mouth.

She glared in suspicion. "What is it?"

"The smart act doesn't work for you. You're not a hard case. You can't pull it off."

"I'm experienced. I've been hating you for two solid hours."

"Trying to."

"Succeeding."

"We'll see." Curling his free hand behind her back, he smothered her moans with a grinding kiss. Driving his tongue between her lips, he claimed her mouth with force, familiarity. His fever was contagious. In spite of her anger, she responded like a lit fuse.

Jack knew the come-on was a cheap shot to stop all the talk. But he couldn't bear to lose her, and this was the quickest fix he could think of. He would have to tell her sometime . . . that he needed her more than she could ever need him. That his conflict of interest between her and the job had grown unbearable.

As glib as he was, Jack had trouble revealing true feelings to those he cared for most. And that had been only a handful of people during his lifetime.

The corners of his mind were as dark as the office as his body temperature rose, but it troubled him that Andrea had come calling in this skimpy dress, to see a private eye in a seedy part of town who could've been primed for anything. Why had she taken such a chance? What had she meant by that researcher crack?

A small but powerful truth slammed him from off center,

like her left-handed swing. Andrea had come here to jerk some jerk's chain for *him.* To protect the defenseless researcher. That's what she'd been most concerned about during their last conversation. That Corbin might find out about him somehow.

Despite his warnings and assurances, she'd gone out on a limb.

Aside from Glory, no one had ever bothered before.

There was a new urgency to Jack's actions. Andrea could feel it. This wasn't going to be just some heavy petting to evade the issues. Jack was in the process of yanking her dress down without a thought to the back zipper. Andrea could feel the elegant garment falling to her waist, lodging on her hipbones. He arched her over the desk, bringing her bared chest into the spill of moonlight. Cradling her in the crook of his arm, he went down on her breasts, with a slow, torturous suckle.

A primal tug shot clear to Andrea's feminine center. She began to squirm with a mounting heat. The moment she began to move her pelvis his hand was there, pushing her dress to the floor, tearing at her silken panties.

There would be no resisting Jack. Not when she knew what was in store. She began to work his belt buckle free, open his khaki pants. His briefs were plain cotton. Laundered to a flat gray. No man could wear them better or would ever lose them faster. Seizing a breath, Andrea freed his engorged penis from its cotton restraint.

"Oh, honey." The endearment was hot and sincere against the curve of her ear. "Keep on trusting me. Please."

Bracing her hands and bottom on the edge of the desk, she opened herself to him, crying out in pleasure as he cupped her vulva in his hand. Gently he tipped her flat on the varnished desktop, still cleared off from Glory's ironing job. Raising her knees, he eased between them, kissing the insides of her thighs, nibbling the moist skin at her intimate opening, inhaling her scent. Time passed in a velvet sweetness as he explored her secrets.

Andrea was dizzy and perspiring when he finally lifted his body over hers and eased his solid flesh inside her. Getting his balance, he glided in and out, once, twice. Picking up speed, he sliced into her hot slick tunnel with quick, hard strokes. With cries of delight she dug her nails into his muscled back.

Climax was explosive. Physical clashed with emotional. Lust, anger, betrayal, doubt went up in one single bottle rocket.

Then it was over. Passions spent, a huffing Andrea sat up, trying to regain her equilibrium. She was still extremely upset with this man. Part of her wanted to kill him where he lay. But mostly she wanted assurances that he could explain it all away, keep her faith intact.

Pushing her hair away from her face, she stared down at him. "I am either the dumbest woman alive or—"

"The only woman alive." Stretched out on his side, Jack reached up to caress her fragile jawline.

Suddenly conscious of her nudity, she sat up straighter, folding her arms across her breasts. "Start talking, Jack. And make it good."

He sat up too, cursing himself for allowing her to get sulky. "I liked you better mad."

"Sad is tougher, I know . . . But dammit, convince me that you don't deserve to hang from a tall tree! When I think of the way I trusted you with—my everything! Oh, Jack, you've made me fall in love with you. And now you're a stranger all over again."

Stunned, he sat up straight. "Say that again. What you just said."

"You are a stranger," she seethed.

He bared his teeth. "Cute. Now I want to hear you say you love me. One more time."

She remained stoic. "*You* were saying?"

"Okay." He took her hand in his, studying its delicacy.

"As you've discovered, Corbin hired me to spy on you. It seemed like a routine divorce job, and the upfront money was good. He painted you as a young opportunist who had married him strictly for gain, biding your time only to take him to the cleaners."

Her gasp of affront stalled him for a moment, then he forged on. "I had no reason not to take him at his word. Of course once I got involved, Corbin's suspicions seemed wacky. You were a bona fide angel, inside and out. By the time I rescued you on the plane, I was half gone on you myself. Then when you told me your story in the bar, I realized just how completely Corbin had twisted things. He was trying to salvage your marriage as he said, but he was the problem, not you."

"Do you always fall for a client's story so easily?"

"He does have a good reputation—"

"So you had heard all the glittering propaganda beforehand!" She snatched her hand back, mimicking his line from the hotel bar. "*I'm not much for fiction.* What bunk!"

"That was a lie, of course, along with some obvious others. Glory is the queen of entertainment junkies. She yammers on for hours about her favorite stars, and backed Corbin up all the way, vouching for his integrity and fine filmmaking."

"Where do your own lies begin and end, Jack? Do they end?"

"Everybody lies."

She looked around, spotting her dress on the floor. "This would be a wonderful time for me to walk out."

He snagged her arm, kept her planted on the desk beside him. "It would be the worst."

"What do you mean?"

"You need me more than ever."

"I don't!" She did wrench free this time and scooped up her clothing. Sorting them out, she stepped into panties, then her dress.

She was going to leave. He talked faster, despite the

lump forming in his throat. "I think I understand what you were trying to do here tonight, honey. It nagged you that Corbin's detective might hear of us and tell him. You wanted to find out for my sake, didn't you?"

She hesitated. "All right, yes. The idea of you meeting with some little accident gave me the chills. And you weren't concerned enough. I just thought, what chance would a market research man have against Corbin's strong-arms?"

"I'm really touched."

She smoothed her dress with a frown, holding it in place with a hand to her rib cage. "Great."

"We are on the same side," he insisted. "And I do intend to see you through this."

She slanted him a doubtful look. "How?"

"He's the one pushing the envelope now. Found that out when I met with him today."

Her gaze sharpened. "What happened?"

"I tried to quit."

"And?"

"He offered me a bonus to stay on."

She gasped in dismay. "Did you agree?"

"Couldn't refuse two million dollars, could I?"

"What can you possibly do to earn that much?"

"I've already done it a couple of times." His eyelids lowered meaningfully.

She covered her face. "Oh, no."

"Corbin's given up on getting you back, and on catching you in the sack by chance. He wants to pay me to seduce you personally and bring back the photographic proof."

"Of course, it would be cheaper to pay you off for such a stunt than it would be to lose big in divorce court."

"And he'd succeed in totally destroying your good name in the bargain. He's quite the devil, your husband. He intends to first smear you in public through the tabloids. You can imagine the headlines: *Famed Producer's Wife Gets*

Down and Dirty Downtown. That initial ploy is meant to brand you persona non grata throughout the business, crack your defenses before you ever get to the courthouse. Then once in court, he'll brand you an adulteress who never loved him in the first place. He was thinking far ahead when he chose a bum like me to tail you; he was after the type who would and could see the second phase through if necessary."

"Gee, for a while, sitting in your chair in this seedy office, I got to thinking that maybe he'd hired you to just eventually kill me."

Jack was offended. "I wouldn't risk jail for a crummy two million."

"Wonder how many years I'd get in the pen for killing you?"

"Simmer down, Lefty. I already have a plan to beat Corbin at his own game. If we're clever, he'll screw himself before it's over."

She sidled over so he could zip her gaping dress. "Can't be done."

"Sure it can." He gave the zipper a reluctant tug, then turned her round to face him. "With a little planning, a little snooping."

"He's bound to be really on his guard from now on—especially with you and me."

"It will take some finesse and patience," he granted. "But while he waits for me to succeed in bedding you, I intend to gather information on him, from the inside of that estate."

"But he knows you by sight."

"Naturally, I can't get close myself."

"You have no operatives."

He traced a finger along her throat. "Still, would it be possible to plant someone on the inside, through Lynn Doanes, maybe?"

"In what capacity?"

"Domestic help, preferably in the nerve center."

''Glory?''

''Yeah.''

She shrugged. ''They're always looking for staff. Corbin's tempermental outbursts drive people away regularly.''

''Call Lynn first thing in the morning. Tell her you have an old tenant in your apartment building who needs some extra dough to make ends meet.''

She thought this over, worry lines drawn at her mouth and eyes. ''Do you intend to give him what he wants, Jack? Photos of us in a compromising situation?''

''Well, I'm going to let him think he's getting them.''

''But you intend to take them.''

His gaze was steady. ''Yes.''

''And I'm to trust you on all this, have faith that you won't ultimately sell me out?''

Her suspicions bit deep, causing him pain. ''We'll be trusting each other, involving people we care for like Glory and Lynn. And you'll have time to decide during the next couple weeks whether I could be the one. As for me, honey, you're already the one and only.'' He placed a feathery kiss on her mouth. ''In the end, if you conclude that I'm just another loser, you'll have your split of the take, a cool million.''

She managed to steel herself against him. Just. ''We're not gaining much of Corbin's fortune.''

''It's enough to hire your hotshot lawyer for the big score. Or''—he rasped against her hair—''it's enough to sail off into the sunset with me. Your choice.''

She gasped softly. ''Why, Jack Taylor, are you making an indecent proposal?''

''If you call the state of matrimony indecent, yes.''

Chapter Nine

What took you so long to answer the door, anyways?''

Glory barged inside Andrea's apartment, dressed in the gray uniform that had been her daily apparel at the Doanes estate for the past three weeks.

Andrea was dressed in a peach satin wrapper, which she cinched tighter as Glory secured the door chain. ''Wasn't expecting you. You haven't come by the past couple days.''

''Well, I can't help it if Lynn Doanes insists on sending me home after work in one of the company cars. Naturally she thinks I live in your building here, since that was the big cover story you gave her.''

''Can't you refuse the ride?''

''Not for the third day in a row, I couldn't. She's been trying especially hard to please this week because they lost another maid. I've been doing more than serving martinis and answering that damn door, I'm into the heavy cleaning.'' Pressing a hand into the small of her back, she groaned. ''I'm so glad it's Friday.''

''I'm sorry, Glory.''

Glory crunched her pudgy face, resembling a bulldog as she sniffed the air. ''You ain't cookin' supper yet?''

Andrea seemed unusually at a loss. ''Why, no, I—''

''You normally are by now. Gee, I did like that macaroni thing you made the other night, with the cheese and chicken. If you have some of that left over, maybe we could stuff it in a pita or something."

"Maybe we could stuff *somebody* in a laundry chute or something." Jack appeared in the doorway, dressed only in his low-slung jeans.

Glory keyed in on his broad bare chest and open belt, then stared beyond him into the bedroom, spying the office 35 mm camera set on its tripod. "Did I interrupt something?"

Self-conscious, Andrea tucked her silken black hair behind her ears, glancing at the floor. "We were taking a few more photos."

"More photos!" Glory boomed. "For crissake, you two have taken enough to fill ten albums."

Jack glared at her. "So what if we find the lens a turn-on."

"And I want only certain kinds of shots taken over to the estate," Andrea asserted. "A little revealing. But tasteful."

Glory grinned. "Whatever."

"You look especially smug." Jack folded his strong arms across his chest, sauntering closer. "Manage to hit the jackpot today?"

Glory nodded, her gray curls bobbing. "Finally got the goods."

They all sat down in the living room on Andrea's sectional furniture. Glory produced a small notebook from her purse. She thumbed through the pages. "Tonight's the night. Doanes is meeting with that redheaded twig at her place for some fun and games."

"Mindi Fellowes," Andrea clarified.

"Right. I was jammed into a sweltering cabana for an hour this afternoon to get the details, but it was worth it."

Jack eagerly leaned forward on his seat, his arms on his knees. "Give."

"I heard 'em making their way to the pool, see, so I ducked outside first, and into one of the cabanas. They lounged around out there in the sun, played grab-ass in the water, then they ducked into the cabana next to mine.''

Andrea gasped. ''Thank God it wasn't your cabana they opened.''

Glory was unfazed. ''Hell, I would've dodged my way out of it easy enough, pretended I was picking up or something. Anyway, they had it off in there, and Mindi was promising Corbin more fun—later that night. Seems Mindi has a hot tub at her town house in the canyon and they've held other *parties* there in the past. In my day we called 'em orgies. Anyway, this one was a fantasy come true for that creep Doanes, because he's to be the only man there.'' She dabbed her blotched face with a tissue. ''Whew! I'm beat.''

''I'll get you some lemonade.'' Andrea popped up and disappeared into the small kitchen.

Jack took the notebook from Glory. ''Excellent.''

''Can I quit the maid gig now?''

''Soon.''

She took a deflating breath. ''I'm getting way too old for this work or any other kind.''

''That's ridiculous,'' Jack scoffed. ''But I do appreciate your going the extra mile with this case and I've found a way to fatten our take another hundred grand. And that, Glory, is going straight to you.''

That perked Glory up in a hurry. She accepted the glass of lemonade from Andrea, raising it to Jack with twinkling eyes. ''That's my boy.''

Andrea winked. ''And mine.''

''Glad you made it. They have the greatest breakfast combos here.'' Jack smiled at Corbin Doanes, hovering over his booth, dressed in a casual beige suit.

Doanes looked around the plain establishment full of working-class patrons. ''At least it's . . . out of the way.''

''Relax. Sit down.''

''Okay, but let's not use any names.''

Jack sipped his coffee, thinking of some names he'd like to use on Andrea's two-bit cheat of a husband.

Corbin settled uneasily into the opposite side of the booth, ordering a cup of coffee from a passing waitress. "You've had some success?"

"See for yourself." Jack handed Corbin a brown envelope. Doanes held on to it as the waitress returned with his coffee. Once she left he slipped open the flap and peeked inside.

"There's only one picture in here."

"It's a sample."

"Can't see her face." Corbin glared. "Only yours."

"Tell me that isn't her."

Setting the envelope on his lap, he took the picture out for a closer look. He looked surprised. "Guess you did manage to bang her."

"Banged her good. She's smiling in a lot of them."

Corbin was clearly enraged beneath the surface. "That's hardly relevant!"

"I wouldn't be too worried about her having a happy future. You intend to destroy that option in short order anyway."

Corbin grew serene. "True."

Jack swallowed some coffee. "Next step will be to arrange the exchange, cash for the photos."

"Naturally, I wasn't going to bring the cash to this section of town."

"Naturally, I wasn't going to bring photos until I have seen the cash."

"You're not as dense as I figured, Taylor."

What happened to no names? Jack wondered. Doanes broke rules as fast as he could make them. "Glad you noticed. Now I've been thinking this deal over—"

"But you are too dense to do any extra thinking."

Jack's eyes glittered hard. "Don't get insulting. I have some useful information for you."

"Such as?"

"For an extra hundred grand I can tell you what Andrea intends to do next."

"I'll be the judge of whether or not it's useful."

"Make that one hundred and twenty-five thousand for rudeness and using my name."

Corbin opened his mouth and clamped it shut again.

"Good move. Now listen; I know something that could change how you're going to handle your smear campaign against your wife. If you're interested, show me your checkbook. I believe it's in the left pocket of your suit jacket. At least it looked a little bottom heavy."

With a grimace Corbin produced the book and a pen.

"Now, write the check to cash and put in the center of the table. If my info isn't worth it, you can take it back."

"Very well." Corbin scribbled in the blanks and peeled off the check. Jack verified the data, then dropped the check between the napkin holder and the creamer.

"Just like you," Jack said softly, "Andrea has plans to go to the tabloids with her story."

"The bitch!"

"The stickler is, she plans to do it Tuesday."

"Tomorrow?" Corbin was wary. "She tell *you* that?"

"C'mon, get real. I'm somebody who picked her up in a bar a week ago. I overheard her on the telephone with her new lawyer."

"Who is the lawyer?"

Jack acted annoyed. "I don't know. But whoever it is approved. They talked of big money, unmasking you."

Doanes sat back on the bench, thoughtful. "She would get smart in the end and hire a shark."

Jack sat back on his seat too, his nerves alive with tension. He hoped he wouldn't have to do more than steer Doanes into the trap.

Luckily, Jack had done enough. Corbin had hold of the bait and went on to enhance the plan he'd confided at the athletic club. "I'll need to act fast. Call a press conference this very afternoon."

"Shouldn't be hard to slip word to the tabloids too, tell your security people to let them pass."

"Done it lots of times, just like that. I'll announce my divorce to all with deep regret. Reluctantly admit that I have some proof of Andrea's infidelity. You can show up during the conference to leak the photos." Corbin's face shone as he schemed, as though putting together his biggest and best production ever. "I'll put Mindi in charge of the money exchange, giving you your cues."

Jack snapped up the check, folded it in half, and stuffed it into the back pocket of his jeans. "Call me with the setup."

"Wear your beeper, Taylor. I've had no luck at all reaching you through your secretary the past few weeks."

How amusing that this smart guy had had his secretary in easy reach for days!

"You know as well as I do how tough it is to keep decent help." With that Jack eased his large frame out of the booth. He dropped some bills on the table to cover his breakfast and sauntered out of the restaurant. Glory's bank was just down the street—by design—and he wanted to deposit her bonus as soon as possible.

When Jack rang the bell at the Doanes estate that afternoon, it was Glory who answered the door. He'd chuckled every time he'd seen her poured into her conversative gray uniform and today was no exception.

"Good day," she chortled. Then on a whisper asked, "Where's Andrea? You smuggle her in via the backseat?"

"Yeah," he whispered back.

"I unlocked the terrace door round the side. She can step right into the crowd of reporters at any time."

Jack winked in approval.

"Come in, sir," Glory said clearly.

"Thank you."

Glory gave his navy linen suit a once-over. "See you ironed your own duds today."

"Bought new. Special occasion."

They both turned as Mindi Fellowes exited a noisy room off the foyer with a briefcase. Using the seconds afforded them wisely, Glory coughed, then mumbled, "Checked, the money's legit."

Jack smiled benignly. "And your savings account now holds an extra one twenty-five."

Glory hissed. "Sweet mercy."

"Mr. Taylor," Mindi greeted him warmly.

"You psychic?"

She laughed. "Security called to alert me."

Jack initiated a handshake, a flash of the redhead naked crossing his mind. It wasn't much of a voyeur's treat, as Mindi was as scrawny as a kid. The actress actually looked far better dressed in today's jade pantsuit.

"I am to take a look at your photos," she announced, staring greedily at the large brown envelope he was carrying.

"While I peek at the money," he murmured charmingly.

They exchanged envelope for briefcase.

Balancing the boxy case on his thighs, Jack undid the twin gold catches. A peek confirmed it was stocked with bills. Mindi, in the meantime was ogling the erotic photographs, taking the time to compare Jack to the stills. "Too bad you're not in the business," she cooed. "Directing or producing."

"What you see is what you get. And let's face it, as is I wouldn't be worth sucking up to."

She stared at him, not sure if he was deliberately being especially nasty. Jack found these arrogant showfolk a constant form of amusement.

"This is how it will play out," Mindi went on a bit more crisply. "You will follow me back into the room, pretend to barge in with a delivery of the photos. Corbin will protest, like a gentleman, then the photos will *accidentally* slip out of the envelope onto the floor. Corbin will act angry that Andrea's dirt is revealed. You will show remorse and meekly take his scolding.''

''Then I can leave, right?''

''Please do.'' Mindi handed him the envelope and reached for the case. ''Now we'll just give the money to Glory for the time being. She can hang on to it until you're making your exit.''

Jack fumbled with the case. It dropped between them. Mindi caught it in mid-air, but not before two packs of five-hundred-dollar bills fell out.

''Idiot!'' Clutching the case, Mindi crouched to retrieve the bills. She quickly stuffed them inside and secured the catches. When she stood up again, Jack was standing by calmly, still holding a brown envelope.

''You sure all the money got back in there?'' he demanded suspiciously. As Jack hoped, she was instantly on the defensive.

''I don't think I like you, after all, Jack.''

''Definitely my loss.''

''Okay,'' she snapped breathlessly. ''Wait sixty seconds and follow me into the conference.''

Jack entered the room full of press, noting that wine and coffee were flowing. It looked more like a party than anything else. Of course everybody was there expecting scoop on Corbin's latest movie, and were thrilled to be so close to rising star Mindi Fellowes. The terrace doors were wide open on the opposite wall, and presumably spotting Jack, Andrea entered in a neat red suit and a large matching hat that concealed her face.

''Oh, Mr. Doanes,'' Jack said clearly and aburptly. ''Maybe I should come back another time.''

''No, no. Come in.'' Corbin clapped him on the back, eyeing the envelope.

''But I hoped for some privacy.''

''Stand by and you'll get it,'' he promised. The stage set, Corbin shushed the group. ''I have brought you here with some sad news. Andrea and I . . .'' He looked mildly distressed. "Well, we're calling it quits." He paused as the groans rose. Jack felt a clench in his gut. Many of these people were openly salivating over the scoop handed them. He was proud of Andrea, who was calmly making her way toward him along the outer rim of the crowd.

"It's a sad decision," Corbin conceded, "but necessary."

A reporter nearby asked the first question. "Is there another person involved?"

"Yes." Corbin sighed. "At least one. But I don't wish to discuss that. I only want you folks to get the story straight from the onset. Try not to place undue blame on anyone. My reputation means the world to me. As always, I am what the public has made me. Without their support of my movies, I'd have no reason to make them." With that he gave Jack a significant look.

"Mr. Doanes," he appealed. "I'll come back later."

"Right, Jack." Corbin nodded covertly, aware that every eye was upon them. Jack stepped away, making sure to catch his foot on the leg of a coffee table. The contents of the envelope went spilling across the white carpeting.

"Oh, no." Corbin's cry of dismay turned to a growl when he realized the photographs were not what he expected. He began to wail as members of the press began to pick them up. "No! Stop! Give me those!"

By this time Andrea was standing beside Jack, clucking at the revealing photo near the toe of her red pump. It showed Corbin tossing Mindi into a giant hot tub full of women. All of them were nude. Someone else was holding up a photo of Corbin stretched out on a patio lounge chair enjoying the sort of *ménage à trois* that he'd tried to lure Andrea into.

"The places you go, Jack Taylor," she tsked. "From now on, you're staying away from hot-tub parties in the canyon."

Jack snagged her arm. "C'mon, before someone recognizes you."

They made for the doorway. Glory was waiting for them in the foyer. ''Here's the case. Now git.''

Jack paused to tear the second envelope, full of the photos of him and Andrea, out of the back of his waistband. ''You can come along now, if you'd like.''

''No, that wouldn't be fair to Lynn Doanes. She isn't home right now, but if I leave with you, someone will piece it all together, blame her for hiring me in the first place. Don't worry, I'll only work through the week and quit then.''

Andrea beamed at her. ''Thanks, Glory. It's what Lynn deserves.''

Corbin's roar echoed through the house. ''Taylor? Anybody seen him?''

Glory eased into the powder room and Jack and Andrea through the front door.

The couple hopped into Jack's old Chevy. Jack tossed the envelope and the briefcase into the back seat and fired up the engine. ''We gotta get through those gates before he alerts security.''

Within two minutes they were off the property and cruising along Banyon Drive.

Andrea slid close to him. ''I love these old cars without bucket seats.''

He spared her a glance. ''How do you feel about private eyes?''

''You know I love you, Jack.''

''Keep telling me so.''

''As often as you like from now on.''

''Do you trust me now, Lefty, for keeps?''

She hesitated. ''Not entirely.''

He gripped the steering wheel. ''But I hoped you'd marry me.''

''Oh, I will. We'll marry as soon as you say.''

''But the trust . . .''

''We'll burn all those compromising photos of us first, then we'll talk about trust.''

"I burned most of them in your kitchen sink this morning."

"Great. And I can easily dispose of the ones in the back seat. But how many others are still floating around loose?"

"Just the one Corbin bought, which only a mother or lover could identify. And another one that belongs to me alone."

"Yours has to go, Jack."

"Even if I swear to keep it all to myself, cherish and protect it?"

Andrea fidgeted nervously. "Where are you storing this precious gem now?"

Jack kept his eyes on the road.

"Answer me!"

With a sigh he flipped down his sun visor. Clipped to the inside of the visor was a head shot of Andrea, snuggled in her pillow, eyes closed, wearing a secret smile.

She stared at it in delighted surprise. "I didn't know you took this."

"There was a single shot left on the roll, and I hated to waste it."

"Well, that one you can keep."

Covetously, he flipped the visor up. "Now as for winning your trust . . ."

She kissed his bristled jawbone. "May you live that long."

The Maine Attraction

Anne Marie Winston

For Karen Solem
Thanks for your faith in me.

Chapter One

The woman was out walking near the water's edge this morning, daintily holding up a long flowing skirt as she picked her way over the gravel and rocks that lined the edge of Swan Lake. Beau had noticed her the day before, when he'd heard a car crunching along the lane that led to the two neighboring cabins as well as the one he rented for his annual vacation along the lake near the Maine coast.

Since the tourist season wound down in August, by September many of the cabins were closed for the winter. Both of the other homes along the lane were vacant, he knew.

He'd been curious enough to peer through the birches and firs toward the little yellow cabin, where she'd been unloading boxes of stuff and carting them into the cottage. She was alone, no man in sight, and his interest level had immediately risen a notch or two. His male eye had noticed that she was slim and her hair was a pretty cornsilk color, but he'd also noticed she was wearing a ridiculously sedate long skirt and that the shining hair had been coiled into a thick bun at the back of her neck.

Repressed, he'd decided. Not the kind of neighbor who might be a good time during the chilly Maine nights for the short time they were both around.

Then Hank Pembroke had come across the lake in his canoe and they'd sat and drank beer, told lies about the women they'd had, and kept an eye on the progress of the latest hurricane of the season as it hovered off the coast of the Carolinas for a couple of hours. By then it was dark and he'd forgotten about his new neighbor.

This morning, Beau was in a good mood. The weather was crisp and glorious, sunny with the promise of warmth later in the morning. He'd started a sculpture commissioned for the state courthouse in Vermont a few days ago and it was coming along beautifully. He could see the image in the wood, and every stroke of the knife, every chip of the chisel, was bringing his vision closer to reality. If he was lucky—and inspired—he could probably have it finished in time to drive it down personally when he left Maine and headed back to Tennessee. That would save him the agony of packing the thing and then worrying himself sick until he got word that it had arrived undamaged at the other end—

Whoa! He damn near spilled the coffee he'd been sipping as he dragged his feet down off the rail and hitched forward in the deck chair for a better look. The woman had appeared at the edge of the lake. She'd pulled up her skirt and was tentatively poking around the water. The skirt was hitched up between her legs and held at her waist like a giant diaper, and the fabric now outlined every slender curve, as well as baring her legs well above the knee.

Fascinated, he leaned forward as she waded farther into the water. There was just enough of a nice little break in the trees to give him a good view of her. Her hair was down this morning too, he realized, as the mild breeze sent a golden banner streaming across her face. With a distinctly impatient gesture, she shoved it away and waded a few steps more.

She moved gingerly, and he'd bet she was barefoot. She'd learn soon enough that an old pair of sneakers did a lot to preserve a person's feet along the rocky shore. Not to mention helping with balance.

He grinned as his new neighbor slipped on an unseen

rock. Her arms flailed wildly and her skirt tumbled down into the water as her hair flew around her head. She almost lost her footing but at the last moment, she managed to right herself. Then, with a shake of her head that conveyed pure disgust with herself, the woman waded carefully out of the water.

Once she'd gotten onto the dry rocks along the tiny beach, he wished he'd made a bet on her shoeless state. She was indeed barefoot. As he continued to watch, she bent forward and gathered the bottom of her long skirt to wring water from the fabric. Her hair fell forward again, and Beau felt his pulse pick up as the shining tresses danced and swayed around her face.

He was a sucker for long, pretty hair.

Then again, he thought, he was a sucker for legs too. And how. His neighbor apparently had wrung out as much water as she could from the lower part of her skirt. Now she gathered up a hefty handful and continued her wringing, pulling the fabric taut against a trim little bottom and baring an extremely interesting length of slender thigh. She obviously thought she was alone, because as she handled the skirt it pulled up, and up, and, *Oh, baby*, he thought, *just a little more . . .*

But she stopped just shy of dragging it higher, leaving him with a tantalizing, shadowed view of the very tops of her legs, where her thighs pressed together, hiding a feminine treasure that he suspected was as breathtaking as her unbound hair.

His body stirred, and he shifted in his seat, enjoying the mild arousal. His yearly trip to Maine was usually a time of solitude, a quiet break from routine. He rarely bothered with women while he was here—well, that was true if he didn't count that little waitress up in Bar Harbor who'd been so . . . accommodating last year. But for the most part, he didn't seek out the fairer sex up here, a fact that would shock the hell out of some of his buddies, most of whom were married and envisioned his lifestyle as one long, lovely orgy of women and parties.

While that wasn't strictly true either, what *was* true was that he had the freedom to indulge whenever he wanted, wherever he wanted, with whoever took his fancy and returned his interest. And so what if he was a lot more discriminating and got laid a lot less than his friends supposed. They got their vicarious thrills through him, he thought with another grin. Why destroy their fun?

And thinking of fun . . . He pushed himself out of the chair, letting it thunk against the deck with a satisfying sound that echoed over the lake. His new neighbor's head jerked up, and he could see her hastily drop her skirt as she looked around for the source of the noise.

If he stood perfectly still, he doubted she'd ever see him, but what the hell. Pursing his lips, he whistled, a long, full wolf whistle that clearly startled her even more. Her head swiveled in his direction, and he tossed up a hand and offered her a jaunty wave.

He could tell the instant she saw him. Though she wasn't close enough for him to make out her features, he could see she had wide eyes that peered at him from beneath the gilt cloud of her hair. They widened even more as she realized he'd been watching her the whole time.

"Don't let me stop you," he called. "I think I'm going to like having you for a neighbor."

There was an instant of silence. Even from this distance he could see her breast rise and fall with the deep, indignant breath she took.

And then she spoke. In a voice as clear as a bell, and as frigid as the water in the bay just a few miles to the southeast, she said, "It's unfortunate that I can't say the same."

He was still laughing as she stomped out of his line of vision and up the steps to her cottage, banging the screen door behind her with such force he could hear it from where he stood.

* * *

Emma thought of the man in the cabin up the hill the following evening as she hurried out to gather the laundry she'd hung on the line that afternoon. There was the skirt she'd dipped in the lake, and her cheeks got warm as she wondered exactly what that man had seen.

It had never occurred to her that anyone was close enough to see her. She hadn't heard a car, a radio, or television since she'd arrived, and she'd assumed the other cottages nearby were empty. Helvi, her editor at the publishing house where her six cookbooks had been published, had offered her the cabin for this week, and she'd mentioned that the lake grew fairly deserted after the start of the school year, when families were done vacationing. A lake house all to herself! The prospect had been tantalizing.

That was the problem, she thought. She was so used to solitude that she *expected* it. The home where she lived, the house she'd shared with her mother until Mother's death a year ago, was on a long isolated lane in a quiet Massachusetts county. When she wanted company, she visited her brother's family or took her culinary creations to friends around Boston for their opinions; otherwise, she spent great quantities of time on her own, especially after Mother had become bedridden.

A hefty gust of wind blasted into her, and a few fat raindrops splattered her. Wow! She hadn't paid any attention to the weather recently. Maybe she'd better turn on the television to one of the two channels Helvi had told her they could get at the cabin and see what the forecast was. Quickly, she pulled down her laundry and bolted indoors as the drops became a deluge and the wind became a living force trying to knock her off her feet.

She settled down in front of the fire with the half-finished baby afghan she was knitting for a neighbor at home and turned on the television.

". . . the eye of the storm currently is centered about twenty miles east of Cape Cod. Most residents of the Vineyard have evacuated, and only a few hardy souls have elected to remain in the resort community . . ." The picture switched from a view of a beach being pounded by huge, whitecapped waves to a weather map, as the meteorologist droned on.

Emma stared at the screen, the information it contained battering at her brain. That was a hurricane! And from the look of things, it was going to come slamming right on up the coast sometime during the night.

". . . expected to reach Portland by midnight tonight. All residents of coastal towns along the Northeastern seaboard are being asked to voluntarily evacuate. Mandatory evacuation plans are in effect already in some areas. Folks, this is one nasty-looking lady. If she behaves, she'll stay offshore and we'll get clipped by the edges. But if Hurricane Sela turns to the northwest, we're going to be right in the path of winds exceeding one hundred miles an hour. Again, everyone who can possibly do so has been asked to evacuate low-lying coastal areas and go inland—"

The television winked off abruptly as did every light in the cabin. Emma gasped and jumped, then immediately felt foolish. It wasn't as if she'd been hurt, just a little startled. Thank heavens she'd made a fire, or she'd be sitting here in darkness.

Rising, she went to the fireplace and took down the oil lamp Helvi had told her was kept for just such occasions. Her editor had been so kind to offer her this cabin. Lord knew it had been years since she'd taken a vacation. To have an entire month in this beautiful haven seemed like the most hedonistic of luxuries. In the kitchen, she picked up the telephone, just to be sure there was no dial tone. As she'd expected, there wasn't.

Well, she wasn't terribly disturbed. True, Swan Lake was less than seven miles inland, but what was the worst that could happen? She'd experienced the winds and rains that went with hurricanes before, and although her home in

Massachusetts wasn't nearly so close to the coast, it couldn't be *that* much worse.

She got herself a glass of water from the water cooler that Helvi had suggested she use rather than drinking the lake water. But she didn't open the freezer for ice, because the power might be off for a while and she didn't want it to defrost any faster if she could prevent it.

As she walked back into the living room, though, she was alarmed to smell smoke—and just as quickly realized the odor was coming from the fireplace. Apparently the force of the wind was pushing it back into the room.

Regretfully, she put out the fire. It got chilly in Maine at night, even this early in September, and there was little she liked less than hopping out of a cozy bed into an icy room. Oh, well, there was really no help for it. Hopefully, by tomorrow the wind would have died down enough for her to get the fire going again. Her watch read nine-thirty and she supposed she might as well go to bed and hope the storm had blown on out to sea by the time she awoke.

She dragged the extra down comforter out of the linen closet and spread it on her bed, then got herself ready and climbed in. She had stocked up on romances by several of her favorite authors before she'd left, and she lay for almost two hours reading, until the oil lamp burned low. No way was she getting out of this nice warm nest to get more oil. It was going to be bad enough getting up in the morning!

Reluctantly, she marked her place and set the book aside, then turned out the lamp and burrowed down into the wealth of quilts spread over the big old iron bed. With nothing to occupy her mind, it was impossible to ignore the howling of the wind, and she tried to suppress the apprehension that rose.

This was one of those times when she felt her solitary lifestyle most keenly. Most of the time, she didn't mourn her lost opportunities, nor regret the choices she'd made.

But tonight, with the storm bearing down and the wind howling, it would be so wonderful to feel strong arms around her, to have someone to comfort her and ease her fears.

After what seemed like hours, she finally drifted into sleep . . .

BOOM!

She was wrenched from a sound sleep by a huge clap of thunder, followed after one heart-stopping second by an ear-hurting, crunching, shattering crash that resembled nothing she'd ever heard in her entire life. In the same instant, she felt herself moving, falling, plunging vertically down, her stomach doing a belly flop that reminded her of her one and only experience on a rollercoaster.

The ride was over in less time than she could take to register it, and she was flung violently into an untidy heap onto something hard while a huge clap of thunder surrounded her again. For a moment, she just lay there, slowly realizing she was still on her back, in a slightly slanted position.

And she was getting wet. Wind howled around her and cold, hard raindrops blew across her body—in seconds she was drenched to the skin.

Confused, dazed, she tried to rise, but banged her forehead—*hard*—on something right above her. Stars spun and she dropped back with a moan. Then it struck her—she was no longer in her bed. Panic rose and she fought it back, taking deep, deliberate breaths, ignoring the wind and stinging rain, forcing herself to *think*.

Whatever had happened, something had disrupted Helvi's cabin in a major way, that much was clear. Poor Helvi and Geoff, they were going to be so upset when she told them their house was damaged—*Emma! Get a grip!* What on earth was she doing, worrying about Helvi's reaction at this point?

It was pitch-dark, so black that she couldn't see a thing. Cautiously, she raised her hands and felt around her. The thing over her head was a beam of some kind—No, not a beam, she corrected herself. A tree branch, judging from the rough texture of the bark and the sloppy, soaking leaves she encountered. The smooth, cold something behind her must be part of her bed, and the sodden fabric piled down near her left hip might be blankets, or a pillow, some part of her bedding.

She continued to feel around her, but unyielding wood and iron were all that she encountered on two sides. The third side, angling off to her right, was open, and that was where the rain was coming from. On the fourth side, a softer, but equally immobile bulk had to be her mattress. Irrational fear overwhelmed her. She was trapped!

A sob rose, then another. She gulped and gasped, trying to breathe deeply again, trying not to let the fright grabbing at her throat overwhelm her.

"Hey, lady! Where are you?" The voice was muffled, but obviously masculine, shouting and impatient, tinged with urgency. A whisper of light slid through a fracture in her prison, and the sight galvanized her out of her shock and fear. "Lady? Answer me if you can."

"Help! Help me, please! I'm under here." The command galvanized her into a response and she used both fists to hammer futilely at the rough wood above her head.

"Where?"

The beam of light slid away, and she shouted frantically, aware that if that small comforting sign left, she would start screaming like a crazy woman. "No! Bring the light back! I'm trapped inside here."

"Okay, calm down, honey. I'll get you out of there."

The light returned, and grew brighter, shining across her from somewhere near her left leg. As it diminished the darkness, she got a look at the walls around her—and was shocked almost into another hysterical attack of sobs.

What she'd assumed was a tree branch was a bit more—like the entire tree. Massive branches had fallen around her and the trunk hovered only inches from her nose. Through the leafy shroud, rain beat down in a steady torrent, occasional gusts of wind flinging it into her little prison. Behind her, when she squirmed to look, was the big iron bed, or a part of it anyway. The tree trunk had hit it squarely, wedging itself into a V-shaped dent in the straight iron bar that had once formed the headboard.

Dimly, she realized her rescuer was speaking, a stream of steady curse words that should have shocked her, but she was already too shocked to do more than fervently, silently agree.

"I think I can get you out of there," he said finally. "Down here there might be a space big enough to pull you out."

"Th-there's an open space to my right," she told him.

There was a brief silence.

"I can't get around to that side," he said. "But I'll take care of you, honey. Hang in there."

"Okay." She clung to the promise. A moment later, she felt movement at her left side, and the wet bulk of fabric was gently pulled away.

"I have to put the light down for a minute." His voice was still loud, because the wind and rain were nearly deafening, but she heard a gentleness in his tone that calmed her.

"All right."

The light disappeared, although a faint glow remained from the hole that her rescuer had created when he moved the blankets. "I'm going to move the mattress," he informed her. "Don't move. Not a muscle. And holler if anything shifts, even a millimeter, in there."

She obeyed, lying perfectly still as the lighted space grew larger and larger until there was a sizable hole down near her feet. An ominous creaking sound overhead made her jerk her gaze upward, fearing that the tree trunk was coming down on her.

"Stop!" she yelled.

"I already did." A hand encircled her ankle, rubbing

gently, and she was so grateful for the simple human contact that her throat closed up again. "I think you can get out. If you wriggle and I tug, we can do it together." There was a moment of silence, and then his voice came again. "Are you hurt anywhere?"

"I—I don't think so." She was afraid to move much, but she didn't feel any unbearable pain anywhere, though her head throbbed from her bump against the trunk. "I can feel all my fingers and toes and I don't think I'm bleeding."

"Thank God." He sounded genuinely relieved. Then she felt his other hand fumbling around her feet, sliding between her calves and along her leg down to the other ankle. Normally, she might have objected to the touch, but there was nothing normal about this situation. "Ready?" he asked her. "On my signal, you try to slide my way and I'll try to pull gently."

On his mark, she began to inch herself down toward the light, toward the man whose rough hands clasped her ankles, then moved higher up, sliding over her calves and knees to clasp her thighs as she felt herself slipping free. To her surprise, she appeared to be above his shoulders, and as her lower body came free, she felt herself starting to slide too fast.

"Put your legs around my waist," her rescuer instructed. "I don't want you to fall or move too much getting out of there. This whole arrangement doesn't look real stable, and I'm not about to have part of you get squashed now."

She bit down on an hysterical giggle and followed his instructions, and he continued to ease her out of her prison, supporting her bottom and back. His body was warm and firm between her thighs, reassuring her in an odd way, and she could feel him straining toward her to counteract the pull of gravity. Finally, all that remained in the hole were her head and shoulders.

The man took her hands in his. "Slide your hands as far up my arms as you can and hold on. When I pull you out, I'm going to try to get my hand behind your head in case you might have hurt your back.''

Again, she obeyed, feeling hard bulges and ridges of muscle as she clutched at his arms. One part of her mind wondered what kind of man had come to her rescue. Maybe he was a local emergency worker. He surely didn't sit behind a desk all day with muscles like that.

Then, before her mind moved in another direction, she was tugged free of the tree. A hand behind her skull dug into her hair as he hauled her up and she automatically threw her arms around his shoulders, pressing her face into his neck. ''Th-thank you,'' she said. And from deep inside where she'd been keeping a tight lid on the box, a sob bubbled up and burst forth.

''Hey, you're safe, sweet thing. Don't cry now.''

She barely registered the concern, or the words, as she clung to what had become the only thing to cling to in this night of horror. He rubbed her back, his fingers massaged her neck and skull for a few moments, and when she began to get the sobs under control again, he said, ''You're freezing. Much as I'm enjoying this, we have to get you out of the rain.''

For a moment, his words made no sense. In the next instant, she became aware of the position she was in, her legs clasped around her rescuer's waist, her arms around his neck, clinging as tightly as she could. Against her inner thighs she could feel the rough fabric of his pants, but that was secondary to the startling, unaccustomed sensation of having a man's hard, warm body between her legs.

Ridiculously distressed by this breach of propriety, she sucked in a breath and a small moan escaped her.

Then, in a sudden movement that made her throbbing head spin, he reached behind him and roughly unclasped her legs, dragging one forward as the other slipped down his hip. Before she could orient herself, he bent and lifted her into his arms. He held the flashlight pointing forward in front of them, and she was too shaken to care where he was going as he began to trudge uphill through the needles of rain that were whipped sideways across them by the winds.

Chapter Two

The woman grew limp in his arms. Beau strode up the hill as fast as he dared in the dark, watching for branches that might trip him up. It was only a few hundred yards from her cabin to his, but it seemed to take hours.

Over and over again, his mind replayed the loud crash that had shaken his bed. Sure, it had been thunder, with such simultaneous lightning he knew there had to be a strike close by. He'd gotten out of bed and walked to the big glass window that looked out over the lake and the neighbor lady's cottage farther down the hill—

And in the next flash of lightning that illuminated the night, the enormous tree that had come down across the house was seared into his brain. He'd stood like an idiot for a moment, unable to believe he'd seen what he'd seen. Then he'd been down the stairs like a shot, shoving his feet into his lake tennis shoes and grabbing the big power light by the door, thinking, *praying*, as he'd raced headlong down the path to the cove, that somehow the pretty blond-haired woman he'd been teasing only the day before had survived—if she hadn't been sleeping in an upstairs bedroom.

Now, he took the steps to his own door two at a time, fumbling with the screen door and shoving the interior one open so hard it crashed back against the wall. Gasping, he kicked the door shut again with one foot and walked over to the couch, dropping the flashlight onto the coffee table with his burden still in his arms. It winked out, but he didn't care. He had to sit for a minute.

Sinking down into the cushions, he let his head fall back against the sofa as he gulped in harsh breaths of air. Adrenaline still pumped through his system and his heart was racing like it did right after he'd finished a marathon bout of sex.

The woman's body was pressed against his and he could feel the soft mounds of her breasts rise and fall in a slow, steady rhythm that reassured him. Reaction and relief set in—an overwhelming thankfulness that made his hands shake as he thought about what could have been.

Then she stirred. Her head had been hanging limp against his chest. Slowly, she began to lift her head, and the fingers of one hand slipped down from his shoulder and fell bonelessly into his lap.

He cleared his throat. "Lady?"

"Thank you." Warm air gusted over his throat.

"You're welcome. How do you feel?"

She exhaled again. "Okay. I think." She was silent for a moment. "What happened to my house?"

"Hurricane Sela." He paused, but she appeared to be waiting for more information. "Apparently, she's a little closer than they'd hoped she'd come and a lot stronger. I think the eye is still offshore, but we're getting nailed now by the second half of her, and the wind is vicious. A tree fell on your cabin."

She shivered convulsively against him, and her hands slid back up to clutch at his neck. "It was a nightmare. If you hadn't come—if you hadn't—" Her breath began to hitch again.

"Shhh. You're safe now." To his way of thinking, there wasn't much that could be more terrifying than a woman in tears. He bent his head and pressed a kiss of comfort to her temple, then carefully shifted her to one side. "I need to get a little light, see if you're hurt anywhere.''

He edged forward and stood, then went to the fireplace and fumbled along the mantel for matches and his lantern. No sense in running down the flashlight batteries when he didn't have to. In a moment, the warm, cheerful light began to dispel the blackness and he lifted the lantern and carried it back to the woman. Setting it on the low table, he knelt beside her and took one hand.

''What are you doing?'' She didn't sound querulous, only curious.

''Making sure you're okay.''

''I'm okay.'' She struggled to sit up. ''Just freezing cold—*ouch*!''

''Sorry.'' He took her other hand, moved the arm up and down, bent the elbow, and then turned her palms so he could see the outside edge of each hand, bloodied and already showing dark bruising beneath the delicate skin. ''How'd you do this?''

She shook her head. ''I have no idea. No, wait, I do know. I panicked when I realized I was trapped, and I think I pounded my fists against the tree to try to get out.''

''You have a pretty hefty bump on your forehead there too,'' he observed, wincing at the knot marring her fair skin. This close, with the light flickering across her face, he could tell that she was pretty. Not drop-dead strikingly gorgeous, but pretty in an old-fashioned way that men today might overlook at first.

Other men, he amended. A self-described connoisseur of the fairer sex, he found the quiet, even arrangement of her features oddly pleasing. Long, dark crescents of eyelash, fine skin, a small straight nose, and arched silky eyebrows over wide dark eyes that might be brown or gray or darkest blue in the morning light. Her mouth was . . . perfect. Pouty lower lip, Cupid's bow centered atop it—a mouth for kissing. Yes, she was definitely pleasing

Then she shivered again, and he realized she was still soaking wet. ''You've got to get out of those wet clothes,'' he said. ''How about if I take you upstairs—''

''No!'' She made an obvious effort to moderate her tone. ''Please, I'd rather stay down here, if it's all right.''

''Sure it's all right. I'll get some blankets and dry clothes of mine and we'll stay down here until the wind dies off.'' He walked to the foot of the stairs, then walked back and looked down at her again. ''I'm Beau Cantrell. Do you have a name?''

''Emma.'' Her eyes were closed, but they slowly opened again, staring up at him. ''Emma Hamaker. Beau . . . you whistled at me.''

He chuckled, recalling the outrage that had stiffened her back at the sound. ''Yep, that was me. Sorry. It was just too good an opportunity to miss.''

''I've never been whistled at before.''

Never been whistled at before? He shook his head as he started up the steps, mulling over what she had said. She must have been kidding. She might try to disguise her charms under shapeless old-fashioned clothes, but there was a truly stupendous figure concealed beneath there. He couldn't possibly have been the only man to notice.

It was a long night. He brought her a dry T-shirt and turned his back like a genuine gentleman while she changed, then tossed her wet clothes into the kitchen sink, grinning at the plain cotton panties and floor-length granny gown. Yep, pretty Emma was as repressed as he'd first guessed. Emma. The name suited her.

He spread a dry comforter on the sofa and draped her in a couple of others, then sat across from her in a chair and dozed, waking around dawn with a crick in his neck and a stiff back. Stretching, he got out of the chair and walked over to the couch to check on his guest.

''Hi.'' Already awake, she offered him a wan smile.

''Hi.'' He was alarmed. There was no color at all in her face. Even her lips were an odd gray-white. ''How do you feel?''

''F-fine. Just a little chilly, still.''

"A little?" He snorted. "That's like saying we had a little storm last night. You're frozen solid, aren't you?"

She nodded, suddenly looking miserable. "I can't get warm. It's silly, under all these blankets, but—what are you doing?"

"Warming you up." He had lifted her, blankets and all, into his arms and was starting up the stairs. "Listen."

"To what?"

Holding her close, he could feel the shivers that shook her, and it scared him. People died of hypothermia. "The storm's died back a lot. Now it's just a hard, miserable rain. You'll be safe up here, I promise." He carried her up the stairs and into his bedroom, setting her down on his bed. The blankets were still thrown to the foot where they'd landed when he'd jumped up in the middle of the night. "Did you sleep at all?"

She shook her head. "Not much. *What are you doing?*"

He paused in the middle of unzipping his pants. "Getting into bed with you. Body heat will help."

"Well, you don't have to be naked!"

He grinned. "Might be fun, though." Stripped down to his briefs, he climbed into bed, laughing as she hitched herself sideways. "Sorry, sweet thing, but you have to get rid of those blankets you're wrapped in. They're probably damp."

He didn't give her time to argue, just yanked them away from her and tossed them to the floor, then pulled up the heavy quilts until they were covered to the chin. But he hadn't missed the way his T-shirt was twisted up around her waist, baring a smooth ivory bottom and endless legs that made a man dream of what it might be like to have those legs snug around his hips while he—Oh, hell, he was getting a hard-on. He was going to scare this poor little thing silly. It was obvious she was nowhere near as used to a man as the women he typically bedded.

The thought only made his unruly body leap and pulse even more. He sighed. What the hell. Reaching out, he slid a hand across her waist and with one quick yank, pulled her close. She yelped, and immediately turned on her side away from him. Which was *more* than fine.

She squeaked, clearly recognizing his state of arousal, and tried to squirm away again, but he spread his hand wide across the soft, flat plane of her belly and held her in place, clenching his jaw against the surge of pure lust that shot through him. It didn't help that the strange tingling heat that he'd noticed before was even stronger now that she was naked against him. Her wriggling moved his hand a little lower and beneath his pinkie finger he could feel the beginnings of silky, springy curls and the slight swell of her feminine mound.

"Relax," he ordered.

"Relax? How can I relax with you—with you—" She sputtered into silence.

"Hard as a rock?" he supplied, grinning into the darkness.

"You are *not* a gentleman," she said, still squirming, trying to pull away.

His amusement faded as the chance words struck a nerve he hadn't even known was exposed. "Any man who leaves two women at the altar is no gentleman," he said between his teeth. "And if you don't stop rubbing against me, you're going to find out just how *un*gentlemanly I can get."

She stilled immediately, freezing like a rabbit spotted by hounds.

Slowly now, he pulled her back into his embrace, tucking her head beneath his chin and forcing himself to ignore the leap of his body as her thighs backed into his and the sweet cleft of her soft, bare bottom gave his hard flesh a snug home. "Ignore it," he advised her, wishing *he* could. "It's just a physical reaction. I've got to get you warm. There's no electricity, so you can't take a hot bath. This is the only way."

"You could make a fire now that the wind's dying down."

"It would take too long to get you warmed up. I'll do it later."

Silence. She didn't move, except to pull the blankets higher, and eventually he felt her relax against him, the tight clench of her thighs and sweet little ass softening, flowing around him even more snugly. The sensation made his cock swell and throb and he didn't dare move because if he did he was liable to flip her over and crawl between her legs before she even knew what hit her.

God, he had to think of something else. Focusing every shred of concentration he had, he began to think about the gorgeous piece of cherry wood he'd picked up last week. He was anxious to get the Vermont piece done now, because that cherry was calling him.

"You're right," she said. "I'm getting warm."

So am I, baby, so am I. "I'm always right," he said with smug satisfaction.

Her head turned fractionally toward him. "If you're always right, why did you jilt two women?"

Now it was his turn to be silent. Finally, he said, "Did you ever hear of 'tact'?"

He felt her belly move up and down as she chuckled. "It's not one of my better qualities, so I'm told."

"By whom?" He was curious.

"Well, my mother, for one. And the other writers in my critique group—"

"You're a writer? What do you write?"

"Cookbooks."

"Cookbooks." It suited her. "Will you cook something spectacular for me tomorrow if you feel all right?"

"I can cook something spectacular even if I feel like I've been run over by a truck."

He chuckled, good humor restored. "And you're modest too."

"Oh, well." She shrugged a shoulder that poked out of his too-big T-shirt and he felt bare, silky skin slide against his chest. ''Nobody's perfect. And don't think I've forgotten about my question.''

''What question?'' Damn, he was sorry he'd brought that up. What a stupid thing to say.

''Why you ditched two women.''

''I didn't 'ditch' them,'' he said defensively. ''Both of them are still my friends. I just realized that marriage wasn't the right thing to do.''

''Exactly how far away from the wedding day did this 'realization' take place?''

''The first time was two months before the wedding day,'' he said.

''And the second?''

''You're a persistent nag.''

''Thank you.''

She waited.

He waited.

She cleared her throat.

''The second time was the day before the wedding.'' And he still felt bad about that one, even though Elsie insisted she'd forgiven him. Hell, she'd wound up marrying his best man, hadn't she?

''You must have cared for them. Why did you decide to break off the weddings?''

There weren't a whole lot of conversations that could be less appealing. He'd made a career out of forgetting each of those occasions, and he mentally kicked himself for mentioning them. His only excuse was that fatigue and the stress of the storm must have short-circuited a few of his brain cells.

''I don't know,'' he said. ''It just didn't feel right.''

''In what way?''

''It was just a weird thing. I looked at them and I couldn't imagine growing old with them, sharing fifty years' worth of memories, raising kids, all that stuff.''

''But you must have—''

''Emma.'' He practically snarled her name. ''Drop it.''

Her body stiffened. But she didn't speak again, which was all he really cared about. So what if she was going to pout now? She'd be out of his hair the next day and things could get back to normal.

Including you, he told the part of him that still ached with the need to be buried inside the tight little channel of the woman pressed against him.

She couldn't believe she'd fallen asleep, under the circumstances. Which, she admitted, she was still under. Literally.

Beau Cantrell, her decidedly unchivalrous rescuer, lay flat on his stomach beside her. They'd both shifted in the few hours they'd slept, and she lay on her back now. His arm was draped heavily across her waist and his head was turned into the curve of her neck. Every time he exhaled she could feel the warm air shiver over her skin. He had a leg thrown over her too, one thigh drawn up so that his knee draped across her thighs and his lower body pressed intimately against her. He didn't feel aroused anymore; in fact, she could feel the soft mass of his genitals against her hip, and she told herself she was relieved.

She'd never lain with a man like this before, and she probably never would again. She'd accepted long ago that she wasn't the type to inspire undying devotion in a man. She might not be the homeliest woman in the world, but she was under no illusions about her looks. ''Plain'' was what her mother had always said.

Yesterday, she hadn't minded her single state. This morning, cuddled under a mountain of quilts while rain beat against the windows and her breath turned into white mist in the frosty air . . . well, she'd never thought much about what it must be like to sleep with a man.

It was nice. Very nice. At least, the actual sleeping part was nice. And she was warm. Last night, she'd thought she'd never be warm again. Suddenly, the night's events shattered her quiet enjoyment and she sat bolt upright in the bed.

"Hey! Wha—?" Beau rolled to one side, a hand coming down hastily to protect himself from her flying limbs. "Jesus! It's freezing in here." He reached for the quilts but Emma was already scrambling out of the bed.

"I've got to go down to my cottage, see if my computer is okay. And my equipment. And I've got to call Helvi if the phones are working."

"Who's Helvi?"

"My editor." She whipped a blanket off a nearby chair and wrapped it around her as she started for the door. "She and her husband own the cabin. They're going to be so upset."

"Wait a minute!" He hopped out of bed and struggled into a pair of pants he whipped from a drawer. He also tossed a pair of gray sweatpants and a matching jacket at her. "You don't even have dry clothes. You got a pretty good knock in the head last night and you almost froze to death. One rescue a month is my limit."

She smiled as she went into his bathroom to pull on the pants and a matching sweatshirt. He was more of a gentleman than he wanted to admit. She used his facilities, then peered into the mirror above his sink and gasped. On her forehead was a goose egg in a lurid shade of purple and her hair looked like someone had whipped it with an eggbeater. There was nothing she could do about her face other than splash cold water over it and gingerly blot it dry. It would take time to restore any kind of order to her hair, so she vacated the bathroom and stood in the bedroom finger-combing it while Beau disappeared into the bathroom.

Then the door opened and he stood framed in the doorway. He still hadn't put on a shirt and she couldn't look away from the sculpted planes of his chest. There wasn't an ounce of fat anywhere on him. His nipples were taut brown buds on solid cushions of gleaming flesh, bisected by a thin line of black curls that arrowed straight down over a flat belly to disappear—

He held a brush out with his left hand. ''Would this help?''

She blushed, she knew she did. Quickly, she averted her gaze. ''Yes, thank you.''

As he tossed her the brush, the phone on the hall table rang, and they both turned in the direction of the sound. Beau had a sweatshirt bunched in the other hand, ready to pull over his head, and he gestured with one bare arm. ''Answer that, will you?''

As if he were used to a woman doing his bidding every day. Still, she walked into the hallway and lifted the receiver. ''Hello?''

''Oh, excuse me. I must have the wrong number,'' said a woman's husky voice. ''I'm trying to reach Beau Cantrell.''

''You have the right number,'' Emma assured her. ''He's right here.''

She held out the phone as he approached, getting her first good look at him in the light of day. He had dark hair, worn too long so that it curled over his collar in the back, and deep brown eyes that were measuring her body absently as he spoke to the caller. When he caught her eye, he grinned, and two deep dimples flashed in his lean cheeks. He was far too handsome for his own good. She'd bet he'd been practicing that grin on women his whole life.

He walked back into the bedroom as he talked, and reappeared a moment later with a pair of thick wool socks that he extended to her. ''Put those on,'' he mouthed.

His shoulders were wide, though he wasn't a husky man, she noted as she sat on a chair and pulled on the socks. And he probably was four or five inches taller than her own five feet eight inches. She knew his arms were thick and muscular, and the rest of his body was just as hard. Her cheeks grew warm as she recalled just how hard he had been last night.

She could not believe she'd lain practically naked in bed with this man half the night! Her mother, bless her heart, would have had a cow if she'd known. Emma hoped those who had moved on to the Great Hereafter didn't have quite such a clear view of life on earth anymore, or her mother would be arguing with Saint Peter to let her back out through the Pearly Gates.

". . . I'm fine, Elsie. Honestly. Yeah, she's all right too. Meet her? Uh, I don't know. Sometime. I'd better get back to her now. Say hi to John and thanks for checking."

She realized she was staring at Beau, and had been for who knew how long. His dark eyes were focused on her and amusement gleamed in their depths. Setting down the phone, he came and took her hand, lifting it to his mouth, and she felt the heat of his breath hot on her skin before he pressed a kiss into her palm. His mouth was firm and warm, pushing her pulse up a notch as her breath caught in her throat. Bemused as she was by the way the simple touch aroused a riot of sensations in her abdomen, she still noticed he was careful to avoid the scraped and bruised areas she'd acquired last night.

"Thanks for the rescue," he said.

She looked up at him questioningly, and he gestured toward the phone.

"I'd have been trying to get off there for an hour if she hadn't thought I had to get back to my woman." He took her elbow and pulled her to her feet then, moving toward the stairs. "Let's get some breakfast before we view the remains."

"Was that your, ah, girlfriend?" She let him tow her down the stairs and stood brushing through her hair as he competently lit a fire in the cold hearth, absently envious of his skill. She'd struggled with hers for two hours before she'd finally gotten it to light properly.

"That was one of my exes." He sounded slightly aggravated. "She's married to my best friend now."

She shivered as he walked into the kitchen and she moved to stand before the steadily growing fire. One of his exes. She'd be wise to remember that he'd had more experience with women than any man she'd ever met.

No matter how attractive he was.

Chapter Three

Lunch was hot soup and cold sandwiches on a break from salvaging what they could from her cabin. Later in the afternoon, he insisted she take a hot bath and relax. They'd gotten everything of hers that hadn't been destroyed, and as Emma sat on his deck drying her hair, Beau idly worked at tying a fishing fly, watching the play of the late sun over her hair.

She was still wearing clothes of his, a T-shirt now with exercise shorts. She'd used a piece of twine around the waist to hold them up, but he lived in hope they'd slide down anyway, baring more of those long, gorgeous legs or, if he got really lucky, a glimpse of smooth ivory thigh. At least she couldn't wear those awful long skirts for another day or so. The clothing they'd retrieved was all soaking wet, hanging tidily on the line behind his cabin.

She'd been thrilled as a little kid with candy when they'd found the kitchen largely undamaged, her wide gray eyes shining with pleasure, and he'd had to resist the urge to grab her and cover her mouth with his. Instead, he'd carried several loads of cooking equipment and her computer up to his cabin. She'd called her friend and reported the catastrophe, assuring her that she was fine, praising the kindness of her neighbor—him—and telling her that she'd probably start home later today or tomorrow.

He cleared his throat. "So, um, when were you thinking of leaving?"

She'd been gazing out over the lake, but her gaze flew to his when he spoke, and she scrambled to her feet. "Oh, I'm sorry! I can get on the road soon. I really appreciate your hospitality—"

"Emma, I wasn't asking you to leave."

She twisted her fingers together nervously, looking at the boards in the deck rather than at him. "All the same, I've imposed enough—"

"I don't mind if you hang out here. There's plenty of space and I could use the company."

Her head shot up, pure surprise etched in her eyes, and he wondered if she was as shocked as he was. What the hell had gotten into him? Hastily, he looked back down at his task. He didn't need a woman driving him crazy, especially a virginal spinster with a great ass and an air of innocence that made him long to teach her about the pleasures her body could give her. He'd opened his mouth to agree with her, he'd swear it, but out had come that invitation . . . he was losing it, no question about that.

Out of the corner of his eye, he could just see her face. She was still staring at him as if she weren't quite sure she'd heard him right.

"You promised to fix me a fantastic meal before you left." He kept his eyes on his fingers fashioning the lure, but he was aware that she stilled.

"I did, didn't I?" she asked.

There was a small silence.

"How do your hands feel?" He noticed she hadn't accepted his invitation, but that could wait. He set down the tiny feathered lure and rose, walking across the deck to her. Her eyes were wide, as deep and gray as the lake on an overcast day, he'd discovered, and though she held her palms up for his inspection, he couldn't seem to look away from those eyes.

"My hands . . . feel fine." She looked away, out over

his shoulder at the water, rippled today by a light breeze.

He forced himself to inspect her hands instead of her face, wincing as he noted the bruising. "You're going to have a hard time doing simple chores until those heal."

"I know." She lifted a hand to indicate her hair. "Even this is a challenge."

Her hairbrush lay on the deck rail, and he reached for it as he pressed her into a seat. "Sit down. I'm pretty handy with ladies' hair."

She cast him a reproving look over her shoulder. "I'm not sure that's something you should brag about."

He laughed. "You sound like somebody's maiden aunt."

"I *am* somebody's maiden aunt," she shot back. "I have two nieces and a nephew."

Her hair was beautiful, and he lifted a handful and let it spill over his palm as he drew the brush through its length. "When I think of a maiden aunt, you sure aren't the first thing that comes to mind."

She was silent. Most of the women he knew would have flirted, coyly angled for more compliments. He wasn't even sure Emma knew he'd meant it as a compliment.

He let the silence hang between them while he brushed her hair until it shone, until there was really no excuse for him to keep on brushing. But Emma was shifting lightly in her seat, a small telltale sign that she wasn't unaware of the attraction between them, and so he continued brushing, stroking over her hair again and again until his body was hard and throbbing at the thought of having all those beautiful tresses wound over and around him, chaining them together while he—

"Beau?" Her voice was breathless.

"Yeah?" Abruptly, he tossed the brush into her lap. He was driving himself crazy.

"I think . . . my hair is dry." She turned her head the slightest bit and he could see her in profile as she licked her lips nervously. No doubt about it, he wasn't the only one affected.

If she stayed, he knew as sure as the sun set he'd have to seduce her. If she left, he was very much afraid he'd have to look her up wherever she went and seduce her there. He hadn't wanted a woman like this since, well, since ever, as far as he could remember. It wasn't a comfortable feeling and he damn sure didn't like it, but that simple fact didn't make it go away.

It didn't get any better as the day slid into evening. Emma watched him from beneath her lashes when she thought he wasn't looking, and when he caught her at it, she flushed a pretty rose and hastily looked away. He was pretty sure she was finding it as hard to take a deep breath as he was. Most women would have acted on the sensual awareness, but not Emma. Innocence was stamped all over her expressive face and he wondered why she seemed so untouched. His erection pressing against her had flustered her far more than it should have last night. Was she a virgin?

She marinated chicken breasts for their dinner and proved she hadn't been kidding about her cooking abilities, serving them with whipped potatoes, fresh steamed carrots, and fantastic corn muffins that she had made without any recipe, as far as he'd seen. She also was the neatest cook he'd ever seen, cleaning up after herself as fast as she used bowls and whisks. When she was finished, he could barely tell she'd just created a meal in his kitchen.

After dinner, while he went to catch the news, she disappeared up the stairs. Curious, he followed her up after a few minutes, and found her in the second bedroom where they'd placed some of her things earlier.

She was packing.

''What are you doing?'' He didn't like the panicked feeling pushing at his chest.

''Getting ready to leave.'' She straightened from the suitcase she'd laid open on the bed. ''Thank you for the invitation, but I really couldn't impose. I'll start back first thing in the morning.''

''I wouldn't have offered if it was an imposition. Why ruin the rest of your vacation?'' He gestured toward the window that faced the lake. ''I told you you could hang out here, enjoy the lake like you planned.''

''I was going to stay for a *month*,'' she said. ''I can't just—''

''It's no trouble,'' he insisted. ''If you cook once in a while, we'll be even.''

She smiled, and again he almost gave in to the impulse to lean forward and cover her lush lips with his own. ''Even? I hardly think so. You saved my life. I'll cook *every* meal—and we still won't be even.''

It was just too good an opening to resist. ''I really don't want you feeling beholden to me,'' he said, grinning. ''Tell you what. I'll let you sleep with me while you're here. Maybe that would even the scales.''

Her pretty eyes darkened even as they widened in shock, and she practically fell over herself backing away from him. ''Very funny.''

''Can I take that as a yes?'' Despite her reaction, he could see the wheels turning in her head, and he knew she was imagining them together, which was exactly what he intended. Trouble was, his own imagination was steadily rolling a vivid scenario in his head, one that had his body reminding him it had been too long since he'd gotten laid.

''No!'' She shook her finger at him, though she wouldn't quite meet his eyes. ''You're just trying to rattle me. Well, it won't work.''

''All right. I guess you can come fishing with me instead. There's only one provision.''

''And what might that be?'' She eyed him mistrustfully and he laughed aloud.

''I catch 'em, you clean 'em.''

''Oh.'' Her brow cleared. ''Now that I can handle.''

''Great.'' He caught her hand and pulled her out of the

room. ''Now come on down to the lake and I'll teach you how to fish after dark.''

A week later, he found her sitting on the big boulder that marked one end of the small cove below the house. It had been a good day. He was inspired, and he'd worked until his hands hurt from chiseling. There was no question in his mind—he'd get the Vermont sculpture done in plenty of time.

She turned her head and smiled at him when she heard his footsteps on the wooden stairs that led to the beach. ''Hello. Are you quitting for the day?''

He nodded. ''You?''

''Yes. I took the insurance adjustor and the contractor to Helvi's cabin today. The repairs should be done in a week. And I'm back on schedule again since I reconstructed the pork roll recipe I was working on when the storm came.''

''Good.'' He kept his voice light as he climbed up and settled beside her. ''Must be my presence inspiring you.''

''It's a wonder you haven't dislocated your shoulder patting yourself on the back.'' She gave him a dry look, then pointed down the shore at a small point of land that stuck out into the lake. ''Oh, look! There's the eagle we saw yesterday.''

He followed the direction of her finger, spotting the enormous bird perched on a branch silhouetted against the sky, but when she turned her head again and her long braid slipped against his shoulder, he grasped the thick hank of hair. ''Why do you always wear your hair up or back like this?''

She shrugged, turning to give him a puzzled glance and her hair slid against his fingers like a caress. ''It keeps it out of the way.''

Without waiting for permission, he removed the elastic from the end of the braid and began to finger-comb it out into a heavy fall. ''I like it better down.''

She didn't answer him, and when he glanced at her, he saw the beginnings of wary arousal in her eyes. Good. He'd been patient for seven long days and even longer nights, waiting for her to start making excuses to spend more time with him, waiting for her to demand more of his attention like women always did . . . but she hadn't.

She shrugged off his come-ons as she just had, by retreating into wary silence. And the next thing she'd do, he knew, was change the topic or get up and leave, letting him know most definitely that she wasn't falling for his charm.

He didn't understand her. Most women got clingy at the least encouragement, and he usually found himself looking for ways to preserve his space, his distance. Emma seemed more than content with the routine they'd established. It didn't appear to bother her that he disappeared for large portions of the day, and she rarely even ventured onto the porch unless there was a phone call for him. Half the time, when he stopped and came in, she was busy in the kitchen, tapping away at her little notebook computer or trying out some recipe and talking under her breath to herself. She didn't even acknowledge his presence unless he spoke to her.

Wryly, he had to admit that he'd never eaten so well. Emma used him as her guinea pig to try out new recipes, or variations on familiar ones. Just yesterday she'd made him sample three different mixtures of lobster bisque and pick out his favorite when he'd stopped for lunch. But he still didn't like the way she seemed to be able to tune him out so easily.

Running his hand up beneath the hair he'd freed from its braid, he massaged the back of her neck, sliding his fingers around the base of her skull, ignoring the way her body stiffened and straightened away from him until she sighed and tilted her head forward.

"That feels wonderful," she said.

He felt himself responding to her warm, soft body so close to his, and he had to stifle the urge to drag her into his arms and carry her back to the cabin. But he didn't want to panic her. He was almost sure now that his pretty Emma was a virgin.

Slowly, he shifted his position, so that he sat behind her with his legs spread wide, bent so that his knees rose into the air, cradling her between them.

"What are you doing?" She turned her head in agitation but he only pointed out at the lake, ignoring the potent lure of her mouth mere inches from his.

"Look," he said into her ear. "Loons."

He felt her shiver but she turned her head to watch the antics of the black water birds. He smiled to himself. Time to tame Emma. He propped his arms on his knees, surrounding her in a near-embrace but not closing his arms around her. "Isn't this nice?" he whispered in her ear.

He felt another tremor move through her, and this time he couldn't stop himself from putting his hands over hers where they lay clasped in her lap. "Very nice," she agreed.

Deliberately, he let the silence stretch between them, keeping her wrapped in his arms, simply watching the end of the day approach. Little by little, he felt her relax, her backbone curving into the arch of his body, hers coming into fuller contact with his, until she was pressed right up against him from the curve of those sweet buttocks to the rounded balls of her shoulder joints.

"Why aren't you married?" he asked.

She stiffened immediately, but he quelled her brief struggle for freedom until she was quiet in his arms again.

"Just curious," he said. "It's not because you aren't attractive, and you're not a bitch on wheels."

She giggled, as he'd meant her to. "That's a relief," she said. There was another silence, and then she sighed. "My mother had multiple sclerosis. As I got older, she became less and less able to care for herself. My brother is older than I am, and he'd already started a family by the time she got really bad." She stopped and exhaled a quiet breath. "There was a man once . . . but my mother was still living and she needed me. And he wasn't willing to share.'' Her shoulders rose and fell in a shrug. ''He wanted me to put Mother in a home after we married so I'd have more time to devote to him, and I wasn't willing to do that. I knew she didn't have long to live and I wasn't about to have her spend her last days alone among strangers. As it turned out, she died of pneumonia the following year, so I was grateful I had the time to be with her when I could.''

''What about your father?''

''He died when I was a baby.''

''My parents aren't living either.'' He shifted on the rock, not sure why he was telling her this. It was painful, and he usually preferred not to think about his past. ''They were killed in a car wreck when I was twenty.''

Emma made a soft sound of sympathy. ''That must have been difficult for you.''

He shrugged. ''I can't pretend it wasn't. But still, I think I'm glad they went together. They were totally devoted to each other and I couldn't even imagine one without the other.''

''That's the kind of love you hear stories about,'' she said. ''It's nice to know that it actually can exist.''

''Did you feel like that about the guy who wanted to marry you?''

She thought about it for a minute. ''No,'' she said finally. ''I didn't.'' Then she half turned in his arms. ''Maybe I'm as bad at commitment as you are.''

He almost opened his mouth in automatic protest before he caught himself. Now why should that make him feel defensive? After all, it was the truth. So instead of denying it, he only nodded. ''That's me. Bad at commitment.''

Better to be sure she knew the score right off the bat, anyway. When they became lovers, he didn't want her getting silly about him, weaving woman-stories in her head about romance. Sex was sex. Period.

''So why aren't *you* married?'' she asked. ''You told me it didn't 'feel right' but you didn't tell me why.''

"My first fiancée was a model," he said. "Gorgeous to look at but not what I wanted for the rest of my life. Unfortunately, we were already engaged by the time I figured that out." Now why had he told her that?

"How did she take it?"

"Not well at first," he said dryly. "I felt bad about it for a long time."

"But not bad enough to keep from doing the same thing a second time."

He exhaled, running his palms up and down the smooth flesh of her arms. "Elsie was ready to be married, and she decided I'd do. At first, I thought I was ready too, but . . . She smothered me," he said. "I couldn't stand having to account for every minute of my time. Having to make sure somebody else knew where I was and who I was with." Abruptly, he shoved himself to his feet and leaped down from the rock, then cupped her elbows and swung her down beside him. "Why don't we have some dinner and find a topic we like better?"

The next afternoon Emma drizzled chocolate sauce over the top of a pan full of crème de menthe brownies, scraping the pot nearly clean before she set it aside. She picked up the pan of brownies, opened the refrigerator door and set them inside. When she straightened, Beau was just coming in the back door from the side porch he used as a wood shop.

He wore faded blue jeans that clung to his long legs and cupped him intimately in a manner that made the bulge below his zipper nearly impossible to ignore, and she had to force herself not to stare. It seemed as if she had done little else but stare at him in the days she'd been here, and she was afraid he knew it.

She'd done her best to give him the space he had told her he needed, had tried to stay out of his way, had made sure her things weren't left scattered around his house. It wasn't difficult. She normally was a neat person, and she certainly had enough to keep her busy. Yes, if she was honest, the arrangement seemed to be working well. Beau certainly didn't indicate in any way that he wished he hadn't issued his invitation.

And she was so grateful. She'd been crushed at the thought of having this vacation cut short before it had really begun. She'd looked forward to it for so long . . . and Beau's invitation really had sounded sincere. She'd promised herself she'd be a model guest. But how many model guests fell in love with their hosts?

It wasn't love, she told herself fiercely. It was mere infatuation. *Infatuation*, that was all. Simple, really. Beau was a gorgeous male animal, and a nice person to boot. She'd had so little exposure to men that it stood to reason that she'd imagine herself in love with the first man with whom she spent a significant amount of time. After all, it had been years since she'd been in such close quarters with a man. That was it. Of course.

Anyway, there would be no point in falling for Beau. He might not know it, but it was clear to her that he was looking for the same kind of love his parents had shared. Why else would he have backed out of marriage twice? He was simply too nice a man to do something so callous without good reason, though she knew he'd flip if he found out she thought he was a nice guy. She struggled with a smile, thinking of how hard he worked on his tough-guy image.

"Something smells pretty fantastic," he said, sniffing as he crossed to the sink and began to wash his hands.

"Brownies." She shot him a deliberately casual smile and indicated the pot sitting on the counter. "You can lick the leftovers if you like. I was just getting ready to wash up."

As he scrubbed the sawdust and wood shavings out of the thick dark hair that covered his forearms, she shifted restlessly. Her body warmed as she watched the water sluice over the muscles that shifted and slid beneath his skin, and for about the millionth time since she'd arrived, she remembered again how it had felt to lie naked with him, to have those arms around her. How would it feel if she let him press those chiseled lips against her own, accepted his embrace and nestled against that hard, tanned body, offered herself for the ecstasy she instinctively knew he would give her?

She knew he'd oblige her if she crawled into his bed.

Beau was a physical person. He was always touching her in some small way, throwing an arm around her shoulders, laying a hand over hers at the table. He'd made a practice of joining her on "her" rock for the past week at the end of their mutual workday, and she'd come to look forward to those intimate minutes when he sat behind her and surrounded her with the heat of his big body.

She wished she were bold enough, reckless enough, to lean back against him, to turn her head and seek out his lips. Sometimes, she was afraid he'd notice how her body quivered at his nearness, afraid her needy longing would communicate itself to him, but he never seemed to find anything odd.

Of course, there was no way she'd ever actually encourage him, mad infatuation or not. She'd accepted her life a long time ago, and though it might be a lonely one at times, she wasn't unhappy. Getting involved with Beau Cantrell would do more than make her unhappy. He would break her heart without ever knowing it.

At the sink, he took a glass from the cupboard and filled it with water from the cooler, then raised it to his lips and drained it in one long draft, the muscles in his strong throat working as he tilted back his head and swallowed. Her breath came faster and her entire body relaxed; her legs felt as if they'd turned to well-cooked pasta.

"Emma?"

She jumped. He was looking at her. Her face grew warm with embarrassment as she realized he'd been watching her watch him for heaven knew how long, and she looked away, then back. He was still watching her, and he gave her a slow smile that made her toes curl inside her sneakers as he swiped a dishtowel carelessly over his arms.

Then he took the two steps that brought him to her side, and when he spoke again, his voice was deep and husky. "Like what you see?"

She couldn't have answered him if her life depended on it. She swallowed.

He reached out one long arm and snagged the spoon from the pot she'd set aside. Slowly, he brought the spoon to his lips and swirled his tongue over the smooth surface, licking off the chocolate that clung to the spoon. His eyes closed, and he made a sound deep in his throat, then he gently tapped the spoon against her lips. "Take a taste."

Obediently, she parted her lips and let him slide the spoon inside, but all she could taste was him, and her eyelids fluttered closed at the intimacy of the action.

"Emma." It was a low whisper as he withdrew the spoon. "Don't you think it's time we stopping dancing around this?"

"A-around what?" The muscles in her own throat felt paralyzed; she could barely force out a sound.

"Around the fact that we want each other. Around the fact that your eyes tell me you want me to touch you here—" He reached out and touched the very tip of her breast with a light finger, "And here." The finger slipped down her body, sliding over her belly and down to the apex of her legs, and she was jolted by the streak of sensation that raced through her.

She wanted desperately to plunge her hands into his hair and drag his head down to hers—and she was very much afraid he knew it.

A primitive smile of satisfaction curved his hard lips and she caught a flash of strong white teeth before his mouth rocked onto hers, and then . . . then she couldn't think at all.

As his warm lips settled onto hers, she gave herself to the heady sensations, sinking against his body and lifting her arms to encircle his neck. He was all hard angles and flat planes, his skin hot beneath her palms, and he set his hands on her hips and pulled her close against him. She was startled by the realization that he was already heavily aroused, and he lifted her on tiptoe, moving her over him until the erection that filled the front of his jeans was snug against the vee of her thighs, throbbing insistently against her.

His tongue flirted with her lips, teasing them apart and then plunging boldly inside, demanding her response, and she found herself helplessly giving it, sliding her hands up to clench in his hair, to cradle his skull and hold his mouth on hers.

He slid a hand up from the swell of her hip, across her belly and on up until he framed a breast in his hand; deftly he whisked a fingertip over the nipple and she gasped against his mouth as it contracted almost painfully into a hard nubbin that radiated streaks of excitement clear down to her womb. Her body twisted against him, rubbing over the hard ridge of flesh sandwiched between them, and he groaned softly.

"Lie down with me," he said against her mouth, his voice almost unrecognizable, deep and guttural.

Lie down with me. The words interrupted the sensual haze that had descended, obscuring her good sense. Though fire raged in her system and a strange restlessness urged her to ignore her own hesitation, she stilled in his arms.

Shaking her head, she backed away from his lips. "No. I—I can't."

Beau's body stilled as well, though he continued to hold her firmly against him. "Sure you can." He tried to capture her lips again. "It's easy."

"No. Beau, stop. I don't want this."

His chest rose and fell as he released an enormous sigh. "Emma, you *do* want this. Are you worried because you're a virgin?"

Her mouth fell open. "How did you know that?"

His eyes were laughing and he had that obnoxious cocky grin on his face again. ''It was just a good guess. Thanks for letting me know.'' Then his face sobered, and a note of sensual urgency took the place of amusement. ''Baby, you don't have anything to worry about. I'll take good care of you, I promise.''

''It's not that.'' Thoroughly unsettled now, she pulled out of his arms and he let her go. ''I know you'd be a wonderful— Oh, never mind!'' She felt the familiar warmth rising to her cheeks. ''I'm not a casual person,'' she said. ''This wouldn't be right for me.''

Beau sighed again. ''Somehow, I knew you were going to say that.'' He reached out and caressed her cheek with his fingers, intently studying her face. Then he heaved a sigh and shook his head before he straightened and began to saunter out of the kitchen. ''I look forward to changing your mind.''

Chapter Four

But she didn't change her mind.

Every evening, she slept in the room next to his. While she slept the sleep of the innocent, he tossed and turned and ached and throbbed and generally cursed women in general for being so cantankerous.

Why did women always have to complicate things? Why wouldn't it be "right" for her? All they were talking about was a simple, sweaty sexual encounter, a mutual scratching of each other's itches, he thought a few nights later.

Well, okay, so maybe "encounter" wasn't the right word for it. Because he sure as hell couldn't imagine that one "encounter" with Miss Emma Hamaker was going to satisfy the need that had been building up in him since the day he'd seen her with her skirt hiked up around her hips down by the lake.

No, it was going to take a while to get her out of his system, and the longer she made him wait, the longer it was going to take. In fact, if she came to him right now, this very instant, and stripped naked for his touch, he doubted he'd be done with her by the time the weeks still remaining of this vacation had ended.

God, he needed her. All he could think about was what her soft breasts would look like, how her nipples would pebble beneath his fingers and her long legs would lift to clasp his hips as he drove into her, how he'd have to be gentle and careful the first couple of times until she was used to taking him—

Beau cursed and shifted, tossing back the sheet that rubbed over his throbbing erection, so aroused that even the drag of the fabric threatened his tenuous control. The air was cool, in fact, the air was *freezing* in the bedroom, but his jutting staff wasn't affected at all. This was nuts. All he had to do was go to a bar, any bar, and the odds were good that he could leave it with a willing woman on his arm. But no other woman would do. He could no sooner have sex with another woman than he could endure this torture for more endless days and nights.

The thought was sobering and he rejected it immediately. Of course another woman would do. It wasn't as if Emma meant anything special to him. After his second engagement had ended, he'd known he just wasn't marriage material. Commitment, emotional intimacy with one woman, it didn't work for him.

That was how he knew these feelings rolling around inside him could only be sexual infatuation. The only reason he was so determined to have her now was because she'd become a challenge.

Yeah, that must be it. It was the challenge.

And once he'd conquered her reserve, learned the secrets of her long, slender body, she'd be just another woman he'd enjoyed for a time. They'd settle into a nice, distant friendship like he had with other women.

Nothing special.

The next morning, the sun was already warming the air by the time Emma had finished eating the toast she'd made herself for breakfast. She worked on a new recipe until nearly noon, then walked down the path to the little cove on the lake.

It was a gorgeous day, the warmest one she'd had since she'd arrived, and she decided not to waste it indoors. After grabbing a quick lunch and leaving a cold sandwich in the refrigerator for Beau, who'd been closeted in his studio on the porch all morning, she went up to her room and slipped into the sedate navy bathing suit she wore when she swam at the local Y at home.

Fastening a skirt around her waist, she headed back down to the cove and sat on one of the logs that rested on either side of the stony ring where summer families apparently made evening fires. Feeling hedonistic and greatly daring, she removed her skirt and lay back. But her hair, twisted up in a practical bun, was uncomfortable at the back of her head, so she slipped out the pins and piled them on the log, shaking out her hair and letting it dance around her in the mild breeze. Then she lay back down with a contented sigh.

The log was warm and wide beneath her; the sun poured down, draining her of any desire to do anything. Closing her eyes, she let herself drowse and drift into daydreaming.

Had she ever been so lazy before in her life?

No. Never. Her father had died before she was born, and ever since Emma could remember, her mother had been frail. She'd grown up worrying about her mother's health, gradually assuming the role of caretaker and eventually, provider. There had been no time for laziness in her life.

And that was a shame, she saw now. This was heavenly, lying here soaking up sunshine. Everyone needed some time like this, time to just relax all the wheels constantly revolving in their brains and—

''Hey, there, Sleeping Beauty.''

The voice was deep and nasal, masculine without any of the toe-curling attraction that underlaid Beau's smooth Southern drawl. Her eyes flew open and she sat up so fast she nearly rolled off the side of the log.

A canoe was approaching rapidly, the two men in it maneuvering right up to the stony beach. One man was chunky; one was thin and round shouldered. Both were openly staring at her, and she felt naked beneath their avid gazes, her bathing suit no cover against ogling eyes.

"Purty day, isn't it?" The speaker was the first man, the big, heavy one. He had lank, greasy dark hair that fell into his eyes as he heaved himself out of the canoe and pulled it up onto the beach, and as he shook his head and flipped it back, an unexpected shiver of revulsion swept over her.

"Yes, it's a lovely day," she said. She didn't have it in her to be too rude, but all the same, she snatched up her skirt and held it against her as she backed toward the wooden steps that suddenly seemed miles away instead of a few yards.

"And it just got purtier," the same man pronounced. He lumbered toward her. "Look at all that hair. I'm Rich and this here's Jamie. We're camped down at the end of the lake. Want to take a little boat ride, honey?"

"Um, no. No, thank you." She swallowed. "I have work to do."

"Aw, c'mon. You don't look busy to me." The man named Rich reached for her hand. He stood between her and the steps now, and even without looking behind her, she knew there was no other way off the beach. There was nothing but a ragged bank probably ten feet high behind her, and boulders at either end of the small cove. Maybe if she were wearing sturdy shoes instead of flimsy sandals, she could try to outrun them, but instinct told her not to turn her back, not to try to flee. She got the distinct feeling that at least one of them would enjoy chasing her down.

"Sorry," she said, stepping backward again, evading the outstretched hand with its grimy nails. "I was just taking a little break. I really do have work to do."

The second man guffawed, and she saw that he was drinking a beer. In fact, there was a cooler in the middle of the canoe and it looked as if quite a few beers had already been consumed. "She don't wanna have nothin' to do with you, Richie. C'mon."

The bigger man's face darkened. "She just needs a little convincin,' " he said to Jamie. His eyes trailed down over her breasts and lower, and he licked his lips.

"Take one more step and I'll be glad to *convince* you to get off my beach."

The steely male voice had everyone's head whipping around, and a relief so intense her knees nearly buckled rushed through her. Beau stood at the top of the steps behind Rich, feet planted and hands hanging loosely at his sides. Though he didn't move, she could practically see waves of male aggression radiating from him and his eyes were lit with a grim light, daring either of the other men to challenge him.

Rich froze, his hand dropping away from her.

She couldn't blame him. Beau was shirtless, and though the other man outweighed him, the sheets of muscle that rippled across his torso, his wide shoulders, and heavy, powerful arms all proclaimed his superior condition.

Then he leaped lightly from the top step to the beach, and Rich's eyes bulged. He staggered backward. "Hey, there," he said. " 'Zis your lady? We was just bein' neighborly." Prudently, he kept edging back toward the canoe.

Beau's lips drew back into what she could only describe as a snarl. "Get out. *Now.*" His voice cracked with sharp authority. "And don't come back, unless you want me to kick your sorry asses into the next state."

Under other circumstances, she might have laughed at the haste with which the two men pushed their canoe off the beach and practically fell over each other getting into it. The canoe bobbled dangerously for a moment then righted itself, and within moments, the hasty splashing of their paddles took them back out into the middle of the lake again.

Beau strode across the rocks to her. "You okay?"

"I—I—yes." She had to swallow the ball of fear that she hadn't realized had lodged in her throat and she took a deep, shuddering breath. "Thank you." She wanted him to hold her, she realized. To cuddle and comfort her until the sick shaking feeling in her limbs died away.

Then she saw the unquenched rage in his eyes as his gaze swept over her, and she steeled herself against the impulse to reach out to him.

"Next time you decide to come down here half-naked and tease the male population of the neighborhood, I might not be around to rescue you," he said in a deep, harsh tone.

"I know. I'm sorry—" But her apology died half-formed as his words sank in. "Excuse me? 'Tease the male population'?" She took a deep breath. "Since when is it a crime for a woman to want to sunbathe—fully clothed—on a private beach?"

A dark red flush started up his neck and if it was possible for his eyes to get any more furious, they did. "I didn't say it was a crime," he said tightly. "But it sure as hell isn't the smartest thing you've done." He reached out and jerked the skirt out of her hands before she knew what he was doing, leaving her standing before him in nothing but her bathing suit and sandals. "You call this fully clothed? Ha! I'd like to be around when you put on underwear."

She was too shocked to answer, shocked, and hurt too by his unexpected antagonism when she'd only wanted to fall into his arms and receive some comfort. She might be an unsophisticated spinster but she knew her clothing was far less revealing than most women's suits. Tears prickled at the backs of her eyes. She opened her mouth, then closed it again without speaking. Stepping carefully around him, she made a beeline for the steps.

She was halfway up them when she realized he still had her skirt, and she was probably giving him an eyeful of her behind. Tough, she told herself. He didn't care. And she didn't care that he didn't. She only wanted to be away from the big boor.

"Where are you going?" he roared from the beach.

She whirled around, goaded beyond restraint by his inexplicable behavior. "To get *fully clothed*," she shot back, marching up the path toward the house.

A second later, she heard his sneakered feet hit the steps. She glanced over her shoulder, and the black rage on his face as he took the steps three at a time and began to sprint up the path toward her was enough to push her internal panic buttons. It might not be smart to turn your back on a predator, but she did anyway, running as fast as she could for the cabin.

She almost made it. But as she reached for the screen door, his palm slapped against it, tearing the handle from her frantic grasp and slamming it with a sharp crack. He used one hand on her arm to spin her around and before she knew what was happening, his hard arms locked around her and his hot mouth came down on hers. She squirmed, pressing against his shoulders, but she might as well have been pushing at granite. As she tried to protest, he took the opportunity to plunge his tongue between her parted lips, demanding her participation, molding her to the unyielding length of his body and drinking from her until she wrenched her mouth from his and took a deep, shuddering breath.

It didn't stop him. When she turned her head away, he pressed scalding kisses down the line of her jaw, his open mouth trailing voraciously down her neck, leaving a moist path behind to mark his possession. He arched her back over one steely arm and his lips traveled down the swell of her breast to close firmly over one nipple beneath the flimsy suit, suckling hard enough to make her rear back and scream in shock.

"Beau! Stop it. You don't want to do this." She tugged desperately at his hair, battered by unfamiliar sensations as her body responded to his primal demands.

"Wanna bet?" He lifted his head enough to look down at her, a heart-stopping grin of genuine amusement lighting the intensity of his features for a moment. He arched his hips against her, letting her feel the straining ridge of his erection surging against her belly. "Does that feel like a man who doesn't want to do this?"

She shuddered, aroused almost beyond coherent thought by his honest response.

Then he let her go.

She was so unprepared that she nearly staggered and fell. Beau hastily put his hands beneath her elbows again, holding her gaze with his. "Look down."

She obeyed, realizing belatedly what he wanted her to look at. His shorts were pushed out of shape, outlining his aroused flesh, and as she watched, the fabric pulsed and moved as he grew even larger.

"I'm tired of aching for you," he said in a low growl. "Tired of walking around like *this*, tired of sleeping alone in that big bed when I could be sharing it with you. Remember how good it felt that first night? All cozy and warm, snuggled together beneath those blankets?"

"I—" She hesitated. "I remember," she whispered. She wanted to reach out and cup that bold male flesh; she wanted it so badly that her palms tingled, and she took a step back, trying desperately to remember all the perfectly valid reasons she had for not wanting to get involved with him.

"Don't pretend you don't want me." She was backed against the door now, and he pressed his body against hers again, capturing her wrists and holding them against the door at either side of her head. Slowly, deliberately, he dropped his head and took her mouth in another deep, hungry kiss.

She knew she should protest, knew she'd regret this. To Beau, she was merely another female in a long parade through his life, to be savored and enjoyed for a time before being firmly set aside. But her body knew the touch of the man she loved, the man she had longed for in the still, dark nights when she'd lain sleepless in the room next to his, wondering if he ever thought of her. Her body knew this might be the only chance in her life she'd experience the compelling demand of a man to whom she could respond totally, completely.

Without conscious thought, her protests became caresses, her arms stopped pushing at his heavy shoulders and clasped him to her, her body stopped straining away from his and melted against him, feeling the heady, rigid heat pillowed against her belly, the press of rock-hard flesh against her sensitized nipples.

Then, when she was clinging to him in mindless surrender, aware only of his mouth, his arms, his tongue demanding a response she was helpless to prevent, he placed his hands beneath her bottom and lifted her feet off the floor, holding her firmly against him while he walked the short distance into the living room. She whimpered as his erection found the snug notch between her thighs, and her own feminine flesh leaped in response. Her fingers slipped through the silky strands of his dark hair to clutch his skull in both hands as she pressed her mouth to his.

When he stood her on her feet again, they were on the thick rug before the fireplace.

He didn't give her time to think, to accept or protest. He simply claimed her mouth again in a sure, sensual kiss, slanting his lips over hers and plunging his tongue deeply, familiarly, into her. She still had her hands in his hair, and she slowly slid them down over his shoulders, molding his hard, naked flesh.

A second later, he took her hands in his and placed them on his chest. "Touch me, Emma," he growled.

She wasn't sure what he wanted, but his skin was hot and burning beneath her palms, and she couldn't resist combing her fingers through the crisp forest of curls over his breastbone. Her hand grazed one flat copper nipple and he sucked in a breath that made her glance up at him in surprise.

Grimly, he smiled down at her. "Don't look so surprised. Doesn't that feel good to you too?"

She felt her cheeks warm. Unable to sustain the intense

eye contact, she focused again on his chest, following the pattern of hair out along his breastbone and this time deliberately brushing her fingers over his nipples.

"God, that feels great," he muttered. His arms moved from around her, and she felt his fingers on the straps of her suit, stripping it away, pushing it down over her hips until it fell in a puddle at her feet. Then he took her hands, drawing back from her and examining what he had uncovered.

She was embarrassed. She was excited. She was so aroused that her skin felt electrified, as if the slightest touch would produce a sizzling reaction. She tried to crowd against him again but he laughed and took her by the shoulders, holding her away. "I want to see you," he said. "All of you."

This time, she stayed where she was as his hungry eyes devoured her. "You're going to kill me," he said, and his voice was so deep and rough she barely recognized it. He put out his hands and covered her breasts with both big palms, and she shuddered at the unfamiliar sensation that streaked from the crest of her nipples down into her woman's mound. Abruptly, he set his hands at her waist and dragged her against him. His head bent as he arched her back over one brawny arm and she gasped, clutching at his shoulders for balance.

Then she gasped again, a harsh sound that died away on a whimper when his lips closed over one stiffened nipple. He sucked at her, and she arched even more, pushing herself against him, needing more contact, more heat, more, more, more—

As her knees buckled, he laid her down on the rug, shucking off his shorts and briefs and coming down beside her in one smooth motion, laying a hand firmly on the aching mound at the junction of her thighs. She made a noise in her throat, biting down on her lip to stifle the scream that wanted to escape, and she saw him smile.

Then he bent his head and took her nipple again, suckling so strongly she *did* scream this time. At the same instant, she felt him slip one stealthy finger downward, sliding along the humid folds of her most intimate flesh. She shifted restlessly, and he shifted too, coming partially over her and inserting a knee between her thighs so she couldn't close them. She clamped them together anyway, firmly gripping that hair-roughened muscled thigh and he groaned as he delved even deeper with his finger. "Come to me, baby," he encouraged her.

Her world was all sensation. His hot breath blasting over the tip of her breast, the unaccustomed heat of hard, silky male flesh throbbing against her thigh, a heavy knee between her legs, and always, always, his hand, shifting, stroking, probing as she writhed, seeking some comfort in a world where shaking, scalding need was all she could find.

His palm settled more firmly over her nest of curls and her eyes flew wide as that questing finger suddenly, shockingly, moved firmly inside her. He was looking down at her, snaring her gaze, holding her with his eyes while her body gave itself to his urging. Her breath caught in her throat, she felt herself hurtling out of control, reaching, rushing toward some unknown destination that only Beau could take her to . . . and then she shattered.

Beau ground the pad of his palm against her, making small urgent circles against the place where her entire being was focused. Her body gathered itself in a great tidal wave of sensation and she surged forward, bucking in his arms. Deep within her womb, a great rolling rhythm thrust her upward again and again as her back arched and her body clutched at that single dexterous finger.

He slid his finger from her and gathered her closer before she could completely relax, his mouth taking hers in a deep, possessive kiss as he pushed her thighs wide. There was an agonizing moment of waiting, and she realized he was donning protection—and then he fitted his body to hers.

Emma's eyes flew wide at the first probe of male flesh against her tender female entrance. Her fingers dug into his shoulders and she tensed as he pushed forward, inexorably stretching her tender, untried entry until she cried out, the sound swallowed by his mouth. At the same instant, he slid past the barrier and buried himself deeply inside her.

Emma froze. He felt huge, impossibly thick, and she wriggled slightly beneath the pinning weight of his hips, trying to find a more comfortable position as panic lapped at the edges of her mind.

Above her, Beau's muscles bunched into hard knots as he fought for control. "I don't want to hurt you," he muttered. "But I can't—I can't—" The words died between his clenched teeth as he began to move inside her, his big body gathering momentum as he withdrew and thrust, withdrew and thrust, faster and faster. He reached down and clasped her buttocks in his hands and tilted her hips up to better receive him, and Emma stifled a shriek into his shoulder at the sudden increase in sensation. She wrapped her legs around his waist, drawing him into even closer contact, clinging to him even though her tender sheath was unbearably stretched and she felt as if she couldn't take another second of his pounding, pummeling ride.

But despite the discomfort, she reveled in her femininity, glorying in the power her body had, in her ability to give Beau the gift of herself. Finally, as his body stiffened and the storm broke, he emptied his seed in a few final bursts of power that left him drained and panting, his face buried in her hair and his body heavily slumped over hers.

She kept her arms around him, hugging him to her until at last, with a heartfelt groan, Beau levered himself away from her. She winced involuntarily as his still-taut erection slid from her body, wishing it didn't have to end, wishing for a return of the moments in which they had been one. He eased down beside her and drew her into his arms, stroking her tangled hair away from her face with one big hand, and the chill she'd felt at their parting vanished.

"You okay?" he asked.

She nodded, smiling faintly. "Fine." Incredibly, she could feel herself blushing and she ducked her head against his chest as he laughed softly.

"Don't get shy on me now." Laying his hand against her jaw, he tilted up her chin with his thumb and inspected her carefully. "Hmm."

"Hmm what?" She wondered if her newly altered state showed on her face. She *felt* as if it must; as if Beau had branded her with his stamp, as if everywhere she went for the rest of her life, she would carry his mark on her, announcing to the world that she was his.

"You look . . . ravished," he decided.

She studied his expression. "Is that bad?"

He laughed, wrapping her in his arms and rolling so that she lay atop him. "Only if there's some unlucky guy out there who's been dying to get you in his bed."

She sniffed as her hair fell around them, curtaining them in a private moment. "Hardly."

Beau's expression changed, his eyes searching her face. "I can't figure you out," he said. "How old are you, anyway?"

"I was thirty in March."

"So why were you still a virgin?"

She shrugged, propping herself on her forearms. "The opportunity to change my, uh, status never really arose, I guess."

Beau shook his head. "The men in Massachusetts must be blind."

While she was digesting his offhand compliment, he rolled again, then heaved himself into a sitting position and drew her up beside him. Instinctively, Emma crossed her arms over her body; when he noticed, Beau rose and snagged an afghan from the back of the sofa, draping it around her shoulders before sitting down behind her as he had so often on "their" rock at the lake, with her cuddled between his knees.

The chief difference, this time, she thought, suppressing a giggle, was that he was stark naked now. She snuggled against him, enjoying the feel of his hair-roughened legs brushing against her. He didn't understand, could never understand what it was like to be . . . ordinary. He'd probably known that women found him irresistible from the time he could walk.

She, on the other hand, had faded into the background for so many years she didn't even question it. Beau might be interested in her here, now, while they were isolated from the world, but if she were stupid enough to follow him back into his real life, he'd lose interest. One look at all the interesting, attractive women that must flock around him and he'd forget she ever existed.

But right now, he was kissing her neck, his hands sliding beneath the blanket to cup her breasts in his big palms and rasp his thumbs gently, steadily back and forth over her nipples. She was going to enjoy every moment, store them all up in her head for the day when this dream ended and she awoke alone.

Alone, as always.

Chapter Five

For maybe the twentieth time in as many minutes, Beau checked the door of the little Christmas shop in Bar Harbor. Emma had gone in there while he'd run an errand across the street. He'd returned to find that he had a perfect view of her through the plate-glass window as she browsed amid rough-hewn wooden Santas and delicate lace angels.

As he watched, she bent forward to examine something more closely, causing her incredible fall of hair to slide over one shoulder. Catching it absently with one hand, she held the long tresses loosely until she straightened, then she gave them a toss back over her shoulder. His breath caught, and he felt a familiar pleasant stirring in his loins. God, he loved that hair.

She'd been leaving it down when she wasn't cooking ever since the first time he'd made love to her. Since then, he'd had to force himself to work for at least part of the day, when all he wanted to do was keep her flat on her back in his bed.

She'd learned fast how to please him, and once her initial shyness had faded away, she'd given him a total hot, sweet response like nothing he'd ever known before. And it hadn't been a hardship to learn what pleased her, what kinds of touches aroused her, what kinds of strokes brought her to a fast, brutal climax, and what kind prolonged her excitement until she was clutching at him, frantically begging him to give her what he'd taught her she needed.

A truck rattled down the street, breaking his absorption. Abruptly, he realized that he was standing on one of the main streets of Bar Harbor with a major bone in his pants, and he forced himself to think of other things.

It wasn't hard to sour his mood at the thought of what they were going to do next. His buddy John had called last night. He and Elsie were on their way to Nova Scotia to visit family and wanted to meet them in Bar Harbor for dinner. Els, John informed him, had been dying to meet his newest lady love ever since she'd spoken to her briefly on the phone. It wasn't that he didn't want to see them. All awkwardness between his former fiancée and him had faded after her marriage to John. It was just . . . well, damn it, he didn't want to share Emma with anyone else. At least not yet.

"Sorry I took so long." Emma stepped out of the shop, waving a package at him. "I got the most gorgeous hand-painted Santa. It's done on a natural slab of birch." She sighed as she reached his side. "I could have spent a fortune in that shop, but how many Christmas decorations does one single woman need?"

Christmas. He knew exactly what he would get her for Christmas. Diamond earrings, for one thing. And she could model them for him wearing absolutely nothing else, he thought smugly as he took her hand and they started down the street. But she'd probably get more excited about the new set of knives, if he knew Emma. She'd waxed enthusiastic to the point of being hilarious one day when he'd caught her sighing over a cutlery catalog; he'd decided then and there that she was going to have those knives.

Then he realized what he was thinking. *Christmas?* It was only September. When was the last time he'd wanted to continue seeing the same woman for four months? To make plans for the future, for God's sake?

Hell. If he ever had, he couldn't remember it. But neither

could he imagine life without Emma again. She'd changed his life, disrupted his routine. No longer could he immerse himself in work for hours on end. Now, he had to stop and seek her out simply for the pleasure of seeing the smile that lit up her pretty face at the sight of him. Half the time he couldn't think for the desire that simmered in his blood every time he caught so much as a glimpse of her walking around in the kitchen or reading on the deck. It was maddening, and he should hate it. But he didn't. If he thought it would stay like that, he'd marry her in a heartbeat.

And that was such a staggering idea that he immediately slammed a mental door on it. Beau Cantrell didn't do permanent women. He'd learned his lesson. Sooner or later, he started feeling panicked, smothered in a relationship. He didn't need long-term hassles.

Although Emma hadn't smothered him so far. Exactly the opposite, in fact. He frequently found himself inventing excuses to interrupt her work, to focus her attention on him. He could only take so many hours away from her, he'd discovered, before his passion for his carving faded and all he could think about was how soon he could reasonably be with her again.

To distract himself from his insane brain, he said, "I'm really sorry about tonight. John's been my friend since we were about thirteen. I didn't feel like I could tell him I didn't want to see him."

Emma looked up at him, a warm smile lighting her eyes. "I don't mind. And you'd hate yourself if you passed up a chance to visit with him and his wife. Didn't you say they live in Michigan now?"

"Yeah." He slipped his arm around her shoulders. "You're probably right." But he'd still rather be sitting in front of the fire with Emma on his lap. Preferably astride his lap, with neither of them wearing a stitch.

Down the hill, a woman in a red sweater and khaki shorts waved energetically. "Beau!" He recognized Elsie, and the tall figure behind her was John.

As he and Emma neared the couple, he stepped forward, enveloping Elsie in a hug that lifted her off her feet as she kissed his cheek enthusiastically. Then he released her and stuck out his hand to John, who promptly used the grip to pull him into a brief, but heartfelt masculine embrace.

"Man, is it good to see you!" his old friend said.

"Likewise." He knew he was grinning like an idiot. "It's damn nice to lay eyes on you two. Glad you called." Then he reached back and drew Emma forward. "This is Emma Hamaker. John and Elsie Breaks," he said to her.

Emma shook hands with each of them, smiling quietly. "It's a pleasure to meet you."

"No, it's *my* pleasure." John Breaks held on to her hand when she would have withdrawn it. "Damn, boy," he said to Beau. "Where do you find 'em?"

Emma flushed, uncomfortable under the frank assessment until Elsie chuckled, a warm sound that invited everyone else to join her. "Don't be offended," she said to Emma. "John always says exactly what he's thinking."

"That's how I caught you, isn't it?" her husband retorted.

The affection between them was clear, and the intimate smile they shared made Emma look away as if it were something that shouldn't have been witnessed.

"Emma already knows the story," Beau informed them. "I was dumb enough to let Elsie get away and John was smart enough to grab her up."

"Or something like that," Elsie drawled. They all laughed then, and Emma was amazed. How could this woman stand there smiling? She'd once been engaged to Beau, had once captured his interest and some part of his heart—and he'd walked away from her.

She, Emma, couldn't imagine calmly smiling at him under such circumstances. Already, her heart ached every time he gave her *that look*, the one that told her, without words, that he wanted her. How many more times would she be cuddled in his embrace, wake to possessive kisses pressed to any part of her body he could reach, see his face drawn taut in the throes of his own release?

Six more nights. That was all.

Her vacation ended in six days, and with it, she knew, would end the single most important relationship she would ever have in her life. She'd never really understood love before, and she almost wished she had never met Beau, because when her six days and nights were up, she'd drive out of the state of Maine with her heart broken into millions of irreparable pieces.

But despite the certain heartache ahead, she knew she wouldn't change a single thing about the past month. Beau had taught her about the beauty of physical closeness, the wonderful earthy, raunchy things people did and said in bed, the intimacies that couldn't be dreamed of unless experienced. And though she knew he hadn't intended it, he'd taught her about love.

". . . starting to get chilly out here. Let's go in and order." Elsie was speaking and Emma gave a small start when Beau put his hand at her waist to move her along.

"What were you dreaming about?" he whispered in her ear while they stood waiting for the hostess to seat them. "Or can I guess?" The look he gave her clearly told her what *he* thought she'd been thinking as he squeezed her waist.

She smiled. "You can guess all you like, but I'm not telling." *Because if I told you I was dreaming of love and marriage and a lifetime together, you'd run screaming.*

They chatted over dinner with John and Elsie and she learned that they owned an imported-car dealership, that they had a two-year-old daughter, and that John's mother drove them crazy begging to baby-sit.

"So we let her have Amanda all week," Elsie said. Her voice wobbled a little at the end, and her husband put a comforting arm around her.

"We needed some time alone," he reminded her. "In about seven months—"

"We'll be a family of four," they finished together.

Beside her, she felt Beau tense for a moment before he stood and reached across the table to congratulate his friends. What was he thinking? she wondered. Did he still love Elsie? Was he sorry he called off his own wedding day? Or was he simply grateful that he wasn't "trapped," like John?

After the hubbub surrounding the announcement subsided, Beau picked up the check the waitress had deposited on the table. "I'm going down to pay this. It's my treat—consider it the first baby gift," he said. John protested and Beau grinned, but she detected a strained quality to his smile.

While the men walked to the cashier's counter, Elsie grabbed Emma by the hand. "I have to find a ladies' room," she confided. "One of the curses of pregnancy."

Emma smiled wistfully. She'd give a lot to suffer that particular curse if it meant she'd be snuggling a baby in her arms at the end of it.

"So how long have you and Beau been in Maine?" Elsie asked from the stall she'd entered.

"Almost a month." Emma didn't bother to explain that they'd only met then.

"Isn't he wonderful?" The toilet flushed, and Elsie emerged. "Oh, I don't love him anymore, but I still think he's the sweetest man alive. He knows how to make a woman feel like a woman." Her eyes twinkled. "Why am I telling you this?"

Emma hesitated. But the question hovering in her mind all evening demanded an answer. "Are you ever sorry you two didn't marry?"

Elsie sobered, and Emma realized she wasn't going to try to pass off a laughing answer. "I was," she said thoughtfully. "Right after he told me he couldn't marry me, I was devastated. Pride, mostly, but honest hurt too. Honestly, though, it wasn't long before I realized he was right, that he and I weren't right for each other." She paused, and then her pretty blue eyes twinkled again. "Of course, having John ask me out a week later and propose within the month helped me get over my pique. And once I fell in love with John, I couldn't imagine being married to Beau. The feelings never compared." She smiled mistily. "I owe Beau a big debt of thanks. For finding John *and* for being smarter than I was about marriage."

Emma smiled and nodded. Privately, she decided Elsie must be mildly mentally impaired. Anyone who would choose *any* other man over Beau had to be missing a circuit or two.

Elsie patted her hands dry with a paper towel as she regarded Emma in the mirror. "You're the first woman Beau's ever lived with, you know. I don't know how you feel but he seems . . . different, to me. Like he belongs with you and he knows it."

Emma rushed to shake her head. "No, I don't think so. Beau and I . . . aren't a permanent thing."

"Okay." Elsie tugged open the bathroom door and started back to join the men, shooting Emma a final grin over her shoulder. "Whatever you say. Just don't forget to invite John and me to the wedding."

On the long drive home from Bar Harbor a little later, Emma laid her head on Beau's shoulder. He'd pulled her across the seat of his truck and fastened the middle seat belt around her, "so I can sneak a kiss at every stop sign," he said.

She wished Elsie were right about the wedding, but she knew the man sitting beside her. He wasn't the kind to be tied down to one woman. This time was all she would ever get. And she'd better enjoy it while it lasted.

He woke her with kisses in the morning, ducking beneath the covers to lightly flick his tongue across one soft breast until the nipple drew into a taut little bud and Emma stirred and reached for him.

Without a word, he covered her, reaching down to tease

open her soft satiny folds and fit himself to her tight little channel. Even after three weeks, she still felt as snug as a virgin around him, and he had to clench his teeth against the need to begin urgently thrusting. As satisfying as it would be for him, he wanted Emma with him. Half the fun of making love to her was watching her dreamy face, her half-closed eyes dazed as she moved to his touch, her arms stroking up and down his muscled back. Only when he felt the first delicate shivers of climax shaking her did he release his iron will and let himself plunge fully into her, and when her rippling internal contractions milked his turgid flesh, he pumped quickly to a wrenching finish, his seed spurting in long, warm jets that left him limp and panting.

After a time, he moved off her and drew her into his arms, and she snuggled against him, her fingers idly combing through the mat of dark hair that spread across his breastbone.

"I've enjoyed this," she whispered.

"Me too. Ready for round two?" Chuckling, he rolled her beneath him and pushed his legs between hers until his hips pressed into hers and she couldn't miss the renewed throbbing of his flesh.

"I didn't just mean *this*," she said, and something in her tone set off his internal alarms. Looking down into her eyes, he saw shadows and sadness there.

"What's wrong, baby?" Propping himself on his elbows, he framed her face with his hands, stroking the hair away from her temples.

"Nothing's wrong." She made an effort to smile, and he was even more alarmed when her lips quivered. "Except that soon it will be time for me to go."

"Go? Go where?" A cold dread knotted his gut. "You still have five days of vacation, right? You don't have to go anywhere yet." He knew his panic showed but he didn't care. Shoving himself to his knees, he rose from the bed and stalked across the room to snag his jeans from a chair. "You can't just leave without talking to me first."

"Talking to you first?" Her tone was incredulous, pain-filled, and the look in her eyes hurt his heart. "Why on earth should I do that? We both knew this was a temporary fling. In fact, you went to great lengths to be sure I understood, as I recall." She rose too, quickly donning her warm flannel robe and belting it with precise motions. "This vacation ends in five days and I have to make plans. I have a life of my own that doesn't include being your convenient sexual outlet." And before he could summon an answer to that, she rushed into the bathroom and slammed the door.

"Emma!" He reached for the knob but she'd locked it from the inside. The shower started to run, and he knew she'd done it on purpose, in order to drown out any more arguments he might have.

"Damn!" He thrust a hand through his hair, sliding down to sit with his back against the bathroom door, trying to think. He had to convince her to stay with him, to come home to Tennessee with him. But a small voice inside taunted him. *Why? So you can have a convenient sexual outlet?* Is that all she thought he wanted?

Of course it was.

The answer hit him with the force of a chisel pounded by a hefty mallet strike. She was right. He'd gone to great lengths to be sure she knew this wasn't a lasting relationship.

Slowly rising to his feet, he turned and paced across the bedroom and back again, over and over, back and forth, walking without purpose, fear clutching at his throat. He'd never felt like this before. Even when he'd decided to end each of his engagements, his feelings had been rational, more a determined relief once he'd known what he had to do. So what was the difference this time? He'd planned on leaving Emma at the end of the month, hadn't he? Planned on going back to Tennessee and resuming his lifestyle, complete with occasional enjoyable liaisons of the sexual sort when the mood struck.

But that mood would never strike again. As if a layer

of blinding fabric had been peeled from his eyes, he saw that his lifestyle would never be the same again. He loved Emma, in a way he'd never thought he'd be able to love anyone. He needed her, and he wanted her for the rest of his life.

The bathroom door opened and he spun around. Emma stood in the doorway, her eyes uncertain. He'd never heard the shower cut off, never heard her moving around. She'd put her robe back on and her hair was still carelessly clipped on top of her head, and suddenly he was furious with himself for putting that look in her eyes.

"Baby." He walked across the room and reached for her hands but she crossed her arms defensively across her chest, pulling away from him.

"Don't, Beau." She shook her head. "Can't we end this with dignity?"

End it? His control snapped. "No, by God, we can't," he roared. Setting his hands at her waist, he yanked her against him. "We're not ending it," he informed her. "Call your editor back and tell her you're moving to Tennessee—"

"No." She didn't try to get away from him but she'd withdrawn into herself, looking down at the floor rather than at him. Her voice was low and intense. "I've got to go, Beau. This time with you has been the most precious time in my entire life, but I have to leave *now*."

"You don't *have* to leave," he said, forcing out the words through a throat so dry he could barely speak. Panic rose as he realized he could lose her. "You're *choosing* to leave. There's a difference."

She shrugged. "Not one that matters."

"But—"

"Beau." She looked up at him. "I saw the look on your face yesterday when John and Elsie told you she was pregnant."

He stilled, sensing this was a key to what was wrong, but not making a connection. "And . . . ?"

"It meant one of two things." Her mouth twisted in a little smile that was more of a sad grimace. "Either you still love Elsie and their news hurt you, or the thought of your buddy being trapped in a family with no way out made you sick."

He was stunned. He opened his mouth, then closed it again without speaking. How could she think that after the things they'd shared? After the way he'd made love to her, how could she think he loved somebody else?

"So you see why I have to leave."

The pain in her voice gentled his rage. "Why?"

She looked away from him again, and he felt about the size of one of the tiny ants that occasionally invaded her kitchen. "Because," she said with bald honesty, "it's not temporary for me anymore. I care too much."

A rush of joy started around his heart and quickly expanded, making him suck in a deep breath of air as he ran his hands up her spine and out to her shoulders. He cleared his throat. "You're not the only one who cares."

There was a moment of dead silence. She shook her head as if she didn't understand. "What?"

He smiled at her confusion. "Emma. You're not going back to Massachusetts without me. Today, we make plans to get married. Today, we decide where we're going to live, and whether or not you want to keep working and how many babies we want to try to make together." His voice deepened. "I always knew when it felt *wrong*, and it took me a while to figure out that this is how it feels when it's *right*. The look you saw on my face yesterday was shock. When John and Elsie told us about their baby, all I could think was that I couldn't wait for the day when I could announce to the world that you were carrying *my* baby. I love you. I think you love me too, and I want us to get married as soon as we can locate a license and a judge."

"Beau, I—" She swallowed. "I—"

"Just say yes," he instructed.

She studied his face for a moment, her gray eyes probing his and finding what she needed. "Yes," she whispered. And then she said it again, louder, in a voice full of feeling. "Yes!"

A relief so intense his knees felt weak washed through him. Slowly, he reached up and removed the clip from her hair, tossing it aside and plunging his hands through the heavy tresses, cradling her jaw and tilting her face up to his.

And as he took her mouth in a celebration of the love he'd waited so long to find, he blessed Mother Nature and the hurricane that had hurled Emma into his arms and his heart. He never intended to let her go.

